The Shifter's Stolen Fae

Wicked Fae, Volume 1

Amelia Shaw

Published by Harley Romance Publishing, 2022.

This is a work of fiction. Similarities to real people, places, or events are entirely coincidental.

THE SHIFTER'S STOLEN FAE

First edition. December 6, 2022.

Copyright © 2022 Amelia Shaw.

Written by Amelia Shaw.

Thank you to my team!

The amazing Lori Grundy for my cover.

And Faedra Rose- my Alpha reader and editor who worked with me to deepen these characters and make everything better!

Chapter 1

Aurelia

I SPRINTED THROUGH the city center, passing the wards into the witch market. My kind weren't welcome in this part of Dallas, but I had little choice in the matter. I pulled my hood lower over my face and did my best to steer clear of the other patrons. The apothecary was my target, and I had no time to waste. As I approached the shop, I pushed open the door, then scurried inside. The woman who owned the store ignored me until I walked up to the counter with my purchase.

"You don't belong here, girl." The woman sneered. "I only serve witches, not filthy beasts like you."

"I need this for my mother," I said firmly with as much calm as I could muster, pushing the purchase across the glass counter toward her.

She knew exactly who my adoptive mother was and wouldn't question the fact I was here to buy something for her. But the shop owner loved to look down on me, and hassled me at every opportunity, anytime I came in on behalf of the woman who'd taken me in.

It's the same song and dance every time.

"One of these days you won't have her to hide behind, mutt," she grumbled but rang up my purchase all the same.

Anger rose in gut, making my fingers tighten into fists and my jaw clench tight.

I'm not a shifter, I wanted to scream but it was easier and safer for everyone to think that. The alternative was far too dangerous for me to even fully contemplate. My wings fluttered at my back quietly, thankfully still glamoured from the sight of prying eyes. I took the bag the woman thrust back at me, then exited the shop without delay.

I need to get home.

I wove through the crowd, careful to keep my wings from brushing against any unsuspecting witches or shifters.

"Watch it," I said as a man bumped into my back. I shivered at the strange pain that came with the move.

Shit, my wings are sensitive today.

"Well, hello there, pretty. I didn't see you there." The man turned to stare at me with a sinister smile as he sniffed the air around me. He was trying to work out what I was, and I couldn't have that.

Not today. Not any day.

I bowed my head and skirted around him, cursing my temper. I should have just kept moving. I should have remained silent.

The man's hand latched around my arm in a bruising grip, stopping me from going any further.

"I don't want any trouble," I ground out between my teeth as a familiar panic welled up inside of me.

His eyes trailed over me as he pulled my hood down. "What are you?" He drew me closer to him.

"I'm none of your concern," I spat like a desperate alley cat and wrenched my arm free of his grip.

"I think you are," he drawled as he reached for me again.

I raced away before he could catch me. Shouts followed me as I pushed through other patrons of the market to escape.

Does he know what I am? How the hell could he smell me like that?

"That shifter girl stole from me," the man bellowed, accusing me from behind. "Stop her!"

Shit, shit, shit.

I rushed through the market, wanting nothing more than to blend in and disappear from sight, but the stranger had caused a stir and more and more witches pointed at me to aid in my capture. There was no love lost between the witches and I, that was for sure and certain.

"I didn't steal anything! He's crazy," I shouted as I passed several women who glared at me and then started screaming to draw attention to me and help the man.

"Freaking witches," I grumbled under my breath before ducking into an alley way.

Several men in black uniforms ran past the opening to the alley.

With no other option, I hid behind a large garbage skip. The scent of rotting garbage made me retch.

Gods, that's disgusting!

I gripped the bag from the apothecary tightly as I stepped out from behind the dumpster and scanned the area for the closest threat.

How do I get out of this mess?

The man who started the chase stepped into the mouth of the alley and grinned at me, blocking off a potential escape route. "You really are a pretty one. You're going to make me some good money." His eyes twinkled with dark mirth as he stepped closer.

"I'm not going to make you anything," I growled at him as I scanned the alley for a second possible exit. There was a fence immediately behind me leading to an alternate alley.

Can I fly over the fence without being seen? He obviously already knows what I am, but what's on the other side? Will humans see me? I can't risk it. Can I?

Something flashed in the man's hand and my eyes widened at the silver weapon.

Is that a gun? Is he going to shoot me with iron?

I shuddered. "Are you going to shoot me?" I asked with a raised brow and a quaver of fear. Being pumped full of iron was not my idea of fun, in fact, for my kind... it could prove lethal.

"This thing?" he asked, flashing me a grin as he waved the gun around. "No, it won't kill you. It will just make you nice and sleepy so I can get you where we're going."

"I'm not going anywhere with you." I sneered and unfurled my wings. He couldn't see them, but it made me feel better to know I could act.

I need to get home. Time is running out!

My mother was waiting for the medicine that I'd bought, and I needed to get it to her before it was too late.

"Oh, but you don't have a choice. Do you know what will happen if the witches see your wings?" he asked with a grin.

My stomach fell as I pulled my wings back to my body in a defensive manner.

He knows what I am, and what the witches will do if they figure it out. Shit.

"You can threaten me all you want, but I can take care of myself," I said, crossing my arms over my chest.

"What if I'm not threatening you?" He asked with a raised brow not unlike my own. "What if all I'm doing is promising you a better life?"

I laughed at his words and pointed to the metal object in his hand. "That looks like enough of a threat to me. I don't need your help or a better life. I'm perfectly fine where I am."

He raised the gun with a frown as if disappointed I'd refused to believe his words.

My gut warned me he had no intention of letting me go. Without further thought I unfurled my wings behind me. I had to take the risk. My freedom was more important than wherever he thought I would have a better life.

Even if I'm outed to the witches, it's still likely a better fate than whatever plans this mercenary has for me.

I crouched down ready to jump into the air. My wings weren't used to flying since I had been forbidden from using them my whole life. But I would use whatever advantage I had to get away from the tranquilizer gun that was pointed squarely at my heart.

"Stop," he shouted and cocked the gun. "I would rather take you in willingly. There are things you should know."

"Bullshit," I said shaking my head. "There's nothing you can tell me that I don't already know—or that I want to know for that matter."

"Really?" He chuckled. "I would have to disagree on that. My employer would very much like to tell you the truth about who and what you are."

I burst into a fit of laughter at his bravado as I bounced on the balls of my feet and jumped into the air.

"Stop," the man shouted, and a soft click sounded a heartbeat later when he pulled the trigger of his weapon.

I soared up above the chain link fence behind me and even higher when a pinch to my shoulder made me flinch. An iron laced dart.

Shit. It got me.

I landed on the dirty concrete at the other end of the alley and stumbled, my head spinning as I leaned against the wall for support.

Don't stop. You have to keep going. He knows where you are.

The mental pep talk barely helped as I desperately tried to shake away the fog from my brain. I took a few unsteady steps forward before gaining my bearings and remembering where I was. I was still inside the wards and only a couple of blocks away from home. I ripped the dart from my shoulder and tossed it aside. The puncture wound would heal soon enough. I'd always healed fast. I just had to act fast.

I can do this!

I pulled my hood back up over my head and slipped out into the bustling crowd, hoping to get lost in the shuffle. I couldn't afford for the man to catch up to me again. I couldn't let him find me—too much was at stake. I needed to get home with the medicine for my mother or I'd be alone in this cruel world. And I sure as shit did not want that.

It only took about fifteen minutes before I finally laid eyes on the quaint little Italian restaurant our apartment sat above. I swayed on my feet as I rounded the corner, heading for the back alley where the fire escape waited. I hauled myself up the ladder, barely able to keep my eyes open. I blinked groggily as the poison of the iron coursed through my system.

How am I going to give Mother her medicine when I can barely keep my eyes open?

With an immense effort I made it onto the small balcony outside our downtown apartment and crawled to the window. My arms were as weak as jelly when I lifted the window and chaotically plunged into the living room. The plush carpet broke my fall, and I groaned wearily as I pushed myself to my knees. I held my head in my hands momentarily as I rubbed my eyes to clear the black spots from my vision.

Just a little while longer. Come on! I need to get the tincture to her.

I dragged myself across the beige carpet of the living room, my sole focus on the door at the end of the hall. My arms shook with exertion, and I slumped to the floor just outside my mother's door.

I'm so weak. I need to sleep.

My vision swirled again as I battled with all my might past the fatigue and strained valiantly for the door handle. To my dismay, I came up short and lost the battle. My eyes closed again and then there was nothing.

6

THE SOUND OF A MUFFLED moan woke me up, and my eyes shot open.

How long have I been asleep and why am I on the floor in the hallway?

My brain was fuzzy as my gaze hit the cream-colored door of my mother's bedroom and my fist tightened, crinkling the small plastic bag in my hand.

The tincture. Shit. Is Mother, okay?

Another muffled moan sounded, and I winced, pulling myself to my feet. "Mother?" I called through the door as I managed to crack it open. The room was dark, just as I left it.

My mother's still form was on the bed.

I took two large steps in her direction holding out the medicine for her but stopped short.

How long was I out because of that tranquilizer? Is she okay?

Mother's chest wasn't rising and falling like it should and pain lanced through my chest, sudden and sharp, stealing my breath away.

No, she can't be gone! She's the only person I have in the world.

Tears blurred my vision as I sat heavily on the edge of her bed, my shoulders sinking. She hadn't been a great mother to me by any stretch of the imagination. Truthfully, I'd been little more than a slave to her, but she had shielded me from those who would have wanted me dead—or for even more nefarious purposes.

Like that man in the market.

I hunched over her body, her skin cold to the touch, and whispered the words of the witches last rites. I hated that she was gone. And it was my fault! If I hadn't gotten caught by that man in the market... she still might be here.

If I ever see him again, I will kill him where he stands.

As I sat gazing at the only mother I'd ever known, it occurred to me she wouldn't have wanted me to waste time. In a circumstance such as this she would have encouraged me to run from those who would suspect me of foul play in her death. She'd often told me that if something were to ever happen to her, I needed to run far and fast.

As tears coursed down my cheeks, I resolved myself to action. It would not do to dwell here and grieve. It would achieve nothing, yet risk everything.

Mother might not have given birth to me, but she had found me and saved me. She'd given me a roof over my head, food, and clothing... and I would not dishonor her memory. I refused to be caught, killed, or used. I would run for my life. I would finally be free, because that's all she had wanted for me. So, for both of our sakes I had to try.

I wiped the tears from my eye as I whispered one last prayer, hoping it would take her into the afterlife, before turning and leaving the room. I didn't know where I was going or how I would survive—but I would. I would do it for her, the one person who ever cared that I could be more than I was perceived to be. Or I would die trying.

As the last of the tranquilizer wore off, I jumped to my feet and marched into the small room that I called my own. It wasn't really a bedroom. It was more of a closet with blankets and some clothes stacked on the floor... but it had been mine. With renewed determination I packed my bag and got ready to leave.

Someone pounded on the front door.

Bang. Bang. Bang.

Shit. Did someone see me? Are they here to take me away?

My head swiveled and I glanced between the front door and my bedroom window, indecision warring within me. In no time flat my own self-preservation won out just as Mother would have wanted. As swiftly and as quietly as I was able, I opened the window, climbing down the narrow, old fire escape and toward an uncertain freedom.

With nowhere to go and little clue of what I was going to do to sustain myself, I had no choice but to run for my life. I could only flee and hope that I'd figure it all out along the way with a wing and a prayer.

Chapter 2

Grey

"WHAT DO YOU MEAN YOU lost her?" I growled at the half-fae bounty hunter standing in front of me.

"She flew out of the alley. She didn't want to be caught." He paced back and forth in front of me, grunting and muttering, and generally carrying on like an idiot.

The scent of his fear permeated the room, nearly making me gag. I leaned back in my chair and tilted my head back, trying to evade the odor so the smell wasn't so bad.

I need patience to deal with idiots. I can't just kill my best bounty hunter.

"Explain to me how an untrained girl got away from you?" I demanded as calmly as I was able. I just couldn't wrap my damn head around it. My people were all well trained—I made sure of it when I brought them in. I didn't waste time with recruits that showed a lack of potential or didn't have some innate ability worth honing like a sharp blade.

"She's not just any untrained girl, Boss. She looks like she's been hiding in plain sight her whole life," he said on a groan.

"How is that even possible?" I wondered aloud.

How does a powerful fae go unnoticed for years, especially among witches and shifters?

"No clue, but I watched her go into an apothecary shop, talk to the staff, and come out with a bag before I was able to confirm what she was." He took a seat, flopping down into the leather chair across from my desk.

Shit. Who is this girl and how do we find her?

A knock sounded on the door.

"Come in," I called, annoyed at the interruption.

"Boss, they're ready for you in the ring," Layla my second-in-command said as she opened the door into my private office.

I stood and buttoned up my suit jacket with a sigh. "Find out everything you can about that girl. I want to know where she has been and who she is by the end of the day," I barked at the bounty-hunter before he scurried from the room to complete his mission.

"Possible new recruit?" Layla asked as she walked by my side through the door.

"Not a possible recruit. She evaded Dan of all people. But she'll work for me one way or another." I stabbed at the button to the elevator.

"You really think you can force her hand?" Layla asked with a raised brow.

The elevator dinged and I stepped inside clenching my fists.

She will come work for me. I won't take no for an answer.

"We'll make sure she is so desperate that she has no other choice," I grunted, crossing my arms as I leaned back against the gleaming wall of the elevator.

"Are you sure that's wise?" Layla pressed, hitting the button for the basement level.

"Are you questioning my authority, Layla?" I turned my glare of annoyance on her. No-one was allowed to question my authority, ever.

Layla's back stiffened and her fear filled the small elevator. "No, Boss. I'm just wondering if that is the right choice, especially if you want the girl to trust you and remain loyal to you."

I sighed, repressing my last nerve. "What do you suggest then?" I asked.

"Have Dan watch her for a couple of days and find out more about her. Then pursue her from there. You don't want to jump the gun and go off half-cocked," she answered as she stepped out of the elevator.

The florescent lights of the basement made me wince. My eyesight was too keen for such harsh lighting, but I needed to be here. It helped boost morale when the boss showed up for challenges.

The large group of supernaturals in the underground space grew quiet at our entrance. Whispers filled the air, but at least the noise level was now bearable to my over-sensitive hearing.

"Who do we have today and what's the grievance?" I asked, my tone one of business-like boredom.

"One of the trolls was disrespected by a shifter and called the challenge." Layla sighed.

"Why am I here over something so petty?" I grumbled and moved closer to the ring.

It's going to be an absolute bloodbath.

The trolls were notoriously stupid and had little magic of their own at their disposal, but what they lacked in magic they more than made up for with brute physical strength.

With my fighting ring canceling out magic, it affected them the least of all the supernaturals.

"It will be a good fight." Layla shrugged, viewing it from a purely logistical standpoint.

She wasn't wrong there. Shifters could still shift inside the ring, so the two would be somewhat evenly matched.

Layla stepped forward and into the ring, then put her hands up to get the attention of the supernaturals in the room. "You know the rules. Once you step into the ring you will not be able to use your magic. If you step out of the ring, you lose the challenge. We don't need anyone to die today, but we go until someone is unable to continue or until someone steps out of the ring," Layla called to the gathered crowd, then waved both contestants into the ring.

I took a seat in the front row, resting my elbow on the arm rest and propping up my chin. I should have been out searching for the fairy that had managed to elude Dan, or up in my sleek office planning the next job. I had artifacts to find and no one who was qualified enough to locate them for me.

The troll and the shifter stepped into the ring and the troll roared out his challenge. The crowd erupted in cheers as the shifter turned into a Siberian tiger.

"The troll challenged Karma?" I asked Layla as she sat down next to me. "Interesting." I leaned forward in my chair, a little more intrigued by the fight now that I recognized our best fighter. The troll *had* to know what he was getting himself into—facing off against a half-witch-half-white-tiger-shifter. And if he didn't, he'd soon learn the hard way.

The troll charged, clearly tired of the formalities, one meaty fist raised in the air as he swung out at the tiger.

Karma easily dodged the blow with her feline grace and flexibility and slashed at the troll's side, opening him up with her razor-sharp claws.

He bellowed in pain as his blood sprayed all over Karma's glorious white fur.

She backed away, skulking then dodging the troll's grasp as he attempted to wrap them around her neck.

"He's too slow." I sighed. "How did he expect to beat Karma with nothing but brute strength? I was hoping he might have a brain cell in that thick skull of his, an idea for tactics perhaps."

Stupid troll is going to die because of his ego.

"We don't need supernaturals like that in the Syndicate," I finished telling Layla with a frown.

"He's a good bodyguard for hire." She shrugged, never taking her eyes from the fight.

A roar filled the air bringing my attention back to the fight.

Karma shook her head as if to clear it and leapt away from the troll's hands once more. She'd clearly copped a blow, but she was just toying with him, like a cat with a mouse.

"Karma just needs to end this already," I said, increasingly irritated, my mind straying elsewhere. I glanced down at my watch, bored with this game she was playing. I didn't have time to burn.

Dan better have information for me soon.

I snapped my gaze back up to the fight as yelling broke out, filling the arena.

Karma had the troll's head lodged firmly between her huge jaws, her enormous, bloodied canines clamped down around his skull ready to finalize the kill.

The troll was slapping the ground, tapping out.

Ugh. Weakness.

I shook my head in disgust and rose from my seat, waving to Layla. *I was done with this bullshit.* "Take him to the cells. He needs to understand the punishment for showing weakness in the Syndicate," I said with venom. I kept only the best.

Layla gave me an affirmative nod as she ran off to do as I commanded.

I dusted imaginary lint from my jacket and turned back to the elevator, checking my phone along the way. We didn't actually get service in the basement, even with the amount of magic we had down here, but if I didn't have a voicemail from Dan by the time I arrived back up in my office... we were going to have a *problem*.

I stabbed at the button for my private elevator and walked in the doors. Then I pushed the button for my floor and rode it to the top of the building. The elevator's *ding* caught my attention just before the doors opened. I strode down the hall to my office and slammed the door behind me, releasing a breath of relief. Silence. Blessed, beautiful silence. My oversensitive hearing could only take so much. The cheering and hollering had been headache inducing.

The shrill ring of my phone made me groan, the irony not lost on me, and I picked it up. "What is it, Dan?" I asked shortly, pinching the bridge of my nose between my fingers.

"I went to the apothecary and asked about the girl," he informed me hesitantly.

"And?" I ground out. I didn't have time to dance around the truth.

Get to the point! I need this girl working for me. I need her now.

"The apothecary said that she's the foster kid of a well-known witch. She gave me the address, but..." he trailed off.

"Dan, if you don't fucking get to the point I'm locking you in the cells for a bloody week on principle," I growled.

"I went to the address," he said quickly. "But there were cops all over the place and a woman was being taken out on a stretcher—dead."

I grinned.

I don't even have to make sure she's desperate. She's already lost the only person who ever cared for her.

"And where was the girl? Was she there?" I asked.

"She's not here, Boss. I think she got spooked when her caregiver died," he said with a disappointed grunt.

"Do you have a name?" I growled.

"I'll, ah, I'll just text it to you, boss," he said, a note of worried in his tone.

Is he being watched? He better not let anything come between me and this fae girl.

"Find her. She can't have gotten far. I doubt she has money or anything of value that could help her. She's going to need the Syndicate. Whether she likes it or not," I said and hung up the phone.

I sat in the chair behind my desk smirking to myself as I opened my laptop. The news about the passing of an influential witch and her ward going missing would already, no doubt, be hitting supe social media.

As soon as Dan texted me the girl's name, I could put out an official order. No one would ignore the king of the Syndicate, that was certain. My word was beyond reproach.

A text came through within seconds.

Aurelia.

I almost salivated as I read the name, tasting it on my tongue like a fine liqueur.

Aurelia is an exquisite name.

I loved it. Without a further second to lose, I got to work on social media. It wasn't regular social media, where anyone could join though. It was my very own encrypted network of supes that would put the word out for me quickly. If anyone saw her, I would be informed. And I made sure that *no one* would dare offer her work or a place to stay. She was mine.

I grinned and sat back in my seat with a self-satisfied smile. It paid to be the king of the Syndicate, but I'd earned my position with blood and an iron-will. No one would cross me, especially not when the stakes were so high. No one would be that foolish. No one who valued their life, at least. The fae girl would soon be mine. I could almost feel it. And I would ensure she remained so—one way or another.

Chapter 3

Aurelia

NO ONE IN THE SUPE areas of the city would help me. Shifters and witches alike could sense that I was different somehow but couldn't pinpoint what it was. It made them feel uneasy around me and bred a natural suspicion that I wasn't able to change. To say it was beyond frustrating to live this way was an understatement.

I walked into yet another supe run motel, this one seedier than the last few I'd tried, and prayed to whatever gods were listening that they would deign to give me a room for the night.

"We don't serve your kind here," the man behind the counter grunted, his face down in a book. He was a shifter, but I couldn't tell what sort.

"And what exactly is my kind?" I asked indignantly as my patience wore thin.

Surely this shifter can't tell what I am.

"Your kind means pampered princesses who aren't shifters," he sneered at me. He sat forward in his chair; his hawk-like nose turned up in disgust.

"Pampered princess?" I scoffed.

What is this shifter's deal? Pampered princess? Yeah, right. I've been practically a slave to my foster mother.

My eyes watered at the thought of her lying cold in her bed as I escaped out the window. I wish I'd had more time to attend to her.

I hope someone gave her the rites that she deserved.

"That's all you heard, girl? You didn't hear me say you aren't a shifter?" He shook his head and waved me off without further argument.

I turned to leave, crestfallen, angry, and tired as all hell.

Turned down again. Rejected again.

He spoke up again unexpectedly as I turned my back. "Wait, come here," he sighed. "What's your name, girl?"

"Aurelia," I answered even though it was probably a bad idea to answer quite so truthfully. Who knew if people were looking for me to ask questions about my mother's death?

"Aurelia, huh? Okay Aurelia, this one night I'll make an exception for you." He nodded and grabbed a key from the wall.

I frowned at him in confusion at his sudden change of heart, but stepped forward anyway, not about to turn down the offer of a place to sleep for the night.

Is this a trap? Am I going to wake up to police at my door or other bad characters like the man from the market?

I shook my head to clear the intrusive thoughts. I couldn't keep thinking about all that *could* happen when my eyes drooping. I was running out of steam fast and desperately needed somewhere to sleep. This was the only place that would give me a room, so as far as I saw it, I had little choice in the matter if I wanted some semblance of safety.

Sleeping on the street is not an option.

Tomorrow, I would have to make money somehow and find a new place to stay, because I doubted this offer would be extended; and remaining in the same place when I was being hunted was not a wise move. But at least for tonight I could have some rest and grieve my mother and the sense of security I had that went with her.

I handed the man some cash to cover the room rate.

He accepted it with a grimace before handing me a key. "Check out is at eleven. I better not see you again until then. Keep a low profile, you hear?"

I grabbed the key with a curt nod before heading back out the door and around the building. It was a normal door key, the kind that had been used for centuries, and not one of those fancy electronic keycards most places used these days. I followed the numbers on the wall until I found a room with the number that matched mine.

The key stuck in the door and I had to jiggle it carefully, so it didn't break. When I finally managed to get it open the musty aroma of the motel room washed over me and I sighed heavily. It wasn't the best place I'd ever stayed, but I couldn't fathom whether it was the worst either, since I had so few memories of where I grew up before coming to live with Mother.

The bed was bigger than I was used to but being that I was used to sleeping on a pile of blankets on the floor it came as no surprise. I flopped down onto the bed—exhausted—and sneezed as dust flew up from the comforter.

If the place is this unused, then why'd he get so huffy about my kind being here? You'd think he'd gladly take my money at the first opportunity.

I shook my head. There really was no point in trying to figure out other people's prejudices, especially when it came to what I was. I just needed a place to rest and regroup.

Surely someone will be willing to help me until I figure out what I'm going to do?

Standing up again, I pulled the comforter off the bed and dropped it in a pile on the floor in the corner before cranking the air-conditioner. It was warm even in the evenings in Dallas during the summer and I had no intention of suffering any more than I absolutely had to; I'd already paid for the room, so its amenities were mine to use.

I sat back down on the bed and pulled my small bag closer. Everything I had in the whole world fit into one small backpack.

Pathetic. I am pathetic.

I fished out an old T-shirt to sleep in. It was far too big and easily covered all of me in case something happened, and I was forced to run. Pushing the thought from my mind, I wandered into the cramped bathroom and turned on the shower, eager to be rid of the sweat and grime of my panicked brush with danger and my very fortunate escape.

Even turned all the way to scalding hot, the water only achieved maybe lukewarm at best.

It will have to do.

I stripped down and stepped under the tepid spray. It does little to help unlock my tired, tense muscles the way it would have if I was at home, and the thought brings tears to my eyes. The only mother I had ever known was dead. She may not have been particularly kind to me, she may not have even loved me, but she had protected me.

I let the tears fall, allowing myself the emotional release to cry for tonight. I permitted myself to be weak in this tiny, dingy motel room because when I left here, I would need to be strong. This sad, musty hovel would be the only place that bore witness to my weakness and fragility. After this, I'd pull it together—somehow—because I had to.

I tilted my head back into the spray, wetting my hair only to realize I hadn't thought to pack my shampoo or other essentials when I left in my frantic hurry.

Damn it.

Cleansing myself as best I could, I shut the water off and reached for the scratchy towel, eyeing it with disdain and cringing. I didn't trust it and decided to use my air magic to dry myself instead. Warm air caressed my skin, and I sighed in relief as my hair dried almost instantly. It was a little wild without any of my hair products, but I couldn't do anything about it at this point in time.

I pulled the large T-shirt over my head and twisted my hair up into a messy bun. It would have to do.

An unexpected knock on the door made me jump, then freeze on the spot.

Who could that be? The shifter at the front desk was serious when he said he didn't want to see me until morning.

I moved instantly into action and shoved my meagre belongings back into my bag without a second's hesitation and scanned the room for another viable exit.

Do I have to jump out another window today?

I slunk quietly around the room, and over to the drab curtains in front of the window. I peeked out the side and into the darkening night. It was eerily still outside but another knock came at the door, more urgent and insistent this time.

Shit. What am I going to do?

Reaching for the window I tried and failed to pull it open. The damn thing was stuck tight, the old wooden frame no doubt swollen into place with age and the damp. Could I use my magic to force it open? What if I broke it? Would I have the motel's landlord chasing me then, too?

"Aurelia, I know you're in there. I just want to talk," someone shouted through the locked door.

I would recognize that voice anywhere. It's the man from the market.

I clenched my fists and pushed down the sudden surge of rage that threatened to boil over. This wasn't the time to lash out at the man who'd inadvertently caused my mother's death. Revenge wasn't worth the risk of being recaptured. I blew out a breath to control my heaving emotions and drew my air magic to me in an attempt to push the window open, but it still wouldn't budge.

Fuck!

"No point in trying the window, Aurelia. I have the place surrounded," the man called out again, clearly ahead of the game.

"Why surround the motel if you just want to talk?" I shouted back at him; angry that he'd somehow found out not only who I was, but where I was staying.

"You have proven slippery, but it doesn't have to be this way. Open the door so we can talk. I know what happened today," he said, his tone softer this time.

Who cares if I break out a window?

There was no way I was trusting that guy. And every second I delayed my escape was a step closer to becoming who knows what?

Someone's slave or whore? Worse?

A shudder rippled through me. I wasn't about to hang around to find out. I let my magic fill me like a storming tempest and a cyclone of air smashed at the window, answering my summons. Shattering glass filled the air around me and shards hit the grimy floor like tinkling diamonds.

"Shit," the man yelled and shouldered his way through the door. "Aurelia, don't! You have nowhere else to go."

"Anywhere is better than wherever you want to take me!" I spat before directing the cyclone toward him. It tore through the room upending furniture as if it were nothing more than kindling and kicked up all the dust as it barreled at its intended target with surprising velocity.

He dived to the side at the last second, narrowly escaping major injury.

I clambered up on the windowsill and leaped out into the humid night air. He was right about one thing. I had nowhere else to go, but I would die before I went with him. My bare feet slapped against the concrete, a jarring sensation racing up my leg. Pain sliced through my tender flesh as glass crunched beneath me.

Fucking ow!

I feverishly brushed the bloodied glass from my feet and sprinted into the night, my poor feet throbbing with each desperate lunge toward freedom. I didn't dare attempt to fly like last time. I would be drawing enough attention to myself simply running through the shifter side of Dallas in an over-sized T-shirt without shoes.

My wings fluttered uselessly at my back, and I tucked them in tighter to me so they wouldn't slow my pace. I ducked down a side street and paused briefly to catch my breath and listen for anyone following me. The night was uncomfortably silent, and the offensive odor of rotting garbage hit me like a freight train, causing me to gag.

Where is he? I know he's still following me.

With my heart pounding in my chest, I chanced peeking around the corner and scanned the street. It was silent. There wasn't a single soul in sight, but I couldn't allow myself to lower my guard or be fooled into a false sense of security like I had at the hotel. I had to keep moving.

Like a thief in the night, I rushed down the side street as silently as I could. I urgently had to get to the human part of the city. No supes would bother me there and I'd heard humans were oblivious to what was right under their noses—so I'd likely be able to fly under the radar there, to speak. The only problem was I had never left the supe side of the city.

How do I even get there?

At the end of the street, lights blared overhead, and I winced. It would be safer to get away from the man who was chasing me, but the way I was dressed would raise all kinds of red flags to anyone who was around and gave me so much as a second glance.

I quickly stepped behind a dumpster and dug through my bag for a pair of leggings and my flip flops. They would be hell to run in but at least they were shoes. I put them on as fast as I could and peeked out into the brightly lit street.

There were people milling around and a bar down the block with patrons spilling out on to the street, talking, and laughing among themselves. It would be the perfect place to get lost in the crowd and plan my next move. It would afford me the luxury of a little time in the very least.

I drew my wings in even tighter to my back, making sure that my glamour was still firmly in place. Then I took a deep breath and stepped out onto the busy street, weaving my way through the crowd and trying my best not to let my wings brush against anyone like I had earlier today.

I kept surreptitiously peeking over my shoulder and scanning the area behind me for any sign of danger. My nervous gaze searched for the man who had ruined my life; the strange who refused to give up his search for me.

What the hell is his deal? Why does he keep looking for me?

I turned around too late and walked right into a brick wall. Well, not an actual brick wall, but the man's chest that I faceplanted into sure as hell felt like it.

"Ow," I said and grabbed my sore nose to soothe the smarting hurt.

"I'm sorry," a rich voice apologized.

I glanced up and into the most mesmerizing blue eyes I'd ever seen. "No, I'm sorry. I wasn't paying attention," I said and chanced a peek over my shoulder again.

A familiar face pushed through the crowd, my eyes widened in shock and dismay.

"Are you okay?" The handsome man enquired, his eyebrows creasing in concern.

"Yes, I'm fine. I'm sorry, I have to go." I tried to rush past him, but he sidestepped into my path.

"What's the rush? Are you in some kind of trouble?" he asked, looking me up and down.

Damn it! Yeah, my clothes completely give it away.

"No, I'm fine. I just really need to go." I glanced over my shoulder again, my heart ready to leap into my throat.

My pursuer was stuck in the crowd but was getting closer every second.

I turned back to those bright blue eyes and groaned. His eyes weren't on me, but over my head, no doubt seeing the man pursuing me most likely.

"I'm sorry. I really need to go," I stressed.

But the blue-eyed brick wall refused to budge. "Let me give you a ride. It's dangerous to walk the streets at night," he said stepping closer to me.

"I'm tougher than I look," I said with a small smile and turned away, my cheeks heating with a blush.

Why am I embarrassed? He's just a man. A gorgeous man with ebony hair that's a little too long and the bluest eyes I have ever seen—but still just a man.

"Please, I insist. I can't in good conscience step aside. My name is Grey," He offered with a dazzling grin as he touched my arm.

"Aurelia," I said as if in a daze and to my own shock I allowed him to lead me away. He seemed protective and well-mannered, and he wasn't *that* guy. What choice did I have? Perhaps the devil I didn't know was better than the one I did?

Shit! What am I thinking? What am I going to do now? He's going to know within minutes that I have nowhere to go! Then what?

So much for having time to figure out my next move...

Chapter 4

Grey

MY SHOULDERS STIFFENED and I drew a surprised shallow breath at the shocking realization of just *what* this fairy was to me. My mind reeled and my whole world view shifted in a single, powerful heartbeat.

Mate.

I peered over my shoulder at Dan and gave him an imperceptible shake of my head as I moved my hand from Aurelia's arm to the small of her back.

She shivered at the contact but didn't step away.

What is that all about?

I couldn't see or feel her wings. Were they out all the time and simply glamoured? Or was it my touch that made her shiver?

"Aurelia, that's a beautiful name," I said with a what I hoped was a comforting and trustworthy smile. "Where are you headed?"

She chewed her lower lip and stared at the ground, clearly uncomfortable. She fidgeted with her hands, wringing them together as if anxious. "I don't know," she whispered. She blinked her big, beautiful green eyes up at me. Tears filled them in an instant, but she set her expression and refused to let them fall.

Our mate is strong, my wolf said in my head.

"Were you just going to wander around the streets of Dallas all night?" I asked, the edge of a growl in my tone unmistakable. I couldn't bear to think she'd be out here, alone, unprotected, and without simple amenities such as food and shelter. It made my stomach lurch.

"I hadn't planned on it. I *had* a place, but I can't go back there now." She frowned, then glared at me with indignation. She wasn't about to stand being called stupid, literally or otherwise.

Her honest reaction made the edges of my lips curl in amusement. It had been literally countless years and years since anyone had dared to look at me like that. "What happened?" I asked.

I know exactly what happened because I sent Dan there to find you. I should have known I'd have to do the job myself.

She was a tricky little thing, far more adept at taking care of herself than I'd given her credit for, and after what had happened in the market today? I should have expected she would try and run from Dan again.

So much for being my best! He's about as subtle as a sledgehammer...

"Nothing," she sighed, licking her lips. "I just can't go back."

"I know of a place that helps people with nowhere else to go," I offered with a shrug, playing at nonchalant. But in reality, I was hanging on her every word. I needed to play this just right if I was going to win her trust. And my wolf would never forgive me if I fucked that up!

"No, that's okay. Really. I'll find somewhere else to go. I'm nothing if not determined." She shook her head and stepped away from me.

I dropped my hand and shook my head, taking my lead from her body language. "I can't leave you out on the streets to fend for yourself. You might be stronger than you look, but the shifters will smell the desperation on you nonetheless."

Aurelia's eyes widened and she gasped, her face paling. She turned her head left, then right, scanning the area for an escape.

My nostrils flared and my wolf beat at my chest from within, excited for a chase. Her instincts screamed at her run, and her fear smelled divine—not *rank* like that of my underlings. With a decidedly concerted effort I schooled my expression to be as neutral as possible, but with my heart hammering away in my chest and adrenaline zinging along my veins with the power of unbridled lightning, it wasn't easy by any stretch of the imagination.

"You're a supe," Aurelia breathed, wringing her hands together more aggressively as her panic reached a fever pitch.

"I am." I nodded, taking a tentative step toward her. I could almost feel the betrayal in her eyes. She'd been hoping I was human, someone safe, oblivious, and easy to brush off when she saw fit.

"Are you with the man chasing me?" she demanded, her voice shaking as she took another step back, which only served to excite my wolf more.

"Stop, Aurelia. I'm barely holding it together and if you run, my wolf will give chase." I held my hands up in mock surrender, willing her listen, to comply to my wishes. I took a large step away from her even though it killed me to do so, affording her the illusion of choice.

"Are you with him?" she bit out between gritted teeth, determined to ascertain the truth.

She's bold. I'll give her that.

"No," I lied. And technically it wasn't a lie. My bounty hunter hadn't known I would be here, and I genuinely hadn't planned on running into the beautiful fairy either. I'd either gotten lucky, or there was an element of fate at play.

"But you knew I was being chased," she pressed. "I watched you look at him over my head." Aurelia crossed her arms over her chest, innocently pushing her breasts up in her ratty, old, over-sized T-shirt.

I swallowed a groan at the sight of nipples peaking against the washed-out fabric. My cock stiffened to the point of pain as she stood before me, oblivious to the effect she was having on me. The leggings and baggy T-shirt did nothing to hide her generous curves from my hungry eyes.

My wolf howled his agreement in my head. He wanted to sink his teeth into her and make her ours. In fact, he wanted to devour her—and in more ways than one.

Not yet, we need her. Don't scare her off! We must exercise restraint.

"I *did* know you were being chased," I admitted. "I'm not blind, nor am I an idiot. I make it a point to be an observant man. It's why I can't let you roam Dallas by yourself tonight. Let me help you," I said softly. I stared down into her eyes and hoped she would be able to recognize my plea.

Please, do not make me chase you.

I didn't want to be the monster she saw Dan as being. And if my wolf had anything to say about Aurelia's role in our future, she would become much more to me than just a means to an end. She would be our mate.

Shit. This is not how I saw all of this playing out.

"I can take care of myself," Aurelia said curtly. "I've escaped him twice today already and I'll do it again if I have to."

"But why is he after you?" I asked.

"I don't know," Aurelia admitted more softly.

"Why would you run if you don't even know what he wants?" I asked with a frown.

He never got the chance to tell her what he wanted? Which meant she wasn't running from the Syndicate, specifically...

She stared at me like I was a goddamned idiot.

That's new.

No one dared look at me the way this fiery woman just did. Not only was she tricky and determined, but she had real courage. She was at every disadvantage there could be right now, and she was still doing her best to doggedly hold her own.

"I'm a woman, for starters, which is a peril in and of itself," she quipped. "And on top of that, no one seems to know what I am; so, when someone figures it out, I bolt. It's safer that way." She shrugged as if that explained everything and turned away from me. She quickly scanned the signs on the cross street we were standing at and stormed down the street to our right without so much as a glance back.

"Aurelia, wait!" I jogged down the street after her.

We're not letting go of her that easily, I promised my wolf when he started rumbling his concern at her rapid departure.

"What did you mean by that?"

"Nothing," Aurelia called over her shoulder, never slowing her pace.

Tamping my wolf's possessive instincts down was trying my patience by the time I finally caught up and touched her arm. Tingles of undeniable pleasure erupted up my spine, sizzling like electricity and I groaned. "Just let me help you," I bit out. "I can give you safety and a job."

"I don't need your pity *or* your charity, thank you," Aurelia said with surprising anger as she spun to poke me in the chest.

"It's not either of those things," I growled in frustration.

Gods this woman is stubborn!

Aurelia flinched away as if stung, her eyes flashing.

I hung my head, breathing deeply to calm myself and my desperate wolf. If I let my alpha dominance out too aggressively, she'd run for the hills. I had to reign it in—fast—or I'd lose her.

"Bullshit, Grey. I'm not a charity case and certainly not yours. I can do this on my own." She spun on her heel and rushed away again.

This fairy was seriously beginning to try my patience. But what choice did I have? My wolf had recognized her as our mate. So, I did the only thing

I could, I ran after her. Blocking her path, I planted my feet and raised my hands in a placating gesture. "At least let me take you somewhere safe to explain my offer. You can think about it overnight and if you are still genuinely not interested, then you can go. Simple as that."

I had no idea what possessed me to offer such a deal to her. There was no way in hell my wolf would ever let her go now he'd caught her scent. I might need her for a job, but he needed her for very different reasons entirely.

Aurelia chewed her lip nervously and her shoulders slumped, dark circles of fatigue visible under her lovely green eyes. "Do you swear that you won't call the police or sell me to someone who will run tests on me?" She crossed her arms over her ample breasts again awaiting my answer.

I had to avert my gaze, before lifting it back to meet her eyes.

This is going to be an exercise in restraint.

"Why would I sell you to be experimented on?" I frowned at her.

Who has been filling her head with this rubbish? We don't experiment on our own people. And if anyone does and I find out about it? They'll be shut down immediately!

"That's why I have to hide!" she said with exasperation. "People hate my kind." She looked away, obviously not wanting to elaborate further on exactly what she was.

"Supes don't experiment on each other, at least not that I have ever heard." I shook my head, equally exasperated. "That would be a disgusting breach of faith between the supe species, and I wouldn't sentence my worst enemy to such a fate."

Aurelia's green gaze slammed into mine at the vehemence behind my words. "All right," she conceded with a heavy swallow. "But I *will* leave if I don't like what you have to say." She raised a brow at me as if to test my oath.

"Of course, I would never hold you against your will. I just want to make sure you're safe tonight and then we'll go from there." I nodded and steered her back the way we came.

"Why do you care?" she asked moving away from me so I couldn't touch her back.

"I told you. I help supernaturals that have nowhere to go. It's what I do. I give them purpose." It wasn't the whole truth, but she didn't need to know the nitty gritty details until she chose of her own free will to join me.

We walked the several blocks to the high-rise which housed my penthouse apartment. I opened the exterior door for her and led her inside, instinctively reaching for her.

She shivered at my hand on her back but kept an artfully blank mask in place.

My wolf whimpered inside me as I contemplated just what kind of life our mate had led up until this point to be so closed-off and independent. I pushed my wolf back down and pulled my keycard from my pocket. I absently slid it over the scanner of my private elevator like I'd done thousands of times before.

She raised an eyebrow at me but stepped inside without protest. A second later Aurelia frowned as the doors closed us in, confining us to an intimate space. There was nowhere she could run. For now, she was trapped whether she liked it or not.

I hit the button for the penthouse, and we rode the elevator in silence.

Aurelia jumped, spooked by the sound when the elevator *dinged* in the quiet space. She smelled like literal heaven, but the scent of her was causing my cock to harden again.

The mate bond between us could be strong, my wolf panted as desire swelled within us.

Heel. We must wait.

I needed to focus on what lay ahead but being in such forced proximity with her made me want to shove her up against the wall and fuck her until we both shattered into a million jagged pieces, like a chandelier smashing into diamond shards on a gleaming ballroom floor. We'd be picking up the fragments of ourselves for weeks.

Her eyes widened as we stepped from the elevator and directly into my living room.

I led her to my plush, black leather couch and waved a hand dismissively for her to sit.

"What am I doing here, Grey?" she asked, scanning my apartment with furtive eyes, like prey assessing an area for potential escape opportunities.

My head spun with the possibilities just hearing my name on her lips. Her lilting tone made it sound exotic. And in an instant, I knew I wanted nothing more than to hear her crying it out, again and again, as I drove myself deep inside her fairy warmth.

My name will be her prayer.

I cleared my throat and the sordid imagery from my mind by sheer force of will. "I thought you might be more comfortable here while you decide whether to take me up on my offer." I shrugged Before I made my way over to the oak bar in the corner of the living space and poured us each a stiff drink. "I have an idea of what you are," I said carefully. "But I want to hear it from you." I casually set one of the glasses in front of her.

Aurelia frowned at the amber liquid in the glass and licked her lips, a sign of her anxiety. "I've never told anyone other than Mother what I am." She chewed her lip as she picked up the glass and sniffed it tentatively. With a grimace, she set the glass back on the table untouched.

"It's just something to help with your nerves, would you prefer something else? Water perhaps?" I asked.

She nodded with a small smile. "Thank you," she said as she blushed and looked away—as if somewhat disarmed by the small demonstration of kindness.

"I understand how difficult it must be for you to trust anyone with what you've evidently been told about supes," I said, moving back to the bar and fetching a bottle of cold water from the mini fridge.

"Everything she ever did was to protect me," she whispered in response, so low even I almost didn't hear it.

"Did?" I asked strolling back to the couch and handing her the water.

"I didn't come here to give you my life story," she said, raising her defenses once more. "You said you had an offer for me," she continued, deflecting the question.

I would have been surprised by her reaction except for the fact that I knew the truth. Her mother had just died yesterday. The turmoil she was going through was obvious and still very raw. "I do, but first I need you to tell me what you are." I sat back on the couch and swirled my drink; happy to wait her out until she broke and divulged.

She took a long drink of her water, clenched her jaw, and glared at me as she set the bottle back down. "Fine," she snapped. "Have it your way. I'm an evil spiteful fairy. Is that what you wanted to hear? Are you going to turn me over to some supernatural testing facility now so they can tear off my wings and siphon my blood for its magic?" She jumped to her feet and rounded the table to the elevator.

Jesus-fucking-Christ!

"No," I said sternly. "I already told you that such hell holes don't exist, and I *don't* think you're evil, Aurelia. You simply have a specific skillset that I need. So, I would like to offer you a job." I stood and blocked her path. "This was not our deal," I reminded her. "You promised to hear me out."

"Fine," she huffed as if she rather be anywhere else in the world. "What kind of job do you have for an evil trickster fae?" She planted her hands on her hips in a silent, attitude-filled challenge.

"Only the trickiest," I retorted with a grin, knowing I had her undivided attention for what felt like the first time.

"And what does that mean pray tell?" She frowned.

This fairy has a quick temper!

"Have you ever heard of the Syndicate?" I asked, cocking a brow in question.

She gasped, taking a step back. "Do you work for the Syndicate?" she asked warily, her gaze back to scanning the room for any possible escape beyond the elevator.

"I don't work for the Syndicate, Aurelia."

She relaxed slightly at those words, but it was a false sense of comfort at best.

I dropped the truth on her like a bomb nailing its target. "I *am* the Syndicate."

"Explain," she demanded in a shaky voice as she took yet another uncertain step back from me.

My wolf perked up again, begging for a chase.

"I told you. My name is Grey, and I own the Syndicate. And the truth is I have been looking for you for a *very* long time—for a job that only *you* can do." I held her gaze as her eyes widened in surprise.

This has to work. I need her to do this for me or I'm back to square one. And I refuse to be this close to my goal and have to start all over again.

My heart raced and my mind whirled. This was it. The pinnacle of my destiny. The point of no return upon which all my hard work hung, precarious as a knife edge and as fragile as a butterfly wing.

She has to agree... because I really don't want to have to force her.

My inner wolf howled.

Chapter 5

Aurelia

SHIT. SHIT. SHIT! I knew I shouldn't have come here.

My anger and panic spiked, and my magic rose to the surface unbidden as my wings spread wide behind me. "You're just like everyone else!" I cried, my voice breaking with emotion.

He just wants to own me... use me! What happens when I'm no longer useful? Will he sell me to the highest bidder? Turn me over to face the communal justice of the witches or shifters who loathed me with every fiber of their being? I can't trust him.

"Aurelia, you need to calm down," Grey said softly, his brilliant blue eyes wide as he held out his hands in placation.

I frowned.

Why is he acting wary all of a sudden?

I followed his line of sight and glanced down at my own hands. "Shit! What that the hell is this?"

A blazing purple ball of living magic swirled just above my palm and my heart leaped in my chest at the startling and unexpected sight.

How do I make it stop?

"Your magic is reacting to your anger and fear. Just focus and breathe with me. In and out. In and out. I need you to calm down before you burn down my apartment with us in it," Grey said in a deliberately soothing tone.

I'd never had this happen before in my life—and I'd *definitely* felt anger and panic before. These feelings were not new to me, not by a long shot. They were basically my bedfellows and constant companions. Fear, anger, and panic were all I knew. How could I know anything else when I'd spent my life so far hiding from those who would use me or harm me?

"You know that telling someone to calm down is the last thing you should do when you want them to actually calm the fuck down, right?" I shrieked as I began to hyperventilate. The ball only grew bigger the more I yelled, the more emotion I allowed to run unchecked.

What is happening? Where has this magic suddenly come from? And why now?

Grey breathed deeply in through his nose and waited for a beat before he blew it back out of his mouth pointedly. "Match my breathing, Aurelia. Focus on my voice. Look into my eyes."

The way he said my name sent a pleasant shiver through my soul and had me feeling slightly calmer. But how the hell was that even possible? He was a shifter and the leader of a corrupt organization, the Syndicate.

Overwhelmed and drowning in panic, I had no choice but to defer to his instruction. While a shuddering effort I managed to match his breathing, sucking in one huge lungful of air after another before blowing it out in time with his. Slowly, *so* painfully slowly, despite the tremble in my bones that refused to abate, I felt a sense of calm descend upon me like an intangible mist.

"Good girl. You're doing so well, princess. Keep going," he coaxed.

I glared at him.

What a stupid nickname!

My magic flared again at his words, undoing my efforts at calming myself. Grey chuckled.

And though it should have further provoked my anger, the sound was like a soothing balm on my skin.

"Okay, okay. No nicknames. Just focus on your breathing and the sound of my voice." He kept his breathing slow and even, coaching me through the storm of fear and anger that threatened to surge up again and swallow me whole.

I matched his breathing once more, listening to his soothing words, losing myself in the deep blue of his incredible eyes, until the magic finally fizzled out, snuffed out like the light of a candle as wet fingers pinched the burning wick.

"You're going to need some serious training to learn to control that, Aurelia," Grey said sternly. "You could accidentally hurt someone—or worse, yourself—with that kind of unchecked magic."

Now, despite the fact he'd just helped me step back from the edge, I desperately wanted to smack him in his smug, gorgeous face. "You think? But there's no one else *like me* to train me though!" I threw my hands up in frustration, before raking my fingers through my long hair.

"Well, what did that woman teach you? Your mother?" Grey shook his head in exasperation.

"Not much of anything, to be honest. I was lucky she even taught me to read and kept me fed," I said narrowing my eyes at him. Did he think I was some kind of a pampered princess? The same way the shifter from the motel seemed to?

"She wasn't your real mother, was she, Aurelia?" he asked with a pointed stare.

"She was the one who counted," I snapped back, turning my back on him. "She didn't *have* to raise me, but she did. She was the only one who ever showed me a scrap of kindness in my whole life as far as I can remember!"

"So, you've never even seen another fae before?" he asked, placing a hand on my lower back and leading me to the couch again.

"There aren't any other fae here." I shrugged. "I'm the only one."

Am I wrong? Did mother lie to me all this time about everything?

The very thought that nothing I potentially knew was real rocked me to my core and left me shaking.

"You're not the only fae in the realm, technically," said Grey with a wince as he trailed off.

"What do you mean by that?" I asked and sat down heavily on the couch, no longer able to support myself under the weight of my emotions and fatigue.

"Full-blooded fae are notoriously elitist snobs. They send their half-fae children to the mortal world more often than not. The fae like having their freedom, but then treat the half-bloods they birth with disdain." Grey sighed and sat in the reclining chair opposite me.

"So, you're telling me that I'm likely only half fairy?" I asked furrowing my brow.

What else could I be? Mother would have told me if I was anything else right?

But the more this night dragged on, the more convinced I was that I knew almost absolutely nothing, not just about myself, but the workings of the supe world, too.

"No, you're definitely a full-blooded fae. With the amount of magic you almost just unleashed upon my living room, there can be no doubt. You summoned that kind of power without even thinking about it, without intention! Half-bloods don't have such gifts, such strength. You're the real deal, Aurelia." He picked up his glass and took a long sip, eyeing me over the top of it.

"Then why was I left here alone to fend for myself? Why am I not in the fae realm?" I asked, unable to hide the hint of sadness and rejection from tainting my voice.

Did my real parents really just abandon me to the human realm? And if so, why? What could I have done to make them not love me? Was I truly bad?

"I don't know," Grey said with a shake of his head. "But I wish I did."

Licking my lips I grasped at straws, at any sense of normalcy, something upon which I could ground myself. I needed a port as much as a ship lost at sea. I needed somewhere to be, to figure all of this out before it spiraled well and truly out of control. "So, you want me to come work for the Syndicate?" I asked, prompting Grey to pick up the threads of the conversation we'd begun earlier.

"I do. I have half-fae who can help you learn control. Not only that, but you'll have a place to stay and money in your pocket for whatever you need." He put his glass down on the table and the ice tinkled against the sides as it settled.

Can I really do this? Mother warned me about the Syndicate. She told me they were the worst of the supernaturals... but Grey has been nothing but kind to me. Is it merely an act to gain my trust? A ploy to get what he wants and nothing more?

Either way, I was stuck between a proverbial rock and a hard place. I had nowhere else to go and that was the stark reality of my situation. I had no one and nothing. My choices seemed limited at best. "I would just have to work for you, that's the catch, right? I'll be your full-blooded fae on staff and will have to do whatever you want me to do, even when I don't agree with it?" I said, grabbing my water.

"The jobs I need your magic for are dangerous, I won't lie to you. But you'll have to train for a while before we can get you started on missions. It will give you the time to learn the skills you need to protect yourself," he said staring in my eyes.

Well, shit. How can I argue with that? It sounds entirely reasonable, all things considered. And I need to learn to protect myself. This world doesn't like my kind.

I just had no idea why. Parched, I cracked the water bottle open again and took a long sip, swallowing slowly. I didn't want to answer too quickly, especially when I wasn't even sure what I wanted. I could definitely use the self-defense skills and the magical control training... but what if he wanted me to do something illegal? Something truly nefarious and wrong?

"If you have half-fae that can help me learn the skills I need, why don't you have them already assigned to these jobs?" I asked with a raised brow. If he didn't have a good answer, I was leaving. I didn't care that I had nowhere else to go.

He said he wouldn't lie, and I want the truth. I'm tired of not knowing!

"They have gone through careful and extensive vetting and none of them have the kind of magic it will take to get the jobs done, Aurelia. If they had I wouldn't have been searching for a full-blooded fae in the first place," he said.

Wait, what?

"Is that why you bumped into me outside the bar?" I said. "Were you on the hunt? You knew what I was from the beginning? How?" I asked angrily and stood again, my temper lending me the strength to leave.

"I was not on the hunt, as you put it, and I was certainly not expecting to bump into you tonight. It was a fortuitous coincidence, but I'm not one to look a gift horse in the mouth. I will always seize the opportunity to get what I want," he said, before moving to block my exit again.

"That's not a good enough answer for me," I bit out angrily and attempted to dodge past him for the elevator.

He gripped my arm lightly, his eyes imploring me to see reason, to give him a chance. "Please, Aurelia, just stay the night. I'll show you where you can sleep and if you still want to leave in the morning, I won't stop you. But don't make me watch you walk out into the dark with nowhere to go. I couldn't bear the thought of what might happen to you."

Something in his gaze and the earnest tone of his voice had me softening, relenting to his wishes. Fatigue weighed heavily on my shoulders, and he was right, I had nowhere to go. What could it really hurt to stay just one night in an apartment that was fancier and no doubt safer than any place I'd ever been? With a sigh, I nodded. I was strong, but the truth remained that I'd be better able to protect myself and run if I was well rested.

Grey smiled in response, and it was devastating.

No, Aurelia. You can't be attracted to the leader of the Syndicate. You are a means to an end for him. Do not *get attached. If anything, even if I accept, this is just a job; a means to an end for myself as much as it is for him. It will be a game of give and take.*

Grey held his hand out to me, his long dark hair gleaming beneath the mood lighting of the penthouse.

Damn, he is gorgeous.

I grimaced, hesitating for several heart beats before taking it.

You really shouldn't be doing this, whispered the only instincts I'd ever known—the ones that had kept me alive and fighting this long. But as I placed my hand in his, all thoughts of running away again evaporated like dew in the sunlight. My spine tingled at the flesh-on-flesh contact, and I gasped, unable to stop myself.

Grey sucked in a ragged breath and led me down a hall.

Did he feel that weird electricity between us too? What was that? I've never felt anything like it.

"That room is mine. It's off-limits," he said, pointing to a door on the left. Then he indicated toward the room in front of him. "You can stay here for tonight. Please, think about what I've said, and I'll see you in the morning."

"Grey?" I asked as he turned down the hall in the direction of the room that was off limits.

"Yes, princess?" He chuckled at my glare.

"What's so important about this job?" I asked, my curiosity getting the better of me.

"It's a project of mine that I've been working on for a very long time," he answered.

With no further clarification forthcoming, I nodded. "Goodnight, Grey," I said. I closed the door behind me, not waiting for a response and not sure if I even wanted one. I flopped onto my back on the large four poster bed. The comforter beneath me was the softest thing I'd ever felt in my life. It felt like I was being swallowed by a cloud.

Don't get used to it, Aurelia. You won't be staying.

Even if I decided to accept his job offer, I doubted his employees lived in his own home. My stomach roiled and my heart thumped. I didn't want to contemplate *why* that fact made me sad, but I had an inkling it had something to do with his touch... with the electricity we shared.

I crawled up the bed and snuggled in under the covers. It felt like a heavenly nest made of angel feathers. My exhaustion stormed in, catching up with me, and I was almost asleep when a ringing sounded from another room down the hall.

Why would someone be calling so late?

I frowned as I pushed the covers off me and made my way on silent feet to the door and pressed my ear to it.

"Hello?" Grey's voice rang out clearly in the hall.

I nearly jumped, scared he would catch me spying on him after he offered me such hospitality.

"No, I can't come out there tonight." His tone was surly and grew louder as he came closer to my door. "I don't give a damn if there's been a challenge, Layla," he barked. "There has been a development."

I nearly raked my fingers down the door at the name Layla. What woman was calling him so late?

Stop it, Aurelia. You don't have a claim on this man, nor do you want one. You are a means to an end.

"This isn't up for debate," he snapped on the other side of my door.

I jumped away from the door with a squeak as Grey threw it open, barely missing me in the process. "What are you doing in here?" I yelled, startled and with no reasonable alternative.

"Did you get the information you desired by spying on me, princess?" He smirked and prowled further through the door.

I backed up until the backs of my knees hit the bed frame, but he just kept stalking closer.

"I'm a predator, Aurelia," he all but purred. "I heard your heart rate pick up when I said Layla's name. Are you jealous of my beta?"

"N-no," I stammered and would have facepalmed right then and there if he hadn't been right up close, invading my personal space.

"You don't sound too sure of that," he said, his eyes glowing with his inner animal as he trailed his nose up my neck, taking a long, deep breath.

Did he just sniff me?

My throat ran dry, and I licked my lips, overwhelmed by his closeness.

His full lips skimmed my jugular, and he growled deep in his throat.

I shuddered beneath him with undeniable desire. "What are you doing?" I groaned and attempted to half-heartedly wiggle away.

I should stop this...

He pushed a little harder, until there was nothing but him.

I fell backwards onto the bed, my eyes wide.

He followed me down, his huge, hot body coming down on top of mine. "You smell like cherries and sunshine. It's intoxicating," he whispered against my skin.

"Grey," I groaned and wiggled my hips, though I some part of me knew that I wanted this—a more prideful part was loathe to admit it.

Something hard grew against my belly as he peered into my eyes. "If you want me, princess, just know that you don't have to be jealous of my second. She's nothing but business. Whereas you will be mine in every conceivable way," he said and nipped my shoulder.

What the hell is he talking about? I can't possibly want this man who is in charge of the fucking supernatural underground, can I?

I rubbed my thighs together, still pinned beneath him. What was going on with my body? I'd never reacted like this to anyone.

With my wings pinned beneath me on the bed he reached his hand up over me, and as if he could see them and ran a hand down their delicate membranes.

My back arched, and I pushed my breasts against his chest. "Grey," I breathed.

"Get some sleep, princess," he crooned. "I have a feeling tomorrow is going to be a very busy day," he said and was suddenly gone, closing the door behind him with a *click*.

With my heart still racing, my breathing ragged, and the depths between my legs aching, I pressed my palms to my eyes and whined in frustration.

What have I gotten myself into?

Groaning, I rolled over to bury my face in the plush pillows where I prayed fervently for sleep to claim me. This was bad. *Really* fucking bad.

Chapter 6

Grey

WHAT THE HELL WAS I thinking?

I'd heard her heart rate unexpectedly pick up last night when I'd admonished Layla, then promptly lost all sense of propriety. I wanted her. Badly. I craved her more than I needed air. Knowing she was my mate and not being able to immediately mark her as mine, and claim her in the flesh, was driving me to distraction.

I still want her.

My wolf was riding me hard to claim her and I'd lost all control when he'd scented her arousal. I could still recall her scent. She smelled of lush, ripe cherries and warm, radiant sunshine. Reliving the memory of last night made my mouth water, but I could only thank the heavens that I'd been able to pull away when I did. The timing wasn't right—not yet.

"Boss?" Layla voice drew me back to reality as she called from the other side of the phone.

"If this is about last night's challenge, then I don't care. I have bigger things to worry about right now," I said with a growl.

"It's not," she assured me. "We have a job for the troll but he's currently in punishment," she explained, sounding exasperated.

"So, send a different bloody troll." I tightened my hand around the phone, nearly snapping it in half.

"He was requested specifically, Boss." She groaned.

"Fine! For fuck's sake, Layla. Let him out for this job. But if he shows any sign of weakness or an ego the way he did before, then he's gone. Got it?" I shook my head.

Why am I the one who has to be interrupted to make this decision? She is perfectly capable of handling this on her own, that's why she's my damned second!

"Next time there's a special request, just handle it, Layla. I have bigger problems than weak trolls." I hung up the phone with a snarl, agitated.

"Why does she call you so often?" A sweet voice asked me from behind.

I told her she doesn't have to be jealous, and why has her scent changed?

"She's my second in command but certain things need my attention," I said as I turned to face Aurelia.

She was adorably rumpled from sleep, her green eyes still groggy, and her blonde curls were wild. She fidgeted at my inspection, no doubt recalling the events of last night.

I smirked. "How did you sleep?" I asked her.

"Very well, thank you." She ducked her head shyly and bounced light from foot to foot as if with pent up energy.

"Come, then. Let's have some breakfast and then we can talk." I rose from my chair and led her into the kitchen where Freya had left breakfast for us. I pulled her chair out for her with a subtle, gentlemanly smile.

She smiled at me in return, her gaze downcast as she mumbled a thank you and sat down.

"Have you gotten a chance to think over my offer?" I asked casually as I scooped up a forkful of fluffy, seasoned eggs.

"I don't know," she answered as she chewed on a piece of bacon. The fact she was purposefully avoiding my gaze did not bode well.

Don't jump to conclusions. She's been through a lot of trauma.

"You don't know if you thought about it, or you don't know if you should take it?" I asked, keeping my tone conversational.

Gods, please. She can't say no. I need her in more ways than one!

"I don't think I should," she clarified, staring at her plate.

How do I convince her?

I wracked my brain for an angle of attack. "Can I ask why? Maybe if you can tell me all the reasons you shouldn't, I can provide you counterbalances as to all the reasons you should," I said picking up my cup of coffee. I took a long sip as I waited for her answer. This had to happen. Now that I'd met Aurelia, now that my wolf and I recognized her as our mate, I really didn't want to have to force her to do what I needed. Ideally, I wanted her to join me willingly. It was the only way I could see all outcomes satisfied.

"I won't be doing anything illegal, will I?" she asked, her tone plaintive and concerned.

I kept my poker face in place, revealing nothing. I needed to be honest with her about what she would be doing, but in the same breath I didn't want to scare her off either. My wolf couldn't stand to lose her. "There are many rumors about the Syndicate and many of them are true. I didn't get to where I am today without breaking a few laws." I shrugged And took another sip of my coffee never taking my eyes from her. She needed to know that I was not a good man, but nothing I did was ever without good reason.

"See, that's the thing. I was always taught to respect the laws and fly under the radar. I don't think I can do that working for you." Aurelia turned her gaze on me, finding strength in her conviction.

"Genuinely, what's the alternative, Aurelia? You have nowhere else to go and the witches will be investigating your mother's death." I drummed my fingers on the table one after another. I took another long sip, watching her with keen eyes.

Her expressive features ran the gamut of emotions, from desperation and worry, to sadness and despair, and then finally settled on anger. She clenched her fist around her glass of fresh orange juice as her gaze hardened. "I don't know, okay? Maybe the witches just want to ask me what happened? Maybe they won't see a need to investigate me too deeply and I won't be a damn pariah anymore." She threw her hands up, sloshing orange juice across the table. "All I've ever done was obey my mother and assist her in all that she asked. Surely the witches will realize that much. I'd never have harmed the only one who ever cared for me!"

"It won't look good that you ran, Aurelia," I said calmly. "In fact, it'll prompt questions that will be hard to answer."

"No, it won't," she agreed. "But it wasn't my fault! That man hit me with a tranquilizer dart in the market and I have no idea why. He said something about how I'd make him good money... I had no choice but to flee. And the truth is that I made it to the hallway outside Mother's room before I lost consciousness." She shook her head, her eyes beginning to water as she relived the memory.

Dan is in some serious shit for pulling that! What the hell was he going to do with an unconscious female in the middle of the market?

I barely contained my growl. "And when you woke up, you found her?" I pulled my phone from my pocket and scrolled through the supernatural news articles. "Shit," I breathed as I found the article I was looking for, the one that would force her to play the only had she had. "This just got really bad for you, Aurelia." I turned the phone in her direction so she could read the headline.

Her eyes widened in horror, and she blanched, the tears she'd been fighting back so valiantly trickling down her cheeks. "But I didn't do it!" she confessed, the lilt of her voice tainted with panic and bordering on desperation. "I was trying to buy her medicine to help her," she whispered roughly, wiping at her eyes.

I moved closer to her and placed a comforting hand on her shoulder, then squeezed it gently. "The article goes on to say she was hexed. Her illness wasn't what killed her... someone else did." I allowed my declaration to hang ominously between us.

"Do you think it was the man who was chasing me?" she whispered as another tear slid down her cheek.

I brushed the tear away with my thumb, hating to see her cry like that. I wanted her to join me, but I didn't want to her hurt any more than she already had. When it came to the woman who would be my mate, I might be manipulative, but I would not be cruel.

I don't think Dan would've have killed her mother, but who else would have known what she was and would want to make her desperate?

"I don't know who did this, but the witches aren't kind to outsiders and will want this crime answered for in blood. And unfortunately, rightly or wrongly, you're their prime suspect. It's not safe for you out there, Aurelia. You can't go back. You don't deserve to be targeted for the actions of another." I gripped her chin, turning her eyes to mine. I didn't need to explicitly mention that the blood they would desire was hers, but the inference was there.

She nodded and licked her lips, her shoulders trembling. "This changes everything," she whispered. "My mother always told me to be wary of them, but this?" Aurelia's green eyes shimmered with unshed tears. "It looks like your job offer is my only option, after all. No one else in this city is going to offer me a safe place to sleep or self-defense training."

My wolf howled in triumph.

She's ours.

"We can start an investigation of our own into who really did this and clear your name," I offered squeezing her shoulder lightly. "If there are answers to be had, we'll find them."

"But only if I come work for you." She shook her head in denial. "Maybe I should just leave the city? I doubt they'll look for me outside the witch part of town."

My poor, beautiful, naïve fairy.

"Aurelia, someone is clearly after you. And until we know why, your safest option is here in the Syndicate. You can learn to protect yourself, how to control your magic, and how to fight. Then we can search for your mother's killer," I said hoping she would see this from my point of view.

"And all it will cost me is my soul, right?" She laughed without humor and shook her head again as she fought a war within herself.

"You will have to come work for me, yes, and it will be dangerous. But not more danger than you currently face alone in the city," I said honestly. I needed her to understand the gravity of the situation. Yes, I was working an angle, but we had no supernatural police force in the city. The witches *would* get blood without a trial. There would be no justice.

"I understand the risks here, Grey, but I'm still not sure. I mean, it's a damn criminal organization! How can you be so at peace with what you do?" The chair screeched loudly across the marble as she stood abruptly, clearly needing space.

"It's not *all* criminal activity," I said as I gripped the arm of my chair. I was doing my best to hold myself back from just shaking some damn sense into her. She wasn't getting the gravity of the situation. Her pure white morals would not serve her in our world. The supernaturals as a whole were fickle, distrusting, and used to doing whatever it took to preserve their way of life. She would not be shown mercy or kindness if she dared venture back out into Dallas alone.

"Really?" she asked exasperated, her tone one of clear disbelief.

"We hire out trolls as bodyguards and provide protection for both humans and supernaturals," I said standing and moving into her path.

This minxy fae isn't escaping on my watch.

"And what would I be doing?" She crossed her arms over her chest and tapped her foot impatiently.

My eyes moved to her chest and back up quickly. Now was not the time to focus on the way that posture pushed her breasts up deliciously. "For now, you would be training and learning your magic, and once you're ready I'll give you an assignment." I reached out and dared to push a golden lock of hair behind her ear.

"You want me to agree to this without even knowing what I'll be doing? You want me to join you, practically blind? Not bloody likely, Grey." She shook her head and scowled, stubborn as ever.

"Fine, how about this? You come and train. You learn your magic and control, and when the time comes... if you don't like the job, you can turn it down." I shoved my hands in my pockets, biting the inner wall of my lip as I waited for her response.

This is risky as fuck.

"You'd really let me do that? You'd train me and then let me turn down the job that you specifically wanted me for?" she scoffed.

"Yes." I nodded, my mask unslipping.

I'll just have to make sure that by the time she is trained and ready she won't want to turn it down.

She didn't trust me. The evidence of that shone in her eyes, but I would make sure when the time came, she would have to trust me. One way or another, I'd win her over. I'd achieve my goals *and* secure my claim on my mate.

Aurelia paced the room, her brows deeply furrowed, and her mouth pinched as she mulled her limited options over. "Okay," she finally said slowly, turning to face me. "I'll train and when the time comes, I'll decide if I want to do this job for you or not."

I kept my stoic mask in place even as my wolf howled his victory in my head. Relief flooded me as I placed a hand on her lower back and led her to the table. "I'm glad to hear it, Aurelia. Let's finish breakfast and then I'll give you a personal tour of the facility." I smiled my most charming smile as I took my seat.

The cat is in the bag!

After breakfast, I strolled into my home office while Aurelia went to shower and change. There was one last thing I needed to handle. One particular detail that could see this all blow up in my damn face.

"Hello?" Dan picked up the phone on the first ring.

"You shot her with a fucking iron tranquilizer dart?" I growled low.

"She was getting ready to fly away, Boss. What was I supposed to do?" he asked.

"You've made everything exceedingly more difficult," I said rubbing a hand over my face.

"What do you mean? You have her, right? So, no harm was done," he said warily.

"She was the perfect scapegoat for whoever murdered her mother when she was passed out in the hall. The witches are out for blood, and she blames *you* for this." I tapped my fingers on my desk in agitation.

"Fucking hell." Dan hissed.

"Exactly. Which means all communication needs to be done over the phone from now on. She's smart and if she sees you at the facility, she will put it all together and we'll be fucked. You'll be the damn reason my carefully laid plans went to shit!" I sat back in my chair.

"What do you want me to do? I've been trying to hunt down a fae for a long time now, isn't my debt paid?" he asked hopefully.

I scoffed. I couldn't believe he'd dare ask that after what he pulled. "You almost ruined everything with this. Like I'm letting you off that easily when I am the one who ended up getting the job done."

"Then what do you need from me?" Dan asked with a sigh.

"I want you to investigate her mother's murder and find anything you can about how she came to live with the witch in the first place." I gripped the phone. Something didn't sit right with me about the story she'd been fed her entire life, and if I was going to get her to trust me, I needed to get her real answers.

"Why would you want me to investigate the witch's murder?" he asked.

"They are blaming her death on Aurelia, you fucking idiot. She will never be safe from them until her mother's real killer is brought to justice." I clenched the phone in my hand tighter.

"Doesn't her being in danger somewhat suit your purposes?" he asked, confused.

"Are you questioning my orders, Dan?" I growled. "Do what you are told and find the killer! Call me when you have the information I need." I hung up the phone and buried my face in my hands.

For fuck's sake! Do I need to start being a ruthless asshole again? Have I been slipping lately?

My oversensitive wolf hearing picked up the shower turning off and I grinned to myself. Everything was in motion, despite the hiccups, and soon I would have exactly what I wanted.

Those who wronged me will pay in blood for what they've done.

I would make sure of it.

Chapter 7

Aurelia

AM I MAKING A TERRIBLE mistake?

My stomach roiled with a storm of butterflies, and I couldn't help but wonder what the hell I was getting myself into as I sat in the back of the sleek black town car.

Grey sat in the seat next to me, his eyes on his phone, no doubt attending to business as we rushed through the city traffic.

I shifted in my seat restlessly, trying in vain to swallow the intangible lump forming in my throat.

"Are you nervous?" Grey asked, resting his hand on my knee to keep me from fidgeting.

My spine tingled at his touch, making my restlessness even worse and bringing back flashbacks of last night. It was hard to banish the sensation of his hard cock pressed again me, and the way he scented my neck. With a shake of my head, I cleared my throat.

Do not fall for the boss of the Syndicate, Aurelia! Seriously.

"I just don't know what to expect, I guess. I've never been out of the supe side of the city," I admitted.

"We're actually going outside the city. It's the only place where I'm able to keep my people off the radar." He didn't so much as look up from his phone as he spoke.

"Maybe this isn't such a good idea?' I said, twisting my fingers together. "Am I going to put your people in danger by being there?'

Maybe I can get out of this if he thinks I will be a threat to his employees? Surely, he wouldn't want the witches attacking his building to find me, right?

"No, you are not going to put my employees in danger," he said and finally peered up from his phone.

"Are you sure?" I asked.

He sighed. "Aurelia, this is the best thing for you until we find your mother's killer and you learn to protect yourself. Just trust me on this." He squeezed my knee reassuringly.

Little *zings* of lightning danced across my skin and my heart beat faster.

Can I trust him though? He's the head of a criminal organization. It would be stupid to trust a man like that, right? So, why am I so damn drawn to him? His touch is practically electric...

I shook my head to clear the unhelpfully sexy thoughts as we drove out of the city and were soon surrounded by countless trees—from horizon to horizon. My eyes widened as the city was blocked from my view, nothing more than a memory as the world took on a new form. An innate sense of peace washed through me, and I couldn't help the infectious grin that spread across my face. I had *never* felt like I belonged anywhere before, but surrounded by nature, I felt calmer than I could ever remember being.

I just wish I could get out of the car and enjoy it! I bet it would feel so wonderful to touch, to be connected to it.

My gaze was fixed firmly on the trees as they rushed by us when something like thousands of ants crawling over me made me shudder. I immediately realized it for what it was. It was much stronger than the wards at the witch market. "That's some seriously powerful magic," I said rubbing my arms to rid myself of the strange sensation lingering on my skin.

"It's a little more extensive than a normal ward," Grey said observing me.

"It doesn't feel very good," I said with a groan, rubbing my hands up and down my arms some more.

"It does take some getting used to, but it keeps everyone safe from the outside world, as long as they stay inside the wards." He squeezed my knee again, his hand lingering.

It wasn't lost on me that he specifically said we were safe from the outside world and not safe from inside.

"Is there something you're not telling me?" I asked with a frown, subtly adjusting my position so that he moved his hand.

"It can be intense in the facility," he offered. "But just keep your head down, train, and you'll be fine." He shrugged and returned his attention to his phone.

What is that supposed to mean?

I shifted in my seat again as the large metal and glass building suddenly rose up into view. A wave of nervous energy spiked in my chest, and I tapped my foot and wrung my hands to avoid what felt like a freak-out just waiting to happen.

"I really think this is a bad idea now," I mumbled mostly to myself.

What exactly am I getting myself into here? Is it too late to change my mind? Maybe I can flee into the forest where it's safe? I could live off-grid, wild and free.

Grey laughed.

The sound had shivers rolling over me again and my nipples tingled beneath my shirt in response. I nibbled on my lower lip and waited for the sensation to pass. Why did that carefree sound make my body react so violently?

Is there something wrong with me? Or is this how all fae feel around other supes?

"You'll be fine, honestly. Try and stay calm. You have more power than any of them and as soon as you learn to harness it, they won't want to fuck with you," Grey said turning my face to his. His gaze flicked down to my lips and his blue eyes glowed with hunger.

I squirmed under his intense scrutiny. My breathing became shallow as an instant heat blossomed between my legs and an undeniable ache grew there.

Holy shit! What is he doing? Is he thinking about last night? Is he about to kiss me? Am I a horrible person because I secretly want him to?

A throat cleared from the front seat.

I'd forgotten all about the driver being there.

Crap.

"Sir, we're about to pull into the garage," the driver said.

Grey reluctantly released me and locked his phone.

I anxiously straightened my spine, desperately trying to ignore the fire the shifter had sparked within me. This was it. I was heading into the unknown.

What was I thinking? This is a terrible idea!

The sun was blocked out by a deep cement garage. The dark stone structure was ominous as we rolled slowly through the space.

Grey put his hand on mine in my lap and threaded our fingers together as if it were the most natural thing in the world, before giving them a gentle squeeze. "You're going to do great here, princess. I just know it," Grey whispered in my ear, his breath warm against my skin.

I shivered in response and squeezed my thighs tightly together as my heart hammered in my chest.

Fuck! I'm glad one of us is confident. Did I just sign up to live with a bunch of criminals who could very well murder me?

"But if I don't, I can leave, right?" I asked, my knuckles whitening.

Grey stiffened. "Once you're out of danger, if that's what you want, then I won't keep you here. I told you I won't hold you against your will." He waved his hand dismissively. But the way he had stiffened at my question told a very different story.

What if he's lying and he never lets me leave? What if all I am is a tool or some kind of weapon to him? How can I trust he'll honor his word?

I scanned the ominous garage for an escape route but came up empty. The place was sealed up like Fort Knox.

What was I thinking?

The memory of the article on Grey's phone came back, hitting me like a sledgehammer. I couldn't go back to Dallas even if I wanted to. I'd draw the attention of the witches in no time and they would be out for my blood. They wouldn't care that I was innocent. They wouldn't even spare me the time to try and explain. The fact was that I was different, and they didn't like or trust outsiders.

My mother had been the only thing shielding me from their wrath and prejudice. The witch side of the city was no longer home, I had to come to terms with that.

I have no home.

The truth smarted like a bee sting, and I grit my teeth together to prevent a sob escaping my throat. I needed to make the best of this new situation and hope to the gods that I hadn't made a terrible mistake. For now, I was alive. I had to focus on that. Every day I spent above ground or not incinerated by witches was a good one.

The car slowed to a stop outside a large, matte metal door. The driver opened his door and exited the vehicle.

I reached for mine.

Grey squeezed my hand and shook his head. "Let him," Grey whispered, and my door opened.

The driver smiled as he held his hand out to me to help me exit the vehicle.

"Thank you," I said shyly as I allowed him. I wasn't used to such treatment and didn't feel worthy of the pampering.

The driver nodded with a small smile. and

Grey squeezed out of the car behind me, brushing my wings as he did so. I had to bite back a moan at the sensation.

"You know, you don't have to keep them hidden here, Aurelia. You can be who you were always meant to be," he whispered close to my ear.

Wait, I don't have to hide anymore?

I glanced back at Grey with a frown. "Are you sure? That seems dangerous. I've hidden my whole life."

"You are far more powerful than you realize, Aurelia. Now it's high time that you see it too." Uninvited, he kissed my neck.

I shuddered and clenched my fists by my sides. How was he able to make me feel like I was on fire? My stomach flipped as his hands landed on my hips, squeezing them gently as he guided me forward.

"It's time to go inside, princess." Grey chuckled.

I scowled at him, but let him lead me to the elevator. This was it, the next chapter of my life if I wanted to survive, and I had no choice but to face it head on.

I plastered a grin on my face and followed Grey into the elevator. My stomach dropped as we ascended into the rest of the building, but I ignored it. I would do this and I would do it with a smile. I would stand as bravely as I could and try my best at whatever was asked of me. If Grey needed me this badly, I must be worthwhile, whether I saw it or not. And whoever I encountered would soon discover the same. I hadn't managed to stay alive this long by being a complete idiot.

The elevator *dinged* and a tall woman with dark brown hair and gleaming amber eyes stepped in. Her eyes were hard as she looked me up and down, inspecting me like a breeder inspects a pedigree pup.

"This is her?" She chuckled. "You want to train her to protect herself? She doesn't look as if she's done a single hard day's work in her *life*."

"Layla," Grey barked.

I narrowed my eyes at the woman. She was his second, the woman who called him so damn much.

"Boss, honestly? I doubt she can be trained for anything battle-centric. She would do better in the breeding center," she said crossing her arms over her chest full of attitude.

Grey moved faster than I'd ever seen anyone move. He became a blur before he rematerialized and picked the woman up by the throat, slamming her into the shiny elevator wall.

I gasped at the unexpected display of violence, but I couldn't blame him. She didn't even know me, yet she'd judged me and determined I was no more than a pretty sow to birth calves for the benefit of the Syndicate. My hands balled into fists at my sides as I stared at the woman gasping for breath. I would have dearly liked to throttle her, myself. Her level of disrespect for me, as Grey's newest recruit, was abominable.

"If you ever speak the words *breeding center* when mentioning Aurelia again, you are gone!" Grey roared in her face, his inner beast rising to the surface and lending his voice to the threat. He dropped the woman with disgust, his rage scarcely contained.

Layla landed lithely on her feet, then bent over coughing and rubbing at her throat.

Grey turned to me, and his eyes widened as if he'd seen a ghost. "Remember what we practiced, Aurelia," he said, his voice dropping to a soothing tone. "You need to breathe." He glanced down pointedly at my hands.

I frowned.

What is he...? Oh shit! Not again.

I nearly shrieked at the purple swirling magic that covered both of my clenched fists.

"What the fuck?" Layla coughed as she looked at my hands with bulging eyes.

"Don't screw with me, bitch," I said through panicked breaths, surprised by my own anger.

Grey grabbed my chin and turned my face toward him. "Eyes on me, princess. Listen to my voice and match my breathing, just like I showed you."

The magic was making me twitchy and I yearned to release it, but I couldn't do that in the small elevator we were on. I didn't need to guess, I knew I'd likely kill us all. I felt it in the blaze of my power. And I wasn't ready to die, especially not by my own hand. I slammed my gaze into his and took a deep, shuddering, and cleansing breath.

"That's it, good girl. Breathe for me, nice and slow. That's it," he soothed, rubbing his hands up and down my arms.

I followed his instructions, listening to his soothing voice and matching my breaths to his. It came a little easier this time, and I felt my magic simmering down.

"What the fuck was that?" Layla shouted, interrupting.

I turned my gaze to hers and the surge returned, sparking back to life like gas poured on a bonfire.

Bitch!

"No, princess, look at me," Grey said pinching my chin and turning my gaze back to him.

I glared at the woman for another second defiantly before flitting my eyes back to his baby blues. Distantly the *ding* of the elevator chimed but I didn't react, I stayed put right where I was, letting Grey's soothing presence calm the raging magic within me.

"Get the fuck out of here, Layla," Grey said, not raising his voice from the gentle cadence he used with me.

"But, Boss!" Layla screeched, clearly indignant and enraged at having been put in her place.

"If you don't want to listen, I'll *let* her test her powers out on you. Now, get out of here." Grey snarled.

The sound of shuffling feet met my ears and I grinned. That bitch had pissed me off, sizing me up like I was less than nothing.

I can't believe she dared imply I'd be good for nothing but breeding!

"I think you may be a little bloodthirsty, after all, princess. And that is something we can definitely work with." Grey grinned as he released my chin.

"I don't like her," I grumbled, glancing away now that my magic was back under control.

"That's going to be a problem, princess. She runs this place when I'm not here." Grey shook his head, chuckling again.

"She runs the place?"

Shit! Have I just painted a giant target on my back? What will I do when Grey's not around to tell her to back off?

"She does," Grey said with a nod.

"Okay, that does it. I've changed my mind. I'll take my chances with the hateful witches instead." I folded my arms over my chest, not missing the way Grey's eyes slid to my breasts at the movement.

"You're going to prove Layla, right? You're going to wave your white flag and admit that you're not cut out for this?" He sighed and shook his head with disappointment.

I don't want that woman to think I'm weak and can't take it, but I have no idea what to expect of this place. I'm like a fucking fish out of water!

I grimaced and huffed out a breath like a frustrated bull seeing red flags.

"Come on, let's get you settled in," said Grey, obviously determining correctly that I wasn't about to play dead, not even for his second in command. He placed a hand on my lower back and led me from the elevator.

The hall we emerged in was a clinical white and there were doors every few feet. We strolled down the hall to a set of doors at the very end.

I furrowed my brows, glancing up at Grey. All the other rooms had only one door, but the set he was currently opening for me were more elaborate. "Grey? What is this?" I asked.

"It's your room," he answered. He frowned down at me as he opened the double doors. "Is it not to your liking?"

"It just looks different... bigger than all the others." I chewed on the inside of my bottom lip, glancing inside the opened doors.

"All of my most valuable employees get rooms like this; you'll get used to it." He grinned and ushered me into the room.

Most valuable employees? Right. I have to remember that he wants me to work for him—and that's all he wants—no matter how he toys with me or how he makes my body feel.

"Won't people think I'm getting special treatment or something?" I asked wringing my hands together as my anxiety reared its ugly head once more.

"You are. Have you forgotten? I have to find a way to get you to stick around once you learn everything you need to know." He nudged me further into the room.

I turned to survey roomy new living space. It was utilitarian but the bed in the center was large, and two doors stood in the far wall, probably a closet and a bathroom.

Don't forget that, Aurelia. He doesn't want you. He only wants what you can do for him. He's just teasing, trying to sweeten the pot. As he said, he's just trying to sway me to stay.

"Grey, I have a feeling that if I stay in this room, I'm going to be a target." I planted my hands on my hips, feeling well out of my depth. If Layla had anything to say about it, that would definitely be the case.

Fuck me. What was I thinking coming here?

Chapter 8

Grey

"HOW IS SHE DOING?" I eyed Layla as she lounged in the chair in front of my desk.

"Aurelia?" she asked with a snide chuckle. "She's far too sunny and happy for this place."

I frowned. That didn't seem right. She was as distrusting as anyone I'd ever met. "But how is her training coming along?" I asked impatiently but kept my tone even and nonchalant. I didn't have time for Layla's bullshit.

What is her deal with Aurelia, anyway? She's almost acting jealous, but that's not possible. That's not the Layla I've always known.

Then again, it seemed more and more of my elite team were acting up and speaking out of turn than usual since Aurelia came into the picture.

"The others are getting irritated by the amount of time she spends in the gym. They're complaining that she's getting special treatment," Layla said with a sneer.

"She is the *one* person who can get me what I have worked for all these years. Of course, she's getting bloody special treatment!" I slammed my hand down on the desk, making Layla jump.

Resettling herself, Layla grumped. "So, what? Am I just supposed to tell them that straight up and watch the challenges roll in? She can't hack it."

"If anyone and I mean anyone threatens her, I will gut them," I growled, the threat clear in my tone. My wolf would not suffer fools when it came to our mate.

Not even Layla will escape punishment if my mate is harmed. She is literally fucking up everything.

"They've always aired their grievances that way. You can't put that kind of target on her by saying she's above the rules," Layla argued.

She's right as much as I hate to admit it. I can't put that kind of target on Aurelia. These are ruthless criminals trained to kill, and the slight will only make things worse for her.

"Fine," I snarled. "But keep an eye on her and tell me how the fuck her training is going! If further challenges are forthcoming, we'll deal with them then," I said.

"She's a quick learner," Layla grumbled like the thought of Aurelia succeeding physically pained her.

"Good. I want weekly reports on her progress." I rose to my feet, buttoning my jacket as I went.

Layla stood and followed me out of the office to the elevator.

"I need to take care of something, call me if there are any problems, I ordered." The words *with her* were left unsaid. Layla knew now not to damn well bother me with anything else but Aurelia. I hit the button for the garage and waited for the doors to close on my grouchy looking second. I needed to get to the witch side of the city and meet with Dan. He had information for me and was adamant that see Aurelia's former home with my own eyes.

Truth be told, I was dreading it. Seeing how my mate used to live, after the things she'd told me, and after the things the witch had taught her about herself... I was certain her life before me was best left forgotten. And I would do everything in my power to ensure it was wonderful from now on; just as soon as she finished her training.

I took my own car instead of bothering my driver. The less people that knew where I was headed, the better. The witches wouldn't appreciate a shifter's interference in their sham of an investigation. But my unwavering need to know what happened to bring her to the human realm in the first place—not to mention what happened to her caregiver—overrode any concern about what the witches might do to me.

Aurelia is a puzzle I need to solve.

I followed the GPS to the Italian restaurant in what the mortals would refer to as downtown Dallas but had been claimed by the witches long ago. Dan stood at the entrance as I parked my car on the street and got out. "This is the place?" I asked with a frown.

"It is. The apartment is above the restaurant. Beware though, the building is predominantly..." He made eyes at the people walking by as he trailed off.

"Got it." I waved to him to go ahead.

He didn't need to say *witches* for me to get what he was saying. Supernaturals did not allow their existence to be known by humans. The fall out of such knowledge would be disastrous. Though, there were a few select humans who closely guarded our secrets.

I followed him up the narrow stairs to the second floor of the building. and

We wove our way around until we came to a plain, unadorned door at the end of the hall. There was nothing there to suggest that this was an active crime scene or that foul play was involved.

"It looks so normal," I said with a small shake of my head and a perplexed frown.

"She was hexed, Boss. I just can't figure out how someone got in. Everyone I spoke to said she was bed-ridden. And if Aurelia was at the apothecary, then how did she answer the door?" Dan scrubbed a hand over his face.

"So, they either had a key or they didn't use the door," I said thoughtfully before pushing the door open. "Are there any signs of forced entry?" I asked as an afterthought.

"Not that I've seen."

The apartment was small but neat. A threadbare sofa sat in front of an archaic box TV set that belonged in the early nineties.

"She died in here," Dan called out, having wandered down the hall.

I trudged toward him, remembering what Aurelia told me about how she finally passed out in the hall, just outside her mother's room.

So close to delivering the medication...

"And that's where Aurelia passed out," I said aloud as I glared at Dan, still pissed off that he thought shooting her with a bloody dart like that had been a smart move.

"I was just trying to get her delivered in one piece. I thought if she was asleep... I mean, how was I supposed to know she would still fly away even with a tranq in her? That dose would knock out a half-fae cold," Dan grumbled.

My wolf growled in my mind at the thought of her stumbling through the city ready to pass out, a dreadfully easy target. He wanted to tear into Dan, but we still needed him *and* there was the small matter of a debt owed.

Dan opened the door to the bedroom and the scent of death still lingered in the air. It had been a week since the witch's death, but the dark presence of finality filled the room like a blanket of suffocating despair.

"She was in her bed when she died." Dan pointed to the rumpled sheets.

"I'm not interested in where she was when she was murdered. What did you actually call me all the way back down here for?" I asked, irritated.

"I thought you might want to see this," he said, and grabbed a small vial off the bedside table.

"It's the medicine from the apothecary, so what?" I took the vial from him and inspected it.

"It was never used. So, the witches that are accusing Aurelia of hexing her mother." He crossed his arms over his chest.

"Explain," I barked, growing impatient with this detective bullshit.

"The woman she bought the medicine from said she left with this specific vial the day of the murder, giving Aurelia a means to kill her." He shook his head and walked past me.

"But it's not poison," I argued. "What was she going to do? Overdose her only caregiver with medication? And if that was her plan, why would she abandon it and use a hex instead? It doesn't make sense. But even if that were the case, and it's a damn stretch, what's her motive?" I asked as I followed him into the hall.

He opened a door to a room that was no bigger than a closet. There were threadbare blankets piled on the floor and a few sets of worn clothes piled in the corner. "They are saying she was being mistreated by the witch and that she had reached her limit. They're suggesting she lashed out when she couldn't take anymore. This was her room," Dan finished with disgust.

This was her bedroom? I hate the fucking dead witch even more than I did before! Bloody hell.

The room was barely fit for a dog. I couldn't believe that a supernatural had treated another supe so poorly, especially one as powerful as Aurelia. "What else have you found? Anything that tells us how she came to live with the witch in the first place, or how she learned to glamor her wings her whole damn life?" I rubbed my temples in consternation.

"There are some legal documents from the human authorities, but that's about it." Dan shrugged as if that were that.

"Show me," I growled.

Obeying my command without question, he wandered from the closet.

I scanned the tiny room again to see if there was anything that she had left behind that she might want. I crouched down next to the pile of clothes, but nothing there was as good as the things that I could get for her to replace them. I stood and followed Dan into a small office. The office was still bigger than the closet that Aurelia had lived in, and I growled, my wolf rearing his head in rage at her evident mistreatment.

Shelves with books and spell ingredients lined the walls and a metal safe sat in the far corner.

"Did you crack the safe or was it like that when you got here?" I questioned.

"It was like that already. Someone got away with whatever they wanted, probably before Aurelia even woke up." Dan crouched in front of the safe. He pulled out a manilla envelope and handed it to me.

This couldn't have been all the witch had on her ward, surely? Was someone else looking for information on Aurelia, and if they were, why leave her passed out on the floor? If she was valuable to another party, why wouldn't they have seized the opportunity themselves to take her?

"None of this makes any sense," I grumbled. "The whole situation is like a tangled ball of yarn." I pulled the papers from the envelope and scanned the topmost one. I frowned at the page as I read the printed words.

"I know," Dan said warily. "How does a small child just show up out of nowhere?"

"I don't know," I answered. "And why would this particular witch take in a child of unknown origins? What was her motive to protect her? This was the first and last time she ever fostered a child. Something just isn't adding up." I shook my head.

"Whoever killed the witch knew what they were looking for and exactly where to find it. Do you think it could it have been a seer?" Dan asked.

I didn't look up from the papers in my hand. "A seer?" I asked. "They are incredibly rare. Almost as rare as Aurelia."

"I know, Boss. But nothing else makes sense. They would have seen every possible scenario involving your fairy and are trying force the future they want into motion." He sat heavily in the chair behind the desk with a frown.

"Well, shit," I said, my skin prickling with unease.

Are we dealing with an evil seer who wants to force us into a situation that we have no control over?

"Yeah, this may be bigger than we expected." Dan sighed at the lack of solid truth to be found.

I pulled my phone from my pocket and dialed Layla. We needed to get someone down here to perform a mimic spell as soon as possible.

"Yeah, boss?" Layla answered on the first ring. She sounded like she was busy, but she could drop whatever she was doing. This situation took precedence.

"I need you to send Karma to witch side," I said vaguely. "I need her witch abilities."

"I'm a little busy breaking up a fight at the moment," she grumbled.

"This is more important than a couple of delinquents fighting over the gym," I yelled, annoyed by Layla's recent spate of incompetence yet again.

"Is it more important than me trying to calm your girl down so she'll put the shifter down that her magic has pinned to the damn wall?" she huffed in response.

I grinned instinctively. I couldn't help it. The mental imagery of my mate kicking ass was just too good.

Aurelia has someone pinned to the wall?

She was learning rather quickly. "The shifter probably got what they deserved. Just send the damn half-witch to the address I am texting you to meet up with Dan. I'll be back at the facility soon." I hung up the phone.

Dan shifted in the chair pulling the papers on the desk close to him and pretending to read them. "Aurelia got into a fight with a shifter?" he asked with a grin that mirrored my own.

"She has And I need to go. Karma will be here soon to do a mimic spell. Get her whatever she needs and see if you can get a look at the person who killed the damn witch," I said and turned to leave.

I took the papers with me, hoping after closer inspection I might find something that would give us a clue. I needed to get back to the facility because there was a very real possibility that the shifter—whoever they were—would be stuck to the wall until I arrived to calm Aurelia down.

The very idea that Layla thought she could even attempt to calm Aurelia down was laughable. Neither woman liked the other.

As fast as I could get away with, I drove back to the facility. My mind loaded with more questions than answers and it royally pissed me off. When I got off the elevator at the training center level, I found Aurelia standing in a swirl of her own magic surrounded by a pack of angry shifters.

They've ganged up on her. On my mate! My wolf roared.

And I lost it. My wolf took control, bursting through my clothes and shredding them to pieces. I jumped at the nearest wolf with a snarl.

"Boss, what the hell?" Layla yelled as she tried to step between me and the shifter.

I took stock of the room, snarling at any shifter that dared get too close. They would *not* gang up on my mate and get away with it.

I will make them pay.

I agreed with my inner wolf whole-heartedly. Aurelia was mine and no one was going to take her from me.

Chapter 9

Aurelia

"OH LOOK, THE BOSS'S pet is hogging the training room *again*," a snide voice called from behind me.

I plastered on my best smile, desperately hoping I could calm this problem down like the others I'd already dealt with. I had been at the Syndicate for a week and Grey had scheduled time for me to practice everything I needed daily, but the other employees were getting upset about how often I had the gym to myself.

I turned to face the guy, ready to talk this out.

Hopefully this won't escalate...

He was probably a foot taller than me, and his muscles had muscles.

"I'm sure that there's enough room for us both to train," I said politely. I'd learned during the week that kindness was often the best way to deal with most of the people in the facility. They were so used to being hostile that my friendly disposition disarmed them.

"That's the thing though. The boss doesn't want anyone bothering you while you train," the shifter sneered.

Well, crap. Grey just painted a giant ass target on my back. Thanks for that, Boss.

"The boss isn't here, so I won't tell him if you don't?" I offered him a smile then shrugged before I turned around to return to my breathing exercises.

The shifter growled. "You dare disrespect me by giving me your back?" he roared.

My eyes widened and I mentally slapped my forehead, realizing too late that I had inadvertently made everything so much worse. I just thought we were done with the conversation—I hadn't meant to insult him. "I'm sorry," I said turning back to the huge man.

Layla stormed into the room, ever the watchful eye.

Immediately my shoulders stiffened. There was no love lost between us.

"Connor, what are you doing in here?" Layla barked, asserting her authority as second.

"The boss's pet just disrespected me," he said as he took a threatening step toward me.

My hands started to tingle with rage. Being called a pet to a shifter was the worst kind of insult, so Connor had my magic flaring.

"Aurelia, stop!" Layla yelled.

I turned my gaze to my hands.

Does she think that's going to help? Her presence alone just makes me angrier.

Purple magic swirled around my hands as the shifter took another step toward me. I threw up my hands in defense, meaning only to fend him off, but my magic seemed to have other ideas. A gust of air blew the shifter back into the wall and sparkling purple light wrapped around one of his ankles, then flipped him upside down.

"You stupid bitch, put me down!" the shifter roared, his spittle flying as his eyes became bloodshot.

I snapped my gaze back to him, glaring hard even though on the inside I was freaking the hell out.

How do I put him down? What is even happening?

"Aurelia!" Layla yelled again. "Put Connor down, now."

"That's not helpful," I gasped out between heaving breaths. My hands shook as I tried to remember Grey's breathing exercises, but Layla screaming orders at me wasn't helping at all. In fact, it was only making things worse. In the next instant a breeze slammed into her, driving her away from me.

"You're attacking me now?" she roared in umbrage.

"I can't control it!" I shrieked back as panic and anger surged within me.

"What have you been practicing in here all week, then?" Layla yelled.

I squeezed my eyes closed tight, attempting to block out Connor and Layla so that I could focus on Grey's breathing techniques when a howl cut through the room.

"Connor, if your friends come in here and gang up on Aurelia do you think the boss is going to be lenient?" Layla said, raising her voice.

My eyes popped open at her words as a new group of shifters prowled into the room. My turbulent air magic blew them back several paces, but they just pushed against the swirling vortex until they were all standing in a semi-circle, acting as a barrier between me and Connor.

"What the fuck are you?" The shifter at the middle of the group growled.

My glamour fizzled out as my powers swirled in overdrive and I knew the moment my iridescent wings became visible by the gasps that echoed throughout the room.

Well shit, I didn't mean for that to happen!

"Wicked Fae," someone whispered.

I closed my eyes blocking out the words. My mother had always warned me that people would call me that. That I was somehow inherently bad simply because of my species. So, I never revealed my wings to anyone.

"Stop fucking around and get her to let me go," Connor yelled.

The shifters began circling me but every time one lunged my air magic protected me, pushing them back again.

I just needed to figure out how to stop the flow of purple magic and put the dickhead bully down. I took a deep breath trying to center myself but movement out of the corner of my eye gave me pause.

Layla managed to break free and charged toward me, probably intent on knocking me out.

I snarled, reacting without thought, and threw her back against the wall too.

"For fuck's sake! Just stop!" Layla yelled.

My gaze went back to the shifters circling me like a school of sharks. "If you want me to put him down, maybe stop threatening me and let me calm down!" I threw my hands up in frustration and Connor flew up to the ceiling, smacking into it with a resounding *crack*.

I winced. That did not look good for me.

The shifters roared and their bodies started to shake, their bones cracking and reforming as they shifted into their wild animals, ready to take this to the next level.

Shit. Only I could piss off an entire pack of wolves by accident!

My magic flared even brighter in response and a shield of transparent, shimmering purple formed around my body.

The wolves circled me, snarling and snapping at the purple shield to no avail.

Without warning a huge snow-white wolf leaped over the others and stood with its back to me, creating another level of protection between me and the angry mob.

Holy shit, he's beautiful.

His head was almost to my chest and his coat was the purest white as he howled at the wolves surrounding me.

"Boss, what the fuck?" Layla shrieked.

Boss? Is that Grey? His wolf is absolutely breathtaking. But why is he standing between me and the others? He's a shifter just like them—they're his employees. Is he protecting them from me? Or me from them?

I frowned in confusion at the bizarre and surreal turn of events, but his presence alone soothed me. I took a deep breath calming my emotions, before I ran my hand through the fur at his back, reveling in its thickness and softness.

I could snuggle up against his coat and dream.

He whined in response.

"Layla, get them out of here. I can't drop the magic if I'm not safe and Grey is just about ready for a bloodbath," I commanded.

"Are you ordering me around?" Layla yelled back. "I'm the second, here!"

"And all you're doing is making things worse, bitch. Now, get them out of here!" I screamed as my magic whipped around me with even more fury.

A purple strand of magic lashed out at Layla like an intangible whip and she yelped in pain.

But I didn't care, I couldn't. She had no interest in helping me personally. She hated me. What I needed was for Grey to shift back so he could help me with my breathing. And he wouldn't do that until these wolves were out of the room and no longer presented a threat—that much was clear.

The shifters circling growled angrily as Layla hit the wall with a *thump*.

"Grey, please shift back," I managed to gasp between breaths. "I can't stop it. I need you."

The white wolf turned his arctic blue eyes on me and whined as he glanced back and forth between me and the threat. Then he growled, staring each of the wolves down one by one until they all showed him their throats in a display of subservience. He *was* the Syndicate, and he was reminding them.

I gripped his soft white fur to keep him from following them as they slunk out the door of the gym.

Grey's wolf shivered under my hand before he shifted back into a man.

A very naked man.

A shudder ran through me as I realized my hand was on the smooth, buff skin of his muscular back.

"Aurelia, eyes up here, princess," and he lifted my chin.

My gaze locked with his.

"See something you like?" he smirked.

"I need your help, Grey. I can't put him down," I answered in a panic, too overwhelmed to dwell on just how incredibly sexy he was, standing there bare as the day he was born, in all his masculine splendor.

"Just keep your eyes on me, listen to my voice, and match my breathing," he coached. He took a deep breath through his nose and out through his mouth, his intense gaze never leaving mine.

I struggled, but eventually matched his deep breaths and my shoulders relaxed slightly.

"That's it, princess, listen to my voice," Grey said soothingly.

"What the fuck is going on here?" Layla shouted, butting in at the most inopportune moment yet *again*.

My gaze snapped to hers and I glared, my shoulders stiffening, and I growled.

"Hey, ignore her. What did I tell you, princess? Don't worry about her. You keep your focus on me and try and drop the shifter." Grey pinched my chin once more turning my gaze back to his.

I focused on Grey and my shoulders relaxed again. I ignored Layla's scoff and finally succeeded in releasing the magic holding the irate shifter. My eyes widened in horror as the man started to fall. My hand flicked up instantly and my air magic cushioned Connor's fall.

Thanks to my instinctual reaction he landed safely on the mat of the training center.

Grey stood in front of me, glaring at the rowdy shifter and Layla.

I stepped in front of him, wanting to protect him from his insubordinate underlings and their misdirected rage.

He chuckled softly behind me as his hands found my hips.

"How could you fucking react like that?" Grey scolded Layla over my head. "She was already angry. The way you handled that was reckless!"

"But, Boss, she..." she trailed off.

"She is no longer your concern," he growled. He wrapped his arm around my waist moving to my side and pulled me along with him.

"What is that supposed to mean?" Layla shrieked moving toward me with unbridled hate in her eyes.

"It means exactly what I said. She is no longer your concern. Now back off Layla." Grey said peering down at my hands.

They started to tingle with magic again, but I continued my deep breathing. I would not let her get to me again. I needed exercise as much control as possible and get away from the psycho bitch.

"Where are you going to take her? Everyone who lives here is my concern!" She spat back, stomping in front of us like she owned the place.

Unwise move, bitch.

Grey glared down at her, unflinching. "I said, *fuck off*." Without sparing Layla another moment of his time he scooped me up and carried me to the elevator like was some kind of jungle man from a storybook.

"Grey! Where are you taking me?" I asked, squirming in his arms.

"My office. I need clothes before I take you home," he grunted and stabbed at the button on the elevator.

"What do you mean take me home?" I pressed, wiggling in his arms defiantly. My hip brushed his hard cock, and I froze as he groaned.

"Don't move or I can't be held responsible for what I do in the elevator once we're inside," he whispered close to my ear.

My eyes widened and I stilled my squirming, swallowing hard.

Grey chuckled as the elevator doors opened. He stomped inside and glared at Layla as she attempted to follow. "Round up those wolves. They are all to be punished for the shit they just pulled." Grey barked at her and hit the button for the top floor. His arms tightened around me protectively, and he pulled me closer.

"Grey? What's going on?" I asked, rubbing his arm soothingly as the doors closed.

"I'm taking you to the penthouse and will arrange for you to be trained there," he said and carefully lowered me to my feet.

"But why?" I asked softly, frowning in confusion.

"When I saw you surrounded by those wolves my animal lost his mind and took over." He pulled my back to his front and leaned his chin on my shoulder.

Something hard poked into my back and I squirmed in surprise.

"Princess, I told you what will happen if you keep rubbing up on me." Grey's moan made liquid heat pool through me moments before he spun me around and slammed my back into the wall of the elevator.

I stared up at him, my heart in my throat, wanting him to kiss me more than I'd ever wanted anything before.

Grey's lips crashed down on mine so hard they bruised me, but in the most wickedly delicious way imaginable. His hands squeezed my hips hard, possession clear in his every move.

I kissed him back, opening my lips to his tongue and moaning as he ground his erect cock against my stomach. I should have been embarrassed by his attentions, but since that first night I'd met him, all I'd been able to think about was how he made me feel. And now, after her shifted to protect me... I felt more certain than ever that I wanted him. King of the Syndicate, bad man, or criminal, it didn't matter. Our intense connection was unmistakable.

He broke our kiss to set his lips near my ear. "See what you're doing to me, princess?" Grey groaned loudly now, making shivers course down my spine. "This is why my wolf freaked out when you were in danger. We need you."

Oh, my gods. Aurelia, you idiot! How could I forget that he needs me for something?

I stiffened in his arms at the thought that I was nothing more than a commodity to him, a valuable commodity, but nothing more than a means to an end.

His head snapped up, his glacial gaze revealing confusion.

"What's wrong?" he asked, pulling me closer and bending down to kiss my neck.

"Is this because of the job?" I whispered.

Could he just be doing all this for me because of the job? Or is there a different reason behind it? Does he want me like I want him?

I scarcely allowed myself to hope for such a thing.

"No! What? Why would you think that?" he asked, kissing my shoulder. "Do you think I get like this for someone who is nothing more than a job to me?" He rubbed his cock against my hip to prove his point.

I moaned, my heart racing.

The elevator *dinged* and the doors opened.

A second later he lifted me up by my ass and carried me from the elevator.

I wrapped my legs around his waist eagerly, knowing this was probably a terrible idea, but when his lips met mine, all thoughts of protest left my brain.

I wanted nothing but Grey and if he truly desired me too, I didn't care what I had to do to get him—and keep him.

I might be his fairy, but he's my wolf.

Chapter 10

Grey

"GODS, YOU'RE BEAUTIFUL, Aurelia," I groaned as I carried her down the empty hall toward my private office.

My wolf howled in the back of my mind. He wanted her just as much as I did, and I wasn't sure I could hold back much longer.

I kicked open my office door and grimaced at the lack of available space to fuck my mate.

Maybe I should just get dressed and take her home? It would be the gentlemanly thing to do... Fuck it. Chivalry be damned! It's not like I'm a knight in shining armor. She knows what I am, and I know what I want.

My lips landed on hers with crushing intensity and I thrust my tongue into her mouth, reveling in her sweet taste and delicious heat. I took two more steps into the office before swinging my foot back. The slam of the door didn't alter the passion of our kiss and only served to make me more desperate.

I sat Aurelia on the desk and broke the kiss, my eyes blazing with desire. "For what do you crave, princess?" I asked, pressing my forehead against hers, my breathing heavy.

"I want you but..." she trailed off, her eyes wide and searching as she gazed up at me.

I reared back. "But what?" I asked, sinking my teeth into my lower lip.

What could she possibly have reservations about?

"I'm a, well..." she turned her head away, her cheeks turning a perfect shade of pink, reminding me of the serene blush of cherry blossoms in spring.

"What, Aurelia?" I pressed, skimming my hands up her hips to her ribs.

A tiny groan escaped her.

"I've never done this before," she said chewing her lip, her furtive gaze finding mine once more.

Damn, that's so hot! My tiny fairy princess is a virgin? Could I get any luckier?

"You've never had sex?" I asked with a grin, my cock aching all the more. "You're really a virgin?"

I raised her face toward mine, letting her know with my smile how happy that made me. I would be the only man that my mate ever knew intimately. It was a gift beyond value. I could have never dared dream the woman I ended up with would truly be *all* mine—completely.

My wolf shivered inside me. An untouched mate appeared to be to his liking too.

"Yes," she said, dragging her gaze to her knees as her cheeks burned a brighter shade of crimson.

"Do you have any idea how sexy that is, princess?" I asked. "I desperately want to fuck you right here on my desk, but that's not the first time you deserve. So, we'll save that for now and I guess I'll just have to make you come instead." I dropped to my knees in front of her without another word.

"What are you doing?" she panicked.

I just grinned and wrapped my hands around her hips before sliding them up under her shirt.

A tiny moan left her as she rolled her head back against her shoulders.

"I'm going to make you come on my tongue and fingers," I growled, the need to brand her, possess her... so impossibly and uncomfortably high. I could scarcely see straight!

I pushed her shirt up over her head and let it fall, my eyes feasting on her perky breasts. She made my mouth water and my wolf salivate like the beast he was. I leaned forward, taking one of her nipples into my mouth and swirling my tongue around its rosy peak.

"Oh gods, Grey," she moaned and squirmed on my desk.

"You like that, princess?" I all but purred as I moved my hands down her sides to the waistband of her leggings.

"Yes," she groaned. "So much."

"Then you will like this even more," I promised and pushed her back on the desk.

She winced momentarily and arched her back, pulling a stapler out from under her before giggling at the ridiculousness of the moment. "Maybe we should have cleaned off your desk first," she suggested but when I pulled her leggings down and discarded them on the floor, the laughter died on her tongue, and she held her breath.

I ran my hands up her thighs, savoring the silkiness of her flesh and leaned in, running my tongue over her soft inner thighs as I pushed them wider.

"Grab the edge of the desk, Aurelia, and don't let go," I commanded, allowing my hot breath to whisper over her pussy.

Aurelia shivered and wiggled her hips with need, her voice plaintive. "Grey, please," she begged.

"What do you need, princess?" I grinned against her skin and moved up, peppered her pretty flower with teasing, feather-light kisses.

"Touch me, Grey. Please," she moaned arching her back again, but she didn't release her firm grip on my desk. Just like I'd told her to do.

Good girl.

I ran a finger up her moist slit to her clit and circled it as I nipped her inner thigh with my teeth. The groan that escaped her had my cock hardening more than I thought possible.

Her pussy juices were soon oozing down her lips and I lapped it up like it was spilled from the holy grail. The taste of her burst across my tongue, igniting every inch of me with fire as my wolf howled in my mind.

Mine. Mate.

My wolf and I were on the same page. There was no way we were letting this delectable virginal female get away. She was ours and we would do anything to keep her—to claim her. And the first part of that wicked plan was to make her come so many times she could never even imagine being with anyone else.

I kneeled on the carpet between her beautiful open thighs and circled her opening with one finger reverently, memorizing its perfection before pushing it slowly inside of her.

Her wet pussy enveloped and squeezed my finger as she gasped softly, her knuckles white as she gripped the desk.

Her readiness had me chaffing at the bit like a stallion rearing to race. I needed sample her heavenly taste again. Leaning forward, I licked at her clit, circling it lazily with my skilled tongue.

"Fuck, Grey," she groaned, before pursing her lips tight, her eyes closing in ecstasy.

"Do you like that, princess? I asked. "The way I worship you with my hands and tongue?"

She didn't answer, her expression one of intense concentration.

I didn't expect her to, honestly. And I was just getting started. I grinned before wrapping my lips around her glorious clit and drew it between my teeth, suckling forcefully like she was the fount of ambrosia—the essence of immortality and the food of the ancient gods.

Aurelia screamed, writhing on my desk as her entire body shook with her first orgasm. Magic flared at her fingers, purple and electric.

But I knew it wouldn't hurt me, so I continued my relentless mission, sucking at her clit.

She screamed for me throughout her entire release, her reactions genuine and unhindered by thought or manipulation. Wave after wave of sensation rippled within her, until finally her body began to relax, and the shivers and shudders of her pleasure subsided.

I sat back on my heels to gaze upon her. She truly was magnificent. "You are perfect, Aurelia." I grinned, the taste of her still slick on my lips as I licked them clean. With a heavy sigh I stood up once more, my cock aching for release. I reached for her hands and pulled her up from the desk and into my arms. "Let's go home."

"What?" she asked with a frown of surprise as she stared down at my cock. "We're stopping?"

My cock jumped at her eyes on it. Her gaze held a hunger that I wanted to explore, but not on my desk. Not for her first time. I wanted her first time to be something she'd remember forever, something that staked my claim on her very soul beyond a shadow of a doubt. "We're going home, princess. Get dressed." I offered her a knee-weakening smirk and then turned to the closet next to my desk.

"But... what about you?" she asked softly looking unsure.

"Trust me, there will be plenty of time for that. But for now, I need to get you away from here," I said glancing at the door.

"Why?" she asked with an adorably naive pout.

"Why do we need to get you out of here? Or why won't I fuck you on my desk?" I asked with a raised brow, pulling a pressed button-down shirt from a hanger. I peered over my shoulder at her, and pink tinted her cheeks as she slowly stood and gathered her clothes from the floor.

"Umm," she said ducking her head with a shy smile. "I guess the first?"

"You've seen how cut-throat this place can be. If we don't go, someone could issue a challenge and I won't be able to stop it," I answered as I pulled my slacks up over my hips.

"But if I'm not staying, then how will they be able to do that?" she asked softly.

"You're still in the building," I said and held out my hand to her. "It's technicality, but they'll demand it be honored. This lot have a code of their own when it suits them."

"What about my things?" she asked, her lips pinched in concern.

"I'll have them sent to the apartment later, but we will get you new things, don't worry, princess." I squeezed her hand in mine to reassure her, wanting her to feel my strength and confidence.

We would get her better clothes than she'd ever had before. She would want for nothing. I would treat her like a real princess. But even as I dreamed of spoiling my fairy rotten, rage tinted my vision red as I remembered where she lived before—In a fucking closet. I wanted to bring the witch back just so I could interrogate her and kill her myself.

Pushing the darkness to the back of my mind, I focused on Aurelia. Leading her through the door and into the hallway, I stabbed at the button for the elevator as we approached. I quickly ushered her into the elevator and pressed the button for the garage. I tapped my foot as we passed the training floor, but thankfully no one got on. I might be the boss, but my people would absolutely riot if I denied a challenge, even if Aurelia was nowhere near ready for such a battle.

Best to get out of here before a challenge is thrown down and shit starts unravelling real fast.

The doors opened at the garage level, and I placed a hand on her lower back, leading her to my car. There was no time to wait for the driver. The faster we made it out of here, the better. I opened the door for her and ushered her into the car when the sound of a distinctly feminine throat cleared behind me. Drawing in a deep, frustrated breath, I closed the door and turned to see Layla watching me, her expression as unreadable as a mask.

"What exactly is going on here, Boss?" she asked, crossing her arms over her chest.

"You forget yourself, Layla. I don't answer to you," I growled.

"So, you're just going to ignore that there's been a challenge against her and leave me with a bunch of enraged criminals?" She scoffed.

"Tell them I've already left," I said, and made my way around the car.

"Half of them are shifters and will smell the lie!" She threw her hands up.

The car door shut with a click and Aurelia got out and stood with her arms folded. "There's been a challenge? Did Connor get his panties in a twist because he got stuck to a ceiling?" Aurelia asked, one defined brow cocked.

"It wasn't Connor," Layla sneered. "Someone else heard about your stunt today and decided they wanted the chance to put you in your place."

"In my place, huh? Considering I'm not staying, I guess they wouldn't know where that is anyway." Aurelia glared and she took a step toward Layla.

I grabbed her arm, halting her forward momentum. "Not a good idea, princess. You've only been training a week," I said pulling her back into my chest.

"Karma is going to start a riot," Layla said and turned back toward the elevator with a nasty smirk.

Karma challenged her? I didn't think the half-witch-half-white-tiger-shifter even liked the wolves that much. Why is she defending them? This must be an ego thing. She's been top cat for so long she probably can't stand the thought of someone being better than her.

"Karma challenged me?" Aurelia asked, her voice softer as her face fell.

Did she think she'd made a friend during her week here? There was no loyalty to be found among thieves and criminals.

Layla burst into laughter.

Aurelia's shoulders stiffened in response and her expression hardened once more.

"Aww, what's wrong little fairy? Did you think you made a friend only for them to have betrayed you?" Layla mock pouted with a wicked gleam in her eye.

"Fuck you. I'll accept the challenge!" Aurelia took a step from my arms toward Layla again.

What is going on with my second? She is usually so much more professional with the employees than this, even the worst of them.

"Aurelia..." I started but trailed off when I saw the determination blazing purple fire in the depths of her green eyes. She needed to do this.

"They think I'm a weak little girl that can't take it just because I smile and don't let bullshit get to me, Grey. I need to prove them wrong." Aurelia stared into my eyes, pleading with me to see her point of view.

"Very well, but *I* pick the date. You're not doing this without more training." I glared pointedly at Layla.

Layla knew how important Aurelia was to my overall plans and I would be damned if her bitchy behavior was going to get in the way of that. She needed to get over whatever the hell this was and focus on being my damn reliable second.

"Fine," Layla spat. "I'll let Karma know." Then she stomped back to the elevator, looking every bit as ridiculous as a toddler having a tantrum.

My shoulders slumped in defeat. How long could I put this off for? Karma was a beast in every sense of the word and a long delay of affairs would be met with considerable outrage. "All right, let's go." I opened the door for Aurelia and helped her back into the car. Closing the door behind her, I rounded the car again. Falling into my seat, I hit the ignition and then the gas, pulling out of the garage. "Are you sure about this?" I asked.

"I have to prove myself," she said absently as she stared out the window at the trees all around us.

"Why? You aren't staying there. You don't owe them anything!" I said.

"Do you think I'll feel good about myself and my worth to *you* if I just run away? I'm no coward, Grey, and I'm powerful." She shook her head as if answering herself.

"I know you're powerful, princess, but that won't matter in the ring." I pursed my lips and sighed. She had no damn idea what she'd just gotten herself into. She may be strong magically, but she was only *just* learning how to protect herself and fight in a physical sense.

"What do you mean that won't matter in the ring?" she asked glancing at me.

"The ring cancels out magic, creating an even playing field for everyone. You won't be more powerful there. Layla shouldn't have baited you the way she did," I said with a growl.

"Mother fucker!" She cursed, clenching her fists in her lap until her knuckles turned white. "That bitch did that on purpose."

I could only nod. I didn't know what Layla's deal was lately, but she was acting *off* and extremely unprofessional. Something had changed, but I couldn't put my finger on what it was.

It couldn't be something as petty as jealousy over Aurelia, could it?

"Can we please stop?" she asked suddenly through a heaving breath.

"Stop?" I asked, confused. "Why? We're in the middle of nowhere."

"I need air," she gasped, her eyes wild and panic stricken.

I stopped the car just inside the wards.

She tore her seat belt off and pushed through the door without another word and ran into the trees, disappearing into the forest, her wings fluttering at her back.

For a terrifying second I lost sight of her, my heart racing. I practically threw myself from the car and took off after her, my wolf howling in my head all the while.

I can't lose her now! I just found her.

And I wasn't sure if I could ever let her go.

Chapter 11

Aurelia

I COULDN'T BREATHE and panic swelled within, threatening to choke the life from me.

Karma wants to fight me without magic? What does that prove to anyone?

The leaves crunched under my shoes as I ran through the trees, the earthy scent of the forest blazing through my senses. I had no idea where I was going. What was I even doing? What would this achieve? As I barreled through the dappled sunlight, a breeze whipped against my face, caressing my skin and easing some of my panic. I slowed to a jog before coming to a complete stand still, took a long, drawn-out breath and let my shoulders slump.

It was peaceful here. More peaceful than I had felt in maybe... forever. I tilted my head back to the sky and let the tiny bit of sun that peeked through the tree branches warm me.

"Aurelia?" Grey whispered from behind me.

I hadn't even heard him coming. "I have never been outside the city before," I admitted. "And when we came to the facility last time, I wanted *so* badly to get out of the car and experience this," I whispered. "It feels so good to be in nature like this. I feel... connected, somehow."

"Why didn't you say something then?" Grey asked.

I turned to peer at him over my shoulder.

He closed the distance between us.

"I didn't think you would care." I shrugged and turned back to the tall trees.

I reached out to touch the one nearest to me. The rough bark was scratchy beneath my palm but felt like home. Something rippled within the tree, and I sucked in a startled breath at the pulse of life flowing beneath the bark.

How is this possible?

"What is it?" Grey asked, moving in closer to my back to observe.

"I can feel the life in it," I answered with a curious frown.

"How do you mean?" Grey asked, placing a comforting hand on my hip.

"There's like... a *pulsing* inside of the tree when I touch it. Something almost akin to a heartbeat or like the cadence of blood flow." I shook my head in wonder and grabbed his hand resting it palm down on the bark. "Do you feel that?" I asked, glancing at him over my shoulder.

He shook his head, his lips pursed as he concentrated. "I don't feel anything, princess."

"That's strange. Do you think it's a fae ability?" I asked, my brows furrowing.

"It might be. It would make sense that the fae possess an affinity with nature beyond other supes." He paused a moment in thought, before looking me in the eye. "Do you want to try something?" he asked moving beside me.

I raised a skeptical brow at him. "What do you mean?"

"Put your hand back on the tree and push your magic into it with intention." He grabbed my hand, laying it against the bark once more.

I tilted my head to the side, listening to the river of life within it. Then closing my eyes, I dug deep into the well of magic swirling at my core.

Grow more leaves.

I pushed a trickle of magic into the tree and instantly felt the pulse grow even stronger. I opened my eyes as a surprised gasp slipped from my lips as I gazed above me. Pink flowers bloomed and fresh green leaves sprouted, fueled by the trickle of magic.

"Wow," Grey said with wide eyes. "That is definitely not like any magic I have seen before."

"What did I do?" I asked rhetorically as I reached up, trailing my fingers over the silky petals of a blushing bud.

"You made it grow and gave it new life," Grey said in awe and squeezed my shoulder.

"I knew I had elemental magic, like air... but this?" I asked shaking my head.

It was all just incredible. Words failed me. And what did this mean? Could I heal sick plants? Is that why I felt so compelled to run into the forest in the first place?

"Come on, I think we should go practice this in a more controlled environment," Grey said as he pulled me away from the tree gently.

I went with him reluctantly, glancing over my shoulder with one last longing look at the bright pink flowers that continued to bloom by the minute.

What the hell else can I do?

Grey opened the door for me as we got back to the car and pulled his phone from his pocket and spoke quietly into it before getting in the driver's seat. "We will get a lock on what you can do and then get your combat training started once we get to the apartment," he said as he revved the engine to a mechanical purr.

The drive back was silent as if we were both lost in thought. My chest ached from the moment we left the forest and made it back into the iron and stone of the city. Maybe there was something to that, like Grey suggested, but I knew very little about fae.

The wicked fae ...

Before long we pulled into an under-ground parking garage and Grey reversed into a spot with a plaque that read: *penthouse*.

I opened the door before Grey could make it around to my side and stepped out.

He glared at me.

"What?" I asked with a frown, perturbed by the unexplained emotional response.

He rounded the car and crowded me against the closed door. "When you're in a vehicle with me, you will wait for someone to open the door for you," he commanded with a throat-deep growl.

"Holy shit. Did you really just growl at me?" I asked, shocked.

"Don't get out of the car without someone opening the door," He reiterated, then pushed me against the car until I was plastered against it and looking up at him, our bodies crushed against one another. "Understood?"

"Okay," I whispered, breathlessly, my heart hammering in my chest at the sudden and aggressive sexual tension that whispered between us and the heat of our bodies. "Understood."

"Good. Now, let's get inside. I want to show you something," Grey said and wrapped an arm around my waist, pulling me along to the elevator like he hadn't just stolen my breath away.

We rode up in the elevator in silence and when the doors opened to the penthouse, I couldn't help but grin. It was *so* different to the last time I was there.

"You didn't have to fill your apartment with plants," I said with an appreciative sigh.

"They're purely for training purposes." He shrugged and walked over to the couch with his arm still around me and sat in front of a slightly wilting plant.

"Are you sure it's just training and not because I felt at home in the forest?" I asked, teasing him a little.

"Heal it," he ordered without preamble. "Do what you did with the tree again."

I raised an eyebrow, but sat down next to him. I held my hand out to the withering plant and stroked one of its sad little leaves that were turning brown.

The leaf perked up immediately at my touch, but the pulsing in the plant was slow and almost labored.

My shoulders slumped at the desperation of the plant. It was dying and unable to do anything about it. It couldn't help itself. "It's so sad," I whispered as I wrapped my hand delicately around the stem. Focusing my intention, I pushed a trickle of magic into it, willing it to live and thrive.

The pulses became noticeably stronger as the leaves slowly perked up. It pulled at my magic a little harder, drawing from me like a baby from the breast.

"It's desperate for life and has latched onto my magic," I said in an awed tone, a gentle smile quirking my lips.

"It what?" Grey demanded and snatched my hand away from the plant roughly and unexpectedly.

I glared at him. "What are you doing?"

Why would he stop me from helping the plant? It's already doing so much better!

My heart went out to it. "I'm healing it, just like you asked me to!" I folded my arms defiantly, irked by his sudden change in temperament.

"It would suck you dry if you allowed it, princess. You need to learn to control the flow of magic, and not let the plant control it." He shook his head and moved the plant away.

At least the plant looked better than it had when I first sat down.

All the same, my shoulders slumped in defeat as the poor plant had no option available to it but to continue to struggle. I wanted to reach out to it and push more magic into it, but irritatingly Grey was right. I wasn't daft. I wanted to heal and help, but I needed to learn to control this new gift before it took advantage of the source unwittingly.

"There will be plenty of time to learn to heal it without putting yourself at risk," he reassured me more gently, squeezing my shoulder.

"Why did you bring so many plants into your home then?" I asked with a confused frown.

"You seemed so at peace in the forest and since we can't be out there, I thought brining some plants to you would help." He shrugged.

If he just wants me for a job, then why does he care how comfortable I am? It doesn't make any sense.

"Thank you," I said with a small smile. "The plants really do make me feel a little better. I appreciate it, Grey."

"Good. There's another thing I wanted to show you as well." He rose to his feet and held out his hand to me.

"What else could there possibly be?" I asked almost to myself and placed my hand in his.

"Come on, and I'll show you." Grey grinned and led me down the hall, past the room I slept in the last time I was there. Then he turned down another hall I hadn't seen before and walked until we were in front of a large pair of metal double doors.

Iron.

I shivered in recognition and took an involuntary step back. It had never bothered me too much before. But after my time in the forest and the way the dying plant had sapped overzealously from me, I could feel the bite of the iron as it pulled at my magic as well and making my shoulders slump. "What is this?" I asked with a frown.

"It's a controlled environment much like the ring at the facility you'll be fighting in. It will make it easier for you to learn to fight and adjust without the use of your magic." Grey opened the doors.

How does he have something like this smack bang in the middle of the city? The power radiating off it is intense. It's already blocking my magic from outside the doors...

I took a tentative step inside, and my limbs felt disturbingly heavy. The oppressive magic neutralizing effects of the room pressed down on me from every side. It felt almost suffocating.

Is this what it feels like in the ring? I'm bloody glad Grey put a stop to the fight happening immediately then. I'd be dead, no doubt about it.

"How do you feel?" Grey asked resting a palm on my lower back.

"I understand what you were talking about now. I would have been at a huge disadvantage if I had gone into the ring without knowing what it felt like." I nodded As I walked around the giant training room and trailed my fingers over the handles of a few gleaming and deadly sharp throwing knives.

The longer I stayed within the confines of the room, the less oppressive the feeling was, and I took a deep cleansing breath. At least it looked like I'd get used to it. "So, what's the plan? I train in here until I'm ready to fight and then I go to the ring?" I asked staring at a bow on display. It was beautiful, with stunningly intricate designs carved into the smooth wood.

"That is part of the plan, but you are going to be doing a lot more training than just this." Grey's hot breath washed over my neck.

I hadn't even heard him move until he was right behind me.

Sneaky wolf.

"What else?" I asked breathless. Shivers skated down my arms at his close proximity. How did just his warm breath on the back of my neck make me feel so achy and needy? It was as delicious as it was frustrating!

"I have another training room that doesn't have the same magic canceling wards. You will train with your magic in there, that way you're covering both bases." He wrapped his arms around my waist.

"Will I get to work with the plants too?" I raised an eyebrow at him over my shoulder.

"Yes, I have some employees who will help you with your plants. They will teach you how to stop the plants from draining you," he said and steered me away from the beautiful bow. He led me from the room and my magic came back immediately.

I rolled my shoulders and pulled them back in relief, the iron no longer pressing down and stifling my magic. I breathed a deep sigh. "That feels much better."

We walked into the kitchen together, and I blinked, mentally questioning what I was seeing.

Two tiny, little glowing sprites were flitting around the space. They were positively enchanting.

I took a tentative step forward, squinting at them. They were glowing green, and their iridescent wings fluttered at the same speed as a hummingbird's wings.

"Fiona, Freya, this is Aurelia," Grey said, addressing the adorable sprites.

Both creatures spun around, and bright smiles bloomed on their faces as they zoomed over to see me. They flew in close, and the flutter of their wings tickled my cheek as one picked up a lock of my unruly hair and tugged on it playfully.

"Hello," I giggled, marveling at their speed and beauty.

Grey grimaced. "You will be helping her with everything she needs, including training, *not* claiming locks of her hair for treasure," he chastised.

The sprites pouted and released my hair.

"Although sprites are known to be mischievous, wicked, little fae creatures they are *very* good with plants and earth magic in general. They will be helping you come to grips with your healing and plant magic," Grey explained.

"You have plants?" a tinkling voice asked excitedly as both sprites zoomed out of the kitchen like streaking balls of glowing light.

A high-pitched squeal met my ears a second later and I laughed.

"They are going to keep you plenty busy during training sessions." Grey shook his head, but a handsome smile tugged at his lips despite the seriousness of his tone.

I didn't care how busy I was. As long as I learned the skills I needed to protect myself, and gain some semblance of freedom, I would do whatever it took and then some.

I can't let Karma win.

Chapter 12

Grey

"WHAT DO YOU HAVE FOR me?" I barked into the phone.

He better have something. It's been hours since I sent Karma to work the damn spell.

"The half-witch-shifter took her sweet ass time getting here," Dan grumbled in response, referring to Karma.

Layla did that on purpose. She knew I needed Karma for a job, and instead, used that opportunity to tell her what Aurelia did, causing no end of problems.

I really don't want to kill my second.

But she was becoming more and more troublesome... "Yeah, there was a bigger issue than I anticipated," I said with a growl. "Did you get anything from the room?" I asked.

"Not really. Whoever it was, wore a hood covering their face and never looked up from the book they grabbed out of the safe," he said.

I tightened my hold on the phone to the point where my knuckles were almost white. "What book?" I grumbled with a frown.

"As much as I don't like Karma, she's good at mimic spells. I got *so* much detail," Dan said, rambling on.

"Get to the point," I growled.

I didn't have time for this. I needed useful, tangible information and to make sure my sprites didn't wear Aurelia out too much while working with the plants. They were overzealous with their desire to train her, and it might ultimately wind up doing more harm than good if I didn't keep an eye on them.

"There was a note on the book. It was in Aurelia's possession when she was found as a child, apparently. I couldn't read the title of the book. It was in a different language, one that I'm not familiar with," Dan said and then sighed in annoyance.

I sat forward in my seat, my back straightening. Could this be what I'd been looking for all along?

How the hell are we going to find it now, though? And how did it end up in Aurelia's possession in the first place?

"This doesn't give us anymore answers, Dan. Only more questions!" I growled, dragging a hand over my face in frustration.

"I wonder if you should have Karma do it again for Aurelia? To see if she recognizes anything, herself," Dan suggested thoughtfully.

"That is not the best idea right now." I grimaced.

Putting the two of them in the same space with the challenge looming overhead was a supremely *bad* idea.

"It may be the only way to find out some real answers though," Dan grumbled right back.

I stood and strolled to the closed door of my office before opening it. A giggle met my ears that had a grin spreading over my face before I could stop it. Aurelia sounded so happy and carefree working with the plants. I didn't even care if I walked into my living room, and it resembled a rainforest to be frank. "Look, just see what else you can find for now. Let me know if you have anything for me, and we might address your suggestion later if there's no other option," I said and hung up the phone.

I walked out into the living room to the sound of buzzing wings and tinkling laughter. I blinked at the plants that had all grown twice their size and had different flowers budding on them that couldn't possibly exist in our world. "What's going on here?" I groaned.

All eyes turned to me, and the sprites tittered.

"Isn't it amazing? Aurelia knows the plants of Faery!" Fiona said clapping her hands excitedly.

My eyes widened and I turned to my mate in surprise.

How could she possibly remember the plants of Faery? She was only a child when she was found. ...was she born there? And if so, who were her real parents and why was she left here?

"You know the plants of Faery?" I asked with a frown of consternation.

"No, I mean not *really*. My magic just does it, like it has living memory. It happened with the tree in the forest today, too. Those pink flowers I encouraged it to grow were not like any of the others." She chewed her lip, shuffling from foot to foot as if plagued by anxiety.

I nodded and moved toward her, placing my hands on her shoulders and bending to peer into her beautiful green eyes.

"Are you sure? Fiona seems to think you know these types of plants. Magic works with knowledge, after all," I said.

Her brow furrowed. "How do you mean?" she asked, confused. "I just focus my intent, and that's what comes of it. I'm not thinking of any specific flower or design. It just occurs."

Freya flew over in between us. "You have to have *seen* something in order to recreate it, Miss Aurelia," she sang excitedly, before she tapped my mate on the nose and shook her head as if the answer were obvious.

"So, wait... you're trying to tell me that I've seen these things before?" Aurelia asked, her eyes widening. "But I've never seen anything like these in Dallas. Nothing so beautiful and magical grows there."

Fiona landed on my shoulder, and I grimaced at her before answering Aurelia. "You must have been in Faery at some point because these don't grow here, as you said."

Fiona was excited, but I needed her to tone it down. They were the only ones who knew the full extent of my plans and if they let them slip, Aurelia may never want to help me.

"I was there? When? How is that even possible?" Aurelia asked softly, furrowing her brow in concentration.

Is she trying to dredge up a long-forgotten memory?

"We'll figure it out, princess. Don't worry. There may very well be a block on your memory," I said and pulled her into my arms without hesitation.

Freya flitted away chittering at me angrily for almost squishing her between us, but Aurelia needed reassurance and Freya had lightning-fast reflexes.

"Is that where I came from, do you think? And if so, why didn't anyone ever coming looking for me? I'm sure a child can't just wander between worlds alone, right?" she asked, whispering her questions against my chest.

"No, a child wouldn't be able to wander between realms on their own. There's a reason you are here and I'm going to find out what it is, one way or another." I patted her back and then stepped away with a small nod.

I couldn't call a witch on my normal payroll to investigate this new development. Karma was the only one with enough skill, and I refused to put her in the same room as Aurelia or give her information she might then use against her. "I'm going to make a call." I sighed and pulled my phone from my pocket.

Freya's wings fluttered excitedly. "Yay! We can work on the plants some more?"

"No. Give Aurelia time to rest. You two are plenty capable of healing the plants without her help." I glared at the sprite. They were overzealous to a fault.

The light around her dimmed at my admonishment, but she nodded her tiny head in understanding.

I didn't want Aurelia to overwork herself, especially if we were going to try and work on her memory block.

Is it even a memory block? Or was she just too young to retain any memories of her home? Did she even have a home?

There were just too many unanswered questions surrounding my mate and it was looking more and more like they all revolved around my plans...

How will she react when she finds out what my plans are?

I was under no illusion that she wouldn't eventually figure them out. She was my mate and a huge part of what I had planned, but I didn't want her to find out the wrong way—or too early, before she was ready.

Fiona jumped from my shoulder and flew right in front of my face. Hovering there, she opened her mouth, probably to say *too much*.

I shook my head. "Don't, Fiona," I said, pinning her with a hard glare. Without further discussion, I stepped around the sprite, and headed back to my office. This new development brought nothing but *more* questions, but maybe I would get some answers once we unlocked her memories.

That is, if it's even possible.

I closed the door behind me then sat at my desk. I leaned my head back against the chair just as my phone buzzed in my hand. I glanced down at the screen.

How does she always know when I need to speak to her? It's kind of creepy.

"Magna, how did you know?" I asked into the phone.

"Know what, Grey?" she answered cryptically.

Is she a seer? She can't be, right? She would never go against me...

"How do you always know when I need your help?" I asked with a muted growl.

"You know that old wives' tale about your nose itching when someone's thinking about you?" she asked with a chuckle.

"Um, sure," I shook my head and rolled my eyes. The woman was eccentric to say the least.

"Think of it as something like that, only imagine it ten times stronger," she said. "Now, what do you need, darling?"

"I found someone who will be able to help me, but I think she has a block on her memory." I rested my head on my hand and blew out a breath.

"This is surely something the hybrid can handle?" she asked, her tone filled with venom at the mention of Karma, my half-witch—half-white-tiger-shifter fighter.

"Not this time. Karma has a massive chip on her shoulder. She's threatened by Aurelia and has already issued a challenge against her, so that option is available to me as far as I can see." I grimaced. It would have been much easier if I could have just called Layla to send Karma, but I couldn't take any chances with this. Too much rested upon it.

"She challenged her?" Magna asked with obvious distaste. "If this fairy is as important as I believe she is... you can't let that stand."

"What do you know about her, Magna?" My spine straightened at her words.

She's telling me what I can and cannot allow, now? How much does she really know about me? This isn't good at all.

"Nothing for certain," she said cryptically. "It's just a gut feeling, but I'm sure we will find out if I'm right soon enough, won't we?"

I sighed again. "How long until you can be here?" I asked, refusing to answer her cryptic question.

"What exactly do you expect me to do, Grey?".

"I think she has a memory block on her. I want you to lift it and see what she can remember." I stood from my chair and began pacing.

"Very well. I will have to gather a few things, but I will be there within the hour," Magna said and hung up the phone promptly.

"What the hell?" I stared at the phone in disbelief.

I should have been used to Magna's eccentricities by now, but that still threw me off. *I* was the one who hung up on people without a word, not the other damn way around. I leaned against the wall in my office, my gaze glued to the ceiling. What had I gotten myself into? What things did Magna need to gather to remove the block?

"Grey?" Aurelia's sweet voice came from the other side of the door before she knocked.

I took a fortifying breath and pushed off the wall. "Yes, princess?" I opened the door, staring down at her pink cheeks. She was so beautiful when she blushed.

"I just got this funny feeling that you needed me. It's weird, I know. I'm sorry for bugging you," she said and turned back toward the jungle that was apparently my living room.

I reached out and pulled her back into my chest. "You aren't bugging me at all. I just got off the phone. I have someone coming to meet you within the hour," I told her, squeezing her hip.

How the hell did she feel that? Magna is half-fae... so is that intuition a fae trait or a witch trait?

I shook my head to clear it of questions that I wasn't likely to get the answers to any time soon. Magna was always cagey when it came to answers about herself, but I wouldn't let her be about this. Aurelia meant too much to me to let Magna get away without divulging absolutely every answer she might find.

"Who is this person? Are they like me?" she asked.

I shook my head.

There is no one in this world like you.

I led her back into the living room and chuckled at the green space. "Did you do *all* this, yourself?"

"Um, I'm sorry. I should have told them to stop... they were only trying to make me happy. Fiona and Freya may have gotten a little carried away." She glanced away, her cheeks becoming pinker by the second.

The leather couch and chairs were covered in a vibrant green moss dotted with bright pink and purple flowers, while lush vines twisted their way elegantly around most available free-standing objects.

"Fiona. Freya. What the hell?" I groaned. "I told you to go easy with this!"

That damn moss better not ruin my furniture.

Fiona buzzed into the living room. "What's the matter, Grey? Don't you like it? Miss Aurelia said she's never really been out of the city, and we thought this would feel more like home to her. We like her smile!"

Fucking sprites. Well played, Fiona. Well played.

I could do nothing but sigh and pull Aurelia into my side more tightly as I surveyed their Faery inspired decorative flair. I couldn't blame them, not really. I'd move mountains to see my mate's smile, too...

Chapter 13

Aurelia

AN UNEXPECTED KNOCK at the door made me jump and I gasped. Turning to look, my gut tightened.

Grey smiled at me as he strode to the door confidently. "Don't worry, princess, it's just Magna. She's the one I've been waiting for."

My shoulders slumped in relief, but I was still on edge. What would the woman think of the way the sprites and I redecorated Grey's living room? What would I remember if she was able to get the memory block off?

Is any of this really important? Why does it even matter that I probably lived in Faery as a child?

I squared my shoulders and exhaled a steadying breath. It would matter, somehow, I knew. Even if I didn't yet understand quite how all of this pieced together. Ultimately, I would have answers as long as this Magna woman could remove the block.

Grey opened the door wide and invited our guest inside.

A wizened old woman hobbled in, her gaze raking over me.

This is Magna? How is she supposed to help me?

Grey reached out a hand to help her into the living room, but she pushed a huge bag at him instead. Grey let out a breath in a *whoosh*, almost as if his patience was already worn thin.

"You must be Aurelia," the elderly woman said as she ambled nearer to me. Her blue eyes were so light they appeared almost milky white. Then she moved closer to me quicker than should have been possible at her age, taking me by surprise. Her hand wrapped around mine and she began to hum.

What in the world is going on here?

I glanced up at Grey with wide, questioning eyes.

"Yes, there is strong magic here," Magna said with a hum of what sounded like disapproval.

I frowned at the woman.

What is she?

"What do you mean?" I asked softly. Was she talking about my magic and how strong it was, or was she saying someone had placed strong magic on me—like the memory block Grey mentioned?

Why would anyone do that to me? What purpose would it serve to make me forget my origins?

"Not your magic, darling." Magna smiled at me and patted my hand like an old friend. "Though, your magic is immense as well."

"Immense?" I asked with a grimace.

My magic sure as hell does not feel immense.

Magna scanned the living room and chuckled at the new living decorations. "You think your magic isn't incredibly strong when you have plants thriving all over poor Grey's furniture?"

I scrunched up my nose at the two sprites whose light dimmed only slightly as I turned my focus on them. "It wasn't *just* me," I said.

"I can feel your magic in every plant in this room, so I don't believe that for a moment. Perhaps you don't realize quite how much you gave of yourself." Magna shook her head and hobbled over to the mossy couch.

The sprites beamed at her and flitted to land on her shoulders.

Cheeky little shits!

They could have at least admitted their part in this green mischief.

Grey set the giant bag Magna had brought on the coffee table and crossed his arms over his chest. "Fiona and Freya, I think there are other things you could be doing?" Grey raised a brow suggestively.

The two sprites tittered between themselves and flew off into the kitchen. It was clear they weren't going to argue with their boss when there was company around.

Magna smiled to herself and leaned forward to open her bag.

Grey sat down next to me and rested his elbows on his knees. "So, what do you need to do this?"

Magna peered over at Grey. "I need space and I need time with Aurelia. I'm sure you can find other things to occupy yourself with too?"

Grey's gaze snapped to Magna and his lips pinched at her sass.

She raised an attitude-filled brow at him and waited.

They sat in a silent stand-off, the one regarding the other, until Grey finally huffed out a breath and stood. "I'll be listening from my office. Let me know if there is anything you need for your spell, Magna." Grey mumbled and left the room.

"There, now that we are alone, how are you holding up, my dear?" Magda turned her perilously light blue gaze on me.

"Holding up?" I asked with a frown. "I don't know what the hell is going on with anything. The only mother I have ever known was murdered, and they're blaming me for it! *Holding up* isn't something I can really wrap my head around right now."

Magna patted my hand and smiled with sympathy. "It is a lot that has been laid upon your shoulders, but I think it's the way it must be," she said cryptically.

What does she mean by that? Why would any of this be the way things were meant to be?

I frowned as my confusion only grew. "Can you tell me if I have a block on my memory?" I asked, pushing those thoughts aside to get her back on track. How did she know so much, anyway? A part of me wanted to move away, but at the same time I also felt a strange kinship with the woman.

"Yes, you have a strong block on you, Aurelia. It's one I'm not even sure I can remove with my magic, alone," Magna said with subtle shake of her head.

"Then what are we doing here?" I tried to remove my hand from her grip in frustration, my temper fast fraying with disappointment. Maybe I was going to get no answers after all?

Magna only squeezed tighter, keeping my hand firmly in her surprisingly strong grip. "I may not be able to use my magic to loosen the block just yet, but maybe I can do something to jog your memory of the time before you were sent to this world?" Magna suggested sternly.

"So, how do you think we can loosen the block, then?" I asked, my chest tightening with apprehension.

If her magic can't do it, then what can she possibly do?

"Never underestimate the power of stories child." She squeezed my hand anew.

"Stories?" I asked softly, my curiosity piqued. "What do you mean?" I flopped back into the soft moss that covered the back of the couch and waited for her explanation. Could she tell me something about Faery?

"I am much older than I look." She grinned. "I remember a time before Faery was closed off from us."

Wait? What the fuck is she talking about? Faery closed itself off from who?

Magna shook her head with a sad smile. "I am but half-fae, and any supernaturals that called Faery their home that weren't pureblooded were expelled and abandoned to hide in the mortal world."

"And you were there?" I asked my gaze locking with hers.

Surely that would make her ancient, right? How can she possibly be that old?

"Please, darling, ask the burning question I see festering in that beautiful head of yours," Magna said with a gentle woman-to-woman shoulder bump.

"There's *way* more than a single question in there," I said and wrapped my hand around hers once more.

"Tell me the most pressing," she prompted.

"Well, for starters, what are you, exactly?" I blurted. "And what did you mean by they kicked us out?"

"I knew that was the question you would latch on to." She squeezed my hand in understanding. "I am a half-breed, child. The Fae did not look kindly on those of us who weren't pure like you," she said, her words without malice or censure.

"But if I am full fae, why not blame me for what was done to you?" I asked, anxiously chewing my lower lip.

"Was it your actions that resulted in us being kicked out of our home-realm hundreds of years ago, child?" she asked as she wrapped an arm around me.

I shook my head.

"I didn't think so, either", she said, her tone warm. "I would have remembered a pretty face like yours if it were that full of hatred and malice."

"Are my kind... evil?" I asked, giving the question that had plagued me my whole existence, life. Could I really be the wicked fae my mother always told me I was? My stomach knotted and I grimaced.

Why did my people make them leave? And are the fae really as bad as everyone says they are?

"Maybe they are not all the wicked fae they have garnered the reputation for, but there are those who went out of their way to actively purify their realm of all half-bloods, shifters, and witches included. They are the ones who are wicked, not you, darling." Magna embraced me with her frail arms.

It did little to make me feel any better about the way my kind had treated the others. It was appalling. Why should any supernatural be cast out of the only home they've ever known? Blood purity, of all things!

Do I want to know about my home anymore? Do I even care?

"It's important to know where you came from, darling. If you don't know that, then you won't know which is the correct path forward," Magna said sagely.

"My people are awful. They kicked you all out of your home because you weren't pure. Why would I ever want to go back there?" I asked.

"Maybe, you can be the one that changes things for the better, darling." Magna's gaze bored into mine with a frightening intensity.

"Why would I matter in any kind of change?" I asked.

She just hummed in response.

What the fuck am I missing here? I was nothing more than a grown-up foster child with a questionable past and an even more uncertain future.

"I think a story is in order. It may help you with your memories, darling," Magna said and shifted on the moss-covered couch beside me.

"What kind of story?" I asked with a raised brow. I loved books whenever I could get my hands on them but that wasn't often.

"A story about Faery," she said happily. "A story about the goodness in the realm and the ancient tales."

"All right," I said with a nod, opening myself to any chance at regaining my memories. "I would love to hear them."

"Millennia ago, Faery was a glorious place where all the supernaturals that live in this realm lived out in the open, in peace, in Faery. They didn't have to hide. In fact, there were always grand dances and parties, both in the wilds of nature and at court. The fae courts were very similar to what you hear about in the human stories," she said with a faraway look in her eyes.

I shifted as I listened to her talk about the beauty of the realm that I was beginning to hate. I glanced at the budding plants that were far too beautiful to belong in this world.

Could they be right and I have been to Faery and because of whatever block is there I just don't remember?

"It was a beautiful place and a beautiful time. But as with all history, it didn't stay that way. The courts were always squabbling, and wars broke out. The Fae Elders' Council determined among themselves that the other supernaturals of the realm were to blame." Magna shook her head.

"How were the shifters and witches to blame for the courts warring?" I asked, my brow furrowing.

"The shifters and witches got along about as well then as they do now, and they were members of rival courts as well." Magna shook her head, pursing her lips at the memory.

That makes sense.

Even I had seen how shifters and witches reacted to each other with utter distrust and a general disdain.

"These courts bordered each other and every time a scuffle broke out along their borders, war would soon follow," Magna said with a sigh.

"So, basically they gave the Elders everything they needed to blame them for the wars that continuously broke out," I reasoned as I rested my elbows on my knees and sat forward. I'd always loved learning about any precious scraps of my history that I could, but this wasn't helping me to remember anything. Still, I kept my silence as she continued her story.

"Eventually the Elders' Council decided that the fae were the only ones who deserved to live in their homeland and searched for a way to expunge all others from their realm. It was, after all, *Faery*."

My whole focus was trained on Magna as she kept me on the edge of my seat with her story. "And they eventually found a way?" I asked and shook my head is dismay.

Of course they did.

"They did and the supernaturals who were not full-blooded fae were ejected from the realm forever." She shook her head sadly as if it pained her to this very day.

"And perhaps the worst part of all is that it's not even a one-way deal…" Magna sat back against the couch.

"What? They can come here, but we can't go there? That hardly seems fair." I covered my face with my hands and closed my eyes tight. There was something *there*, niggling at me, just out of reach… but the more I tried to grab for it, the farther away it seemed to slip.

"Nothing about being kicked out of our home was fair, child," Magna said.

"Right. Well, I don't think this is working, Magna." I shook my head in defeat.

"Close your eyes again, and clear your mind, darling. And just listen to the sound of my voice," she coached softly.

I can do that.

It was much like Grey had taught me do when I was calming down to control my magic. I took a deep breath and focused myself, preparing for whatever was to come.

"Think back to your first memories," she said, her voice soothing.

I did as instructed, and the memory of being found walking the streets of Dallas hit me like a speeding freight train and I shivered as I remembered the chill in the air and the utter sense of despair that had plagued me like a shadow.

"That's good," she coaxed. "Now, push back farther."

I concentrated, but there was a wall there. I couldn't go back any further. Grimacing, I tapped at it in my mind, testing its permeability with tendrils of my magic—but it was rock solid. "I found the block," I said aloud, and then with all my mental strength I punched a hole straight through it. No one was keeping my secrets from me, not when I had the power to do something about it.

Chapter 14

Grey

A STRANGLED, HAIR-RAISING scream tore through the apartment, chilling my very soul. I jumped up from my seat behind my desk and rushed from the room, practically knocking over everything in my path in my haste to reach my mate. "What the fuck happened?" I asked Magna with a protective growl, my urge to shift almost overwhelming me.

"I don't know," she said, her voice tinged with concern. That spoke *volumes*. The old half-fae had scarcely revealed her true emotions to anyone in all the time I'd known her. She was a woman of mystery and hidden truths, and always kept her guards high. "She told me she had found the block and mere breaths later she started screaming." Magna's face crumpled with a deep frown.

"I thought *you* were supposed to be removing the block?" I hissed as I kneeled on the mossy floor next to her.

"It was stronger than my magic could overcome, Grey. So, I tried another tactic." Magna held her hands over Aurelia's head and a faint green glow emitted from her palms as she focused, her eyes closed.

I trailed my fingers down the side of Aurelia's cheek and pushed an errant lock of hair behind her ear.

What the fuck happened, Aurelia? Why did you just start screaming? Are you all right?

"The block appears to have been damaged," Magna sighed, before directing her words at my mate. "What on earth did you do, child?"

"What do you mean?" I asked turning my glare on the old woman.

"She did something to the magic maintaining the memory block. I didn't tell her to do that," Magna whispered in response, her lips pinched as she sat back; the glow leaving her hands.

"What does that really mean, though? Does it mean you can't heal her?" I asked, pulling my unconscious mate into my arms from the moss-laden couch.

"She's not physically injured." Magna shook her head. "And no, I can't heal her mind. That magic is beyond the reach of a half-blood. We have our limits."

"Are you telling me that she's somehow fractured her damn mind, and you can't do a thing to fix it?" I growled, cradling my mate.

"I don't think it's fractured, but *she* will need to heal herself and face whatever is in her past before she wakes again," Magna said with a shake of her head.

What the fuck does that even mean? Face what's in her past? I hate it when she talks in riddles!

"Now, the time has come for you to tell me what you think Aurelia *is* to you and your plans," Magna said with a raised brow.

"You know I can't tell you that, Magna. Neither of us can risk it. It could paint a target square on your back. I don't need that complication, nor do I want you lost as collateral damage. You don't deserve that, Magna." I held Aurelia closer to my chest and her soft, unconscious sigh tickled my neck.

"She may not be happy with your plans, Grey, once she realizes the role she is to play in this game of revenge. Are you prepared to face that?" Magna asked, her eyes shining with an air of knowledge.

This fae woman always knows way too much.

I sighed. It was bloody vexing at the best of times, but even more so given the circumstances. "What do you know?" I asked.

"I know that she thinks she's evil because of what her people did to us all, and she doesn't want to go back to the fae realm because of it," Magna said, shocking me. "She's taken the guilt of an entire people, who came long before she was ever born, upon her shoulders. I can only imagine that weight feels… crushing."

"I don't know what you *think* you know about my plans, Magna, but that won't be a problem." I rose from the floor with my precious burden and stormed down the hall, my temper fraying as I tried to keep myself in check.

The sprites flitted around me in bursts of bright pink and green, their wings fluttering furiously as they darted to and fro.

I kicked open the door to Aurelia's room and laid her gently on the bed with a grimace.

"Miss Aurelia's room needs plants!" Fiona gasped, clapping her hands together.

"Not now," I grunted and sat next to Aurelia on the bed, my heart aching as it twisted in my chest. I brushed her wild hair away from her face with my fingertips. She was *so* beautiful—even in sleep—that it hurt.

I can't believe she's mine.

Mate, my wolf simpered.

"Master Grey," Freya interjected softly. "Is she going to be okay?"

"According to Magna, she's just working through her memories, the ones that came before we met her... but I don't know what that will ultimately mean for us." I scrubbed an anxious hand over my face.

Fuck! What if she wakes up and remembers who she is and how to get back to Faery? She's a full-blooded fairy. There would be nothing to stop her from crossing over. Will she leave us all here to rot once she rediscovers herself?

Hiding from the humans in plain sight all the time was painful beyond the ability of words to accurately explain. Especially when many of us still remembered what it had been like to be free of all of that. We could shift out in the open without fear, cast magic, and travel as we wanted. We lived our best lives—and then it was stolen away from us. I couldn't imagine what it would feel like to be able to reclaim that...

And what if truly Aurelia can? She may well be the key in more ways than one if we mean anything to her at all. But who knows how she'll feel when she wakes... I stood abruptly and stomped back into my redecorated living room, pushing a curtain of greenery aside as I went.

Bloody sprites.

"How long do you think it will take for her to wake up?" I asked Magna.

"I don't know, honestly." Magna pursed her lips and wrung her hands together. "It could be minutes or hours. Maybe more. There's no way to know how she will fare on this journey of the Self. It is hers to walk alone."

I slumped down on the couch next to the wizened half-fae woman with a frustrated huff. "You know more than you are letting on," I accused, crossing my arms over my chest.

"I always know more." Magna smiled.

Could she be the seer that took the book from the witch's house?

I had to find out. Sitting up straighter, I interlocked my fingers and licked my lips. There was no beating about the bush, here. "What do you know about Aurelia and her past?" I asked with a raised brow, hoping I didn't come across as confrontational as I felt.

"I know she's important, Grey. Far more important than even you know," she said quietly. "She is a rare creature."

"Do you always have to be *so* fucking cryptic?" I grumbled. "I *need* answers."

"How would you like me to be, darling? If I tell you *anything* it could potentially change *everything*." Magna stood, her expression terse. "The future cannot be jeopardized."

"You are a seer!" I jumped to my feet, my tone triumphant. I had been right all along!

My inner wolf howled, his hackles rising.

My suspicions had finally proven true, and vindication never felt so sweet.

Her nearly white eyes turned on me with an intense glare. "That's not common knowledge, Grey," she said evenly, her gaze suddenly more dangerous.

"Were you at her home the day her witch caretaker was murdered?" I marched over to the door and blocked her exit. There was no way she was leaving without answering me.

There are too few seers for this to be a coincidence.

"No," she growled, affronted by the mere suggestion. "I would never!"

"Do you know what book was found?" I asked, pressing forward with determination.

"Book?" she asked, confusion contorting her face as the edges of her anger instantly softened. Her eyes clouded over and she swayed on her feet, before her knees buckled and gave way.

I lunged for her on instinct, my reflexes as an Alpha wolf shifter comparable to lightning. She didn't weigh much, and I lifted her with ease, laying her down on the mossy couch she had just risen from.

What is happening right now? Is she okay? I can't have her unconscious too!

The sprites buzzed into the room frantically, their voices high-pitched and shrill.

"Don't touch her, Master Grey!" Fiona fluttered in front of me, her eyes wide and worried.

"Why the hell not?" I asked, frowning. "I had to catch her!"

"She's having a vision, right now," Freya whispered to me, her tone filled with awe.

"Have you seen this before? What could happen?" I asked, taking a step further away from Magna.

"She could accidentally pull you into her vision," Freya warned and wrung her tiny hands together, her entire being riddled with nervous energy.

"And, after what she just said, if I know what she sees... it could spell disaster." I nodded.

Fucking hell. I can't catch a break, here!

I understood, but the not knowing had an irrational anger bubbling to the surface of my mind. It was a toxic feeling, so I pushed it back with a concerted effort. That would serve no one right now, least of all Aurelia.

Anger makes you stupid.

And when your head wasn't in the game, you screwed up and there were some things you could never take back. I took a steadying breath and allowed the roar of my anger to simmer down.

I need to save my anger for those that deserve it...

A groan filled the quiet space, snatching me from my thoughts.

I turned away from the frantic sprites and back to the wizened woman. "Magna, did you see something?" I asked as her eyes cleared of whatever she'd just witnessed in her vision.

"Not much, I'm afraid," she grumbled and rubbed her forehead as if in pain. "There's another seer blocking me, I can feel it. And I worry they're after Aurelia."

"Who's after me?" came Aurelia's sweet, familiar voice from the hall.

Startled, I spun around with a broad smile. "You're okay!" I rushed to her and cupped her pale cheeks in my hands.

My wolf was pushing at the surface, ecstatic that our mate had awoken, but he was threatening my control as I stared into her eyes.

"Yeah, I think so. What happened?" Aurelia asked with a shaky sigh.

Magna sat forward with a glare, again shocking me with her uncharacteristic forthrightness. "You weren't supposed to touch the block."

"What are you talking about?" Aurelia asked as she rubbed at her temples.

Strange.

"Princess, what did you do when you found the block on your memories?" I asked, guiding her back to the couch. I sat her down beside Magna and took a seat in front of her on the coffee table.

Aurelia frowned and closed her eyes in concentration as if searching for something internally. "It's gone," she said, her voice barely above a whisper.

"What do you mean it's gone?" I asked. "Does that mean you remember everything?" I needed to know about the book and how it fitted into this bizarre puzzle that was Aurelia's life. It could have ramifications on my plan and it was obviously important. A seer would never have risked exposure for something that wasn't.

"It's still a little fuzzy," she admitted. "But the block is gone." She opened her green eyes and stared directly into mine.

"Do you remember anything about a book?" I asked, leaning forward.

"Grey," Magna warned me with a glare, her tone like cracking ice.

"I was just asking a question, woman." I shook my head at the old woman and pursed my lips in annoyance, probably giving me the appearance of someone who'd just sucked on a wickedly sour lemon.

"Forcing her memories to the surface before she's ready isn't good for anyone," Magna scolded before patting Aurelia's arm like she was a small child.

"Hello? I'm sitting right *here*!" Aurelia threw her hands up in exasperation. "Can you please not talk about me, when you can talk *to* me?" she stressed.

"What's the first thing you remember, Aurelia?" Magna queried gently, squeezing her arm in a more familiar and comforting gesture.

Aurelia sighed, then closed her eyes again.

I leaned closer. I wasn't going to miss a single thing. Anything could be worth noting at this point, even if my mate didn't yet realize it.

"It's cold," she said with a tangible shiver. "And I'm huddled in an ally way that I don't remember seeing before. A person in a long dark cloak with a hood approaches me."

Shit. Could it be the same seer Dan and Karma saw in the mimic spell?

"I said something to them in a language I don't even know if I understand," Aurelia continued as she scrunched her brows together in deeper concentration.

"You don't know what language it was, or what you said?" I prompted and turned my surprised gaze toward Magna as we observed Aurelia's memory recall.

"I think I said that I want to go home," Aurelia whispered. She opened her eyes and stared at me, her gaze plaintive and confused. "How did I understand that when I have never heard it before? It's so strange."

"What did the cloaked person do when you said that?" Magna coaxed, keeping the track of discovery on the straight and narrow.

"They shook their head at me and said something." She shook her own head as if warring for understanding. "You can't. I think they said I couldn't go home."

"How old were you?" I asked squeezing her knee, piecing the timeline together.

"I look to be maybe six or seven years old? But how is it that I forgot all this? It's not like I was *that* young. That's school aged... I *should* be able to remember." She slumped back onto the couch, her face a conflicted array of emotions.

"Aurelia, there was a block on your memory," I said. "It's not your fault. They were purposely hidden from you."

"Why would that person tell me I couldn't go home? They seemed familiar to me in the memory, like I knew them or something," she said and tilted her head back to stare at the ceiling.

"You knew them? If you saw them again, do you think you could identify them? Point them out, maybe?" I asked, getting excited that we had straws to grasp at.

Could she tell us who this person was and how to find the book? This could be the lead we've been looking for, and it's all just been locked away in her mind!

"I probably could, eventually, but my head is still fuzzy. I feel like I'm trying to remember a dream, the way you do when you're waking and it's slipping away with every second your eyes are open." Aurelia shook her head, her lower lip trembling.

"Not to worry," Magna said and patted Aurelia's hand. "You can't push too far, too fast, or you could hurt yourself, darling. It's not worth the pain." Magna shot me another stern glare to make her point.

My wolf growled angrily in my head, but not at the half-fae seer woman. He was growling at *me*.

I was putting our mate at risk by being so impatient. I couldn't hide my excitement. I might soon have the answers I needed and be closer to my goals than ever before. But where was my game? I was a master of my damn poker face, and I was forgetting myself; getting swept up in the thrill of learning like a child.

"I feel like I'm failing you, Grey... by not being able to remember," Aurelia said softly.

I could hear her heart in her throat. "No," I growled. "You are not failing me, princess." I cupped her cheek and pressed my lips to hers softly, regardless of our present company.

"Are you sure? I could try harder," she said, breaking the kiss, her eyes shimmering.

"No, I don't want you to hurt yourself. You've had a long day. It's time you rested. Your trainers will be here early in the morning, anyway. You need to recover." I kissed her forehead and stood, pulling her up with me. I shared a covert look with Magna and nodded toward my office.

I moved through the hall to Aurelia's room and opened the door for her.

Her tinkling laughter filled the space as she scanned the room I'd given her.

"Fiona and Freya," I growled, wanting to smack myself in the head.

Overzealous sprites! I told them not to go crazy.

The blanket was a lush expanse of soft moss draped over the bed, and there were garlands of fragrant, blooming flowers draped around the headboard. They wanted Aurelia to feel at home and at peace.

I shook my head and kissed Aurelia on the cheek. "I need to have a chat with Magna and some overzealous sprites. Get some sleep." Strolling from the room, I closed the door behind me. I needed to talk to Magna. She once again knew more than she was letting on. And even though the future could be at stake, I couldn't be left in the dark. Aurelia was in my care after all.

I raced down the hall to my office and pushed through the door. "What do you think is happening, Magna?"

"I think we need to tread very carefully here," she answered without preamble. "Whoever was in the witch's apartment is going to come after Aurelia. That is the truth, Grey. She's not safe." Magna turned to raise an eyebrow at me, no doubt wondering as to my next move.

"I know that! It's why I'm getting her trained to use her magic *and* protect herself without it. I knew she was special the moment I met her, Magna. I felt it in my bones—literally." I sat behind my desk, my fingers steepled.

"I don't think you quite understand what I'm saying. The future is uncertain. This person could be a danger to her as much as a danger to your own carefully laid plans." Magna had a faraway look in her eyes as she spoke, seeing or feeling who knows what.

"So, you're saying that she could still take the other side on this? The potential exists that we could wind up as enemies?" I asked shaking my head as the wind was knocked from my sails.

I can't let that happen. I can't let this psycho seer near her.

There was no way in the world I was going to lose my mate. Losing her would be akin to having my heart torn from my chest and thrown in a blender. I'd never recover from it. There was no healing to be had when your destined mate was lost. I'd be no more than a husk, a shell of myself.

And I can't let that happen, either.

Chapter 15

Aurelia

"AGAIN!" THE MAMMOTH of a man training me roared from the other side of the makeshift ring, his expression darkening with intimidating intensity as he took up his stance once more.

This guy is absolutely relentless!

"Water," I gasped, small stars dancing before my eyes as my head swooned with the fuzzy onset of dehydration. He'd been working me like a juggernaut in Grey's magic canceling room for hours and it felt as though I was fast approaching my limit for the day. I'd never felt so physically sore or fatigued—not even after being tranq'd by that bastard back in the alley the day Mother died.

"When you're fighting for your life do you think your opponent will let you stop for a water break?" Max shouted with a cocked brow. "Again," he repeated sternly and without apology.

He's really not going to let this go.

Sucking in a deep breath, I scowled and crouched back into a fighting stance, mirroring my trainer. Allowing my frustration and anger to lend me strength, I waited for Max to come at me again. Having been at this for hours I was basically one giant living, breathing bruise. I had muscle aches in places I didn't even know I had muscles, but I kept going. I had to. My challenge fight with Karma was fast approaching and I was damned if I was going to lose to that bitch. There was no world in which I could live with that shame.

I'll prove myself and make her rue the day she decided to fuck with me.

As Max closed the distance between us, faster than I'd anticipated, I slammed one fist into the pad on his hand and spun in a circle, executing a pretty impressive roundhouse kick.

Max's other hand blocked my foot effortlessly and he pushed it away with a disapproving smirk. "You're slow," he taunted.

"I'm not used to this much exercise," I growled back, every fiber of my being crying out for reprieve as my muscles burned with agony. I had never done much exercise in general, but over the last week since my mother's death Grey had insisted on a rigorous and grueling training schedule. My hours of proverbial torture had been steadily increasing by the day and Max wasn't about to let up on it either. He knew what was at stake just as well as I did, and he wasn't about to fail his employer or allow me to fail myself, either.

"You need to get used to it," he snarled. "You are a sitting duck in a fight. Try harder, be faster!" Max shook his head, clearly tired of my bullshit excuses.

"In a fight I will have my magic," I huffed, scrunching my nose as my brows furrowed in annoyance.

"Will you have your magic in the ring?" Max glared at me, making his point clear. This wasn't about surviving in a general sense; it was about somehow overcoming Grey's best fighter in a ring that suppressed all magic. "Again!"

I kicked out at him again and spun, bringing my elbow down hard on his side,

Max blocked it easily.

I jumped back, ready to go again, forcing my body to obey my will.

He swiped out with the pad, swatting at me as if I were a pesky fly and no more than a mere annoyance. "You need to start a daily run to help increase your stamina," Max said with a shake of his head. "In this room. Make it five miles before I get here every morning."

My face fell, his words almost like a tangible slap to the face. "Are you kidding me? You want me to run five miles *before* the ass crack of dawn and *before* you beat the crap out of me?" I stressed with a scowl and moved to snatch up my water bottle.

"I'll make sure Grey is aware of the adjustment to your training program and you won't have a choice. I heard the sprites can be very convincing," Max said.

"You wouldn't!" I spun on him, my jaw falling open. "You sure like to play dirty."

"One day, you will thank me for it. You need to be fast. Karma will use everything she has at her disposal, including her ability to shift. And if you hadn't already noticed... that kitty has big claws. Now, grab a weapon. You're going to need to be proficient." Max pointed to the weapons wall.

With a renewed surge of energy like a second wind, I bounced excitedly on the balls of my feet. I had been just dying for a chance to learn a weapon. I eyed a beautiful bow, intrigued, and took a step toward it.

Max stopped me with a cluck of his tongue. "Not the bow, at least not yet. You need to learn close combat first," he warned. "Karma isn't going to allow you're the mercy of distance and time."

My shoulders slumped as I ran my fingers over the glittering selection of small knives on display. "What about this?" I asked, watching my reflection shift and distort over its polished blade as I passed.

"No. Not that one, either. That's a throwing knife and you never want to throw away your only weapon," Max snarled as if that should have been damn obvious to a beginner like me. He stomped over to the rack and pulled a sturdy looking dagger from it before placing the perfectly balanced blade in my hand.

I gripped it, tight. The dagger felt good in my grasp, and I slashed out with it experimentally. It felt like a natural extension of myself. "It's perfect," I murmured mostly to myself. The metal glinted under the harsh and unforgiving fluorescent lighting, its beauty as stoic as it was cruel.

"Come at me with it," Max ordered gruffly.

I raised an eyebrow at his empty hands and instinctively twirled the blade in my hand as if it were something I'd done a thousand times before. I'd never really worked with a blade, but it just felt *so* natural. I widened my stance and slashed out as fast as I dared.

Max twirled away from me, too quick for me to strike him. "You must be faster than this! Karma will *not* go easy on you. I expect better. I demand better. Again!" he barked.

I crouched down once more, adopting the fighting stance Max had so ardently spent two hours perfecting. He'd knocked me on my ass so many times that he finally drilled it into my head. Taking a chance, I faked left and then corrected, slashing at him from the right. but

Unfortunately for my thinly veiled sense of hope, Max was smarter than that. "You drop your weight to your right foot before you feint to the left. It's a tell, and any opponent worth their salt will pick up on it immediately," Max said as he spun behind me and jabbed me firmly in the kidney with his elbow.

I dropped onto the mat with a cry of frustration and pain.

Fucker isn't pulling his punches. That hurt!

The blade pressed into the mat beneath me as I caught my breath, prostrate on my hands and knees. A towel dropped down next to me, signaling the end of foray with weaponry for the day. I picked it up gratefully and swiped at my forehead and neck as I sat back on my heels, hurting all over again.

I need to get fitter.

"Time for a cool down or your muscles will seize up and you won't be able to crawl out of bed in the morning. So, get on it. I want a one-mile jog on the treadmill," Max ordered and he stomped out of the room.

The door slammed shut behind him, and I fell back on the mat like a starfish, stretching out my aching limbs. The only sound to be heard in the whole training room was that of my own heaving breaths. "Why the fuck did Grey hire such a sadist to train me?" I mumbled to myself, permitting myself a micro pity party.

"*Now*, Aurelia!" Max barked from the other side of the thick iron door.

"Mother fucker has super hearing too," grumbled as I shook my head and peeled myself bodily from the mat. With a half-hearted sigh I ran the towel over the back of my neck and trudged over to the treadmill.

This sucks.

I pushed the buttons, programming in a slow jog with a subtle incline and my muscles screamed in protest as I started my one mile cool down.

Grey's going to pay for this. What does he expect me to do? I'm doing my best, but this is murder.

I gulped down water as I did what I was told. I wasn't going to give up or quit training, but I sure as hell not going to show up with a smile on my face and a kiss-ass attitude. Aside from discovering my magic and Grey, so much of my situation sucked. My humble life had become dangerous and complicated overnight and if I was being honest, most days I still found myself reeling with the whiplash of it all. I'd gone from being an outcast fairy hiding in plain sight, to being more powerful than I knew how to handle—and that painted a *big* target on my back with neon lights.

As I mused, my muscles slowly worked free of their stiffness. I jogged for about ten minutes, completing my mile, and sighed in relief when it was done and dusted, taking a breather before drinking the last of my water.

Grey had been even more adamant about starting my training off strong after the revelations of the old fairy's visit. I still couldn't remember much from before the alley, and I had no idea what language I'd been speaking in that memory. The only thing that made any sense was that I was speaking the native tongue of the fae.

I turned the treadmill off with a sigh and stretched my arms over my head before trudging out into the hall beyond; relieved to be outside the heavy, anti-magic wards of the training room. I really needed a shower, but it didn't make sense to do that until after I'd finished all my training for the day which included my magic session. Exhausted, I flopped into a chair by the kitchen island as the sprites flitted around.

How do they cook when they are so tiny?

They flew about the kitchen glowing a beautiful bright green that reminded me of the forest. Magic trailed behind them in their wake, sparkling like the tail of a glittering comet.

Fiona turned to me with a tiny grin. "Miss Aurelia, how was your training?" Fiona asked.

Freya gasped and turned to me, startled from her busyness.

"Terrible," I said shaking my head, before resting my chin on my upturned palm. A tall glass suddenly appeared in front of me with something thick and green inside of it and I grimaced in response, heaving a heavy sigh.

"Don't look at me like that!" Freya wagged a finger at me. "It will help heal your sore muscles."

"What is it?" I asked, picking up the glass and sniffing at its suspicious contents. I didn't completely trust the mischievous sprites. They were good-natured but could have very well given me something that tasted like ass just to titter and joke about the prank they pulled off. It didn't smell terrible though. It smelled like berries and something vaguely floral.

Both sprites gazed attentively at me, waiting. as

I took a tentative sip and warmth washed through me like a river of sunshine and honey. I groaned in gratitude and gulped it down without further fuss. My muscles relaxed instantly, uncoiling like the tension on a spring released, and the pain from my bruises mercifully ebbed away. "Thank you," I grinned at them, emptying the glass.

"That will teach you to trust us, Miss Aurelia. We would never give you anything that would harm you," Freya whispered, the tone of her voice belaying horror at the mere thought of such a thing.

"I'm sorry, girls. I just had a *really* tough training session with Max." I pushed the empty glass across the counter feeling a hundred times better already.

"Here," said Freya. "You need to refuel for your magic training after being in that gods-awful box for hours!" A moment later a plate full of sandwiches appeared on the counter in front of me.

"How do you do that?" I asked, picking up a sandwich. My stomach let out an unholy growl and I grimaced in embarrassment.

"Magic," Freya giggled by way of an answer and flitted away without another word.

I shrugged and bit into the sandwich. Clearly, I wasn't getting any more of an explanation than that.

Grey strolled into the kitchen, bent down, and kissed my sweaty cheek.

"Ew. Don't touch me right now. I'm all gross!" I leaned away from him in an effort to escape his affections.

"Did you have a good training session?" Grey asked chuckling and shaking his head.

"No," I huffed. "You hired a complete sadist." I scowled at him.

"He's the best trainer available." He took the stool next to me and reached for a sandwich, too.

Fiona smacked his hand away without hesitation.

Grey took a leaf out of my book and scowled back at her.

"Those are for Miss Aurelia. She needs to refuel, or she won't be able to perform her." The sprite waggled her finger at Grey with a stern expression, reminding me of a nanny swatting at a naughty child trying to steal another cookie from the cookie jar.

"I can't eat all of these, Fiona!" My eyes widened. There were several rounds piled high, all filled to overflowing with the works; fresh meat and salad, coupled with a variety of pickles and spiced relishes that smelled absolutely mouth-watering.

But there's so much! Do they really expect me to eat all of them? They can't be serious?

My stomach growled again at the thought, and I shrugged. I wasn't going to argue with my body. I trusted it to know what it needed.

Well, shit. Maybe I can eat it all, after all.

A plate appeared in front of Grey a heartbeat later and he nodded with approval, the scowl turning to something that definitely teased at affection for the sprite.

"Yes, Miss Aurelia. You must eat to refuel. The fae eat *a lot* especially after having their magic drained the way that bloody box does!" Fiona glared at Grey to make her point.

"Hey, don't glare at me. She was the one who agreed to the fight with Karma. This is all just helping her learn to fight without her magic." Grey threw his hands up in surrender.

The sprite shot back a stern glare, obviously unimpressed with his answer. She didn't like the training sessions or the aftermath any more than I did.

I snickered at the little sprite's loyalty, touched that she'd stand up to a great big and powerful shifter like Grey, the Syndicate itself.

"Please eat, Miss Aurelia. You need your strength. The fae burn through their energy rapidly." Fiona nodded to the plate of sandwiches.

She's not going to let me leave the counter until I have cleared my whole plate, is she? Bossy little thing.

I finished the sandwich with a dramatic sigh and picked up another, realizing I really was far hungrier than I'd thought.

"Is Magna coming by today?" I asked after swallowing my mouthful, reveling in the heady mix of flavors assaulting my tongue. "I wanted to talk to her about the block on my memories again sometime."

"No," Grey said, but didn't elaborate.

I unconsciously tapped my foot. "Do you know when she might be back?" I asked. I needed answers and Magna seemed like the one most likely to get them for me. She was ancient and knew more about Faery than anyone we knew—at least that I was aware of.

"She's working on finding the cloaked individual you met as a child," he said cryptically.

My shoulders stiffened at his words. Why did I not like the sound of that? The person had felt somehow familiar in my memory. They had felt almost like family.

It feels like a bad idea to let Grey anywhere near that person, but why? Who am I trying to protect, Grey, myself, or the hooded figure?

"What's wrong?" Grey asked, not missing my reaction.

"I guess it's just... do you think it's a good idea to look for them? They could be dangerous," I said, the white lie leaving my lips before I could think better of it.

Grey sniffed the air, then frowned at me. "You don't believe that the words coming out of your own mouth, princess. Why don't you want me to find them, really?" He turned me to face him in the chair, his level gaze pinning me down with its intensity.

I shoved the last piece of my sandwich into my mouth and then grabbed the last one from the plate in an attempt to buy myself time.

What the hell do I say? I don't even understand what I feel... it's confusing.

"Aurelia?" Grey asked, directing my eyes to his.

"I'm not sure," I began hesitantly. "Whoever they are, they felt familiar to me. But I have this horrible feeling that if the two of you were to ever be in the same room as each other it would be bad for everyone." I shrugged and glanced away, unable to express more clearly what I was feeling.

"We need to find them," Grey said with a sigh. "I have reason to believe they killed the witch who raised you."

I gasped at his words and turned my gaze back to him. He wasn't lying and the way he didn't refer to her as my mother wasn't lost on me. Could he know how I lived before? And what more did he know?

But that's not possible. He would have had to have gone to my old apartment.

"Grey, what do you mean?" I asked slowly, swallowing the lump that threatened to swell uncomfortably in my throat.

"I had a witch perform a mimic spell to help clear your name of the murder. But the figure revealed in the apartment by the magic was cloaked. They wore a hood over their head; like they had something to hide. Then they stole a book from the witch's safe. One that was meant for you," he finished.

What book could he be talking about? I don't remember any damn book.

"What was so special about this book?" I asked, my brow creasing in consternation. Mother had never mentioned any book, and certainly not one I was supposed to inherit.

"There was a note that the book was with you when you were originally found. Whoever the hooded figure was, I think it's the same person that abandoned you in that alley all those years ago, before the witch fostered you." Grey steepled his hands on the counter in front of him, allowing me time to make sense of it all.

Something about that explanation didn't sit right with me, though I wasn't sure why and I closed my eyes in thought, dredging through what little memories I possessed.

Could I be wrong about the hooded figure? Could they be out to hurt me?

The intangible feelings of familiarity pulled at me. Who was this mysterious figure and why did they leave me to a life of hiding among the witches? A strange sensation fluttered in my belly and an intense heat flushed through me, though I couldn't pinpoint why or from where the sensation originated.

Ultimately, I wasn't sure of anyone's true intentions, Grey's included. But I knew somewhere deep down, in a place I couldn't quite reach, that I didn't want to think so. But if was true and I trusted the wrong person... everything could be destroyed. My future wasn't the only one at stake. After what Magna had revealed, I felt connected to Faery in a way that almost frightened me.

I don't know what part I'm to play in all of this, but something tells me I'm at the center of something big.

I just needed to find out what it was before it was too late to take action, and I certainly wasn't going to be able to do it alone.

Chapter 16

Grey

WITHOUT WARNING AURELIA slumped to the side, almost taking a tumble from her stool at the kitchen island.

Thanks to my lightning-fast shifter reflexes, I managed to grab and stabilize her before she fell to the marble tiles.

"Don't!" Fiona shouted; her voice shrill as she darted forward.

But it was too late. My eyes closed and suddenly I was mentally whisked away to an unfamiliar place—a dark alley, cold and alone, huddled on the ground in nothing but a thin coat with rain pelting my skin.

"Are you listening, child?" My eyes widened as a male voice that was somehow strangely familiar sounded in the dirty alley nearby.

Is this Aurelia's memory? How am I seeing this?

"I want to go home!" I pleaded, but it wasn't my voice. It was that of a child's, crying because she was cold and afraid.

"You can't go home. You have a part to play in all this," the hooded man said firmly as he shook his head.

"I don't care about my part. It's cold and lonely here," the girl whimpered.

I knew the fae were cruel, but this is some next level shit. They abandoned Aurelia. For what, some unknown mission or greater plan?

I growled but the sound never left my mind. I wasn't here to change things. It was just a memory, and I was merely as observer of the past.

Maybe this is the reason she forgot her past. Did I inadvertently make her relive this past trauma by pushing too hard? She clearly blocked all of this out for a reason.

"You must remember your purpose, Aurelia. A small amount of discomfort now will all be worth it in the end," the hooded man assured her.

She was a small, delicate child starving and freezing, exposed to the cruelty of the elements and he wanted her to remember some grand purpose?

What bullshit!

"I hate it here! How am I supposed to live like this?" she asked in a small, panicked voice, cowering away from the man as he remained utterly impassive.

"Do you have the book?" the man asked, completely ignoring her outburst.

The bastard was unfeeling and cold and didn't seem to give a damn that Aurelia was suffering. This wasn't some minor discomfort. Human, fae, shifter, or witch... if something didn't change, she would die on these streets, cold, alone, and without even the smallest of mercies.

I tried to remind myself that something *did* happen, and she went on to survive the elements. But my wolf was snarling in my mind, instinctively wanting to curl up around her and keep the child warm until help could be found, or we could get out of this place. He didn't understand this wasn't real—all he could see was that our mate was suffering, and we were doing nothing to protect her.

"Yes, I have the book," she answered. Little Aurelia shifted, pulling the thin coat tighter around her small shoulders.

"Do you remember what to do with it?" the man pressed.

"I need to hide it until the time is right," she said, her voice almost a whisper.

What is that supposed to mean and how did it eventually end up in the hands of the witch? Did Aurelia hide it in the safe, herself? And who was the note that Dan saw from?

"Good. Do not fail me, Aurelia. Everything hinges on this. You must be stronger than you've ever been before," the man said cryptically, and the memory faded.

I still clutched Aurelia tightly and squeezed her a little tighter as she began to stir in my arms.

"What happened?" she asked with a frown, blinking her eyes open. She pulled away from me cautiously and sat straighter on her stool.

Fiona flitted around the kitchen in a frantic buzz and then another plate of fresh sandwiches appeared in front of Aurelia, this time in an array of sweet marmalades, chocolate spreads, and jams.

"Eat, Miss Aurelia! You need sugar, fast. Using so much magic just after having been in the training room is draining," Fiona fussed.

"What do you mean?" Aurelia asked, still a little dazed as she came back to reality but picked up another sandwich as she'd been told to.

"You relived a memory," I told her as evenly as I was able. "But once again it just leaves us with more questions than answers." I clenched my hand into a fist on the counter. I needed to calm the down, but rage bubbled up inside of me after seeing the memory for myself. I'd gotten to know my mate in the present, as an adult... but having witnessed her plight as a child, it served only to make me and my wolf even more protective and possessive than ever before.

So much conflicting information. How do I protect her and execute my plan?

"Wait, what do you mean? How do you know?" Aurelia asked rubbing a hand over her forehead.

Freya settled on the counter, her eyes full of empathy and concern for my mate as a cold glass of water materialized within Aurelia's reach.

"You pulled me in, princess. I saw the memory for myself, as if it were my own." I reached out and tucked a lock of hair behind her ear.

"What was the memory?" she asked with a confused frown. "I don't remember that." She shook her head and took another bite of her sandwich before taking a sip of water.

"I think it was more of the same memory you saw previously. You were freezing in the alley and talking to the man in the hood."

My wolf growled in my mind. He still didn't like that one bit but neither did I.

"How was I able to do that?" She stared down at her hands, fiddling with the bread.

Fiona fluttered closer. "By touch, Miss Aurelia. I tried to warn Master Grey, but it was too late. He wouldn't let you fall!"

I pursed my lips and continued. "You don't remember anything about your purpose or the part you're supposed to play?" I asked. "The memories aren't ringing any bells for you yet?"

She shook her head. "I don't know. It's all still fuzzy. I can't help but wonder if there's a reason I can't remember though, and perhaps it's for the better that I don't?" Aurelia chewed her lip nervously.

Indecision warred within me as I pondered if she could be right. In response my conversation with Magna came back to haunt me.

So, you're saying that she could still take the other side on this? The potential exists that we could wind up as enemies?

"I need to make some calls." I stood from the island and pushed another lock of hair behind her ear affectionately, admiring Aurelia's strength and beauty before taking my leave.

I can't allow her to change her mind. I can't lose my mate and my plans all in one fell swoop. I don't think she would leave us here to rot, but can I really be sure about anything?

I needed to talk to Magna as soon as possible. Careful not to panic or stress her further, I rushed down the hall on light feet and quietly closed the door to my office. My phone rang immediately, and I shook my head as I picked it up.

She really does know more than I ever will.

"Magna," I sighed into the phone as I took my seat, drumming my fingers on my mahogany desk.

"I don't have anything more than you do, Grey. The future is still uncertain. I can't tell you what to do," Magna said sounding just as exasperated as me.

"I know you can't, but have you seen anything that can point me in the direction of the book?" I asked running a hand down my face. The book was meant to be in her possession. She should have hidden it, but somehow the witch had gotten a hold of it.

"Just focus on her training and try not to intrude on any more of her memories, that's all I can say," Magna warned.

"It was an accident, for fuck's sake! Should I have let her fall?" I growled at the old seer.

"No, of course not. Your wolf never would have allowed that," she said, then went quiet for a moment. "Grey, speak with Dan. I believe he has something that may be of help."

The call ended and I growled. The old woman was getting on my nerves hanging up on me like that all the time.

She has some seriously big lady balls.

I slumped into my chair and dialed Dan, my angst making me feel unreasonably snappy.

He picked up on the first ring.

"Report," I barked into the phone, wincing at my own tone.

"I think I have a lead. Meet me shifter side, Boss," Dan said excitedly.

"Shifter side? But the woman murdered was a witch," I reminded him, shaking my head and rolling my eyes.

"I know but there's been another murder that matches the same MO," Dan said with a groan.

What the ...? There's been another murder?

"How does a shifter getting topped have anything to do with Aurelia?" I asked sitting forward in my chair as I tried to piece the puzzle together.

"It's the guy who ran the motel," he explained. "That cheap shit hole that I chased her from. He was a hawk shifter and he was murdered in the motel not long after she'd been there. There's got to be a connection," Dan said.

Is someone murdering supernaturals who dared show her a scrap of kindness? What purpose would that serve?

I'd have to wait and see. "I'll be there in twenty minutes," I grumbled and hung up the phone. Rising from my comfortable leather chair, I stormed from my office and into the kitchen, but Aurelia wasn't there. Changing direction, I made my way toward the training room where she'd likely be focusing on her magic lessons.

She stood in the middle of the room, purple magic pooling in her hands as she closed her eyes in concentration.

"Sorry to interrupt. I need to head out for a while," I said.

Aurelia spun on me, and her magic went wild, bursting out in all directions; but before it could touch me, it fizzled out, losing its momentum.

"Grey! You scared the shit out of me!" Aurelia yelled in exasperation, throwing her hands up in the air.

"Sorry," I apologized, offering her a sidelong grimace. "I have to go. Don't open the door for anyone." I raised a brow at her to make my point.

She nodded and heaved a sigh, turning her back on me to return to her training.

At least she's showing some serious dedication. She's going to need all the training she can get before she faces off against Karma.

I rushed out of the apartment and within ten minutes was striding up to the skeezy motel that Aurelia had paid for a room at. I grimaced; the place was as dingy as motels came and not fit for a human let alone shifters, and especially not my mate.

What had she been thinking, opting for a place like this?

I flinched at my own judgmental thoughts when her memory played out behind my eyes again. She likely had no choice. I sighed with a shudder and my wolf whined.

She's stayed in worse than this.

"Hey Boss."

Dan's voice startled me from my thoughts.

"Where was he found?" I asked and moved toward him.

He had dark purple bags under his eyes, and he looked somber. He was clearly exhausted. "It's bad, Boss. I know she didn't do it because she was with you, but no one in the supe community does and they are calling her a wannabe serial killer." He shook his head.

"Show me," I barked, just about ready to start slitting throats.

Dan led me into the motel lobby and through a door that went out to the back. He pulled a key from his pocket. He stopped in front of a door with a boarded-up window. "This is the exact room she was in when I found her. There was a note of her name and room number at the front desk, too." Dan put the key in the lock and wiggled it until the lock clicked open.

"Get a hold of management after we're done here and make sure this place is closed down until upgrades can be made. This is a right shithole." I shook my head and stepped inside behind him.

"Yes, Boss. I'll see it done," Dan said and followed me inside.

"What the fuck?" I asked with wide eyes as I stared at the macabre sight that greeted me. "I thought you said it was the same MO, Dan?" I folded my arms across my chest.

"Blaming Aurelia is the same MO, right?" he answered. "Last time they left her on the floor to take the blame... and this time, well *this*." He grimaced as if the situation explained itself.

Aurelia's name was written in blood above the headboard on the wall.

Why would the shifters assume this was done by her, when it was clearly left as a warning directed at her?

"That wasn't done with the intention of blaming her, Dan. It's a warning *to* her. She's not safe. Whoever murdered the witch, and the shifter are dangerous. This is no coincidence." I took a step deeper into the room and pulled my phone out of my pocket.

I don't care if calling the facility is ill advised. I need to know what happened here. Right now, and I only know one person who can do that.

"Boss?" Layla asked when she picked up the phone.

"I'm sending you an address. I need Karma to do another mimic spell and if I have to wait as long as the two of you made Dan wait last time, then you'll both be punished for your insolence and it won't be pretty," I said and hung up the phone promptly.

I scanned the room, engaging my keen wolf senses and walked around to the other side of the bed. My gaze immediately locked on a small slip of paper which was dropped on the floor, partially hidden by the shadow of the bed in the dim lighting. I bent over and picked it up. The flowing script was in a language I recognized but had never learned how to read. Aurelia's name was written on it in, but that was all I could make out. "Whoever did this, is Fae," I growled, my gut burning with a smoldering rage.

Could it be the same hooded figure from Aurelia's memory? What purpose would this stunt serve when he was the one who abandoned her to our realm in the first place? Or at least I think he's the one who sent her here... but why?

I pulled the camera up on my phone and snapped a quick picture of the note, sending it to Magna instantly. Maybe she would be able to read the language better than I could.

Dan wandered out twenty minutes later to await Karma's arrival.

She and Layla walked in minutes later with shocked expressions on their faces.

"What is that?" Karma, the half-witch-half-white-tiger-shifter asked pointing at the name drawn in blood.

"What does it look like you idiot?" I barked. "Just do what I asked."

Layla raised a brow at me in response, but I was beyond both of their bullshit.

Karma wandered around the room shaking her head. "Shit," she said. "I can't believe she did this."

My temper flared even brighter. "For fuck's sake, woman. She didn't do it! Have shifters lost their collective commonsense over night?" I crossed my arms over my chest, simmering.

It's clearly a threat directed at Aurelia! Why would she write her own name in blood?

"Are you sure?" she retorted with more attitude than was wise. "The signature is the same. It smells like her in here, too."

Layla took a step forward, following after Karma.

"She hasn't left the bloody apartment and before that she was at the facility. It wasn't her!" I shook my head.

I've really got to tighten up my vetting process. What good are strong fighters to the Syndicate when they're morons?

My phone buzzed in my hand, and I peered down at it with a curse.

It was Magna.

SOS. You need to get home! Now.

My back straightened, and I growled low in my throat, my hackles going up. Something was wrong at the apartment! A chill shivered up my spine and a sense of foreboding dread slithered into my soul.

Fuck.

If I didn't get there soon, would I lose my mate forever? There was no way on Earth I was going to wait around to find out. Without a word of explanation to my crew, I turned and ran like the very fires of Hell were on my tail.

Chapter 17

Aurelia

MY INSTRUCTOR FOR MAGIC control training was not as much of a sadist as Max was.

Thank the gods.

I didn't think I could put up with being butchered for a second time in one day—physically then magically.

Talk about punishment.

"Center yourself, Aurelia. Remember, you control the flow of your magic, not your emotions," Reah offered softly.

She'd figured out pretty quickly that if she raised her voice at me when my eyes were closed, that it didn't go so well. It turned out that I lost control with more than just Grey and his shifters and it was something that needed to be remedied.

I took a deep breath and pulled my magic back. I wasn't sure how this would help me in a fight, though. If I was fighting with my magic, I wouldn't be able to close my eyes and center myself to control it.

I should be learning how to manipulate my magic on the fly. I should be able to wield it no matter how I feel. Angry, sad, panicked, elated—it shouldn't matter. What use is my magic at all if I can't use it at will, whenever I need to, no matter the situation? This is frustrating as hell.

"Aurelia, you are losing focus. Concentrate," Reah said, interrupting my train of thought calmly.

I banished the thoughts from my mind and tried again to focus on the flow of my magic. It had gotten out of control again. Reigning back in, I allowed myself to adjust to how it felt. The way it flowed through me, sparking like lightning, before whispering along my veins to erupt in my palms.

Shit. Don't lose focus. You've got this, Aurelia. I need to do this for me, and I need to make progress for Grey and the Syndicate. I help him and he helps me...

"Okay, now I want you to attack me with your magic," Reah instructed.

I cracked an eye open, my brows knitting as I tried my best to maintain my focus while also holding a conversation. "Um, are you sure about that, Re? Shouldn't I use a target or something, instead, first?" I asked incredulously. "I don't want to hurt you."

"Don't worry, sweetheart. I'm a lot faster than I look." She smirked, looking like an absolute bad ass with a case of serious over-confidence.

She's not a sadist! She's a bloody masochist. What was Grey thinking when he hired these people? They are both freaking insane.

Sucking in a deep breath, I sighed.

All right. Have it your way. Let it be forever on the record that I tried to warn you!

Narrowing my focus to a pinpoint, I let my magic pool in my palm and stared down at the crackling purple spark of magic, willing it to grow and expand. My powers answered my summons eagerly and the glittering mass grew to the size of a golf ball before I flung it at Reah.

The woman disappeared just before my magic would have connected with her chest, likely searing a blazing hole straight through her—though I had no way of knowing what the effects of my magic were just yet. I hadn't had an occasion to use it that way to find out.

"Too slow!" she taunted.

I spun around at the sound of her voice, almost throwing myself off balance in my haste.

Damn it. How did she do that? She literally just disappeared right before my eyes and then reappeared like a rabbit being pulled from a bloody magician's hat!

"With enough practice, you will be able to do the same," Reah assured me with a bright grin. "It's early days. You're only just beginning to learn what you're capable of."

"Can you read my mind now, too?" I asked in frustration.

I'm in so deep over my head here.

Refusing to permit my failure to drag me down, I threw another ball of magic before she could answer me.

She disappeared again without a trace, without so much as even a blur of motion, and her giggle soon met my ears from somewhere to the left.

"No, I can't read your mind, Aurelia. But your question was written all over your face," she called. "You're going to have to practice your poker face, too!"

I turned to her and faked a throw, keeping the sizzling spark of my purple magic firmly in hand.

Just as I had hoped, she disappeared from sight, reacting to my move, pre-empting my strike.

I spun around to my other side and launched my magic in the opposite direction, releasing it as it grew with my intent.

Reah reappeared, only to throw up a shield-wall in front of her at the last second, my magic shattering against the glowing forcefield like purple diamond dust.

"Good!" she sang with a smile. "You're starting to think like a real fighter and you're anticipating my next move. It's not something that can be taught that easily." Reah nodded to me, happy to bequeath her approval and congratulate me on my fast learning.

I'd literally almost just lit her up with magic and she was praising me? What the hell.

She really is insane.

"Um, thanks?" I answered, though it was more of a question.

"Let's go again," my instructor encouraged as she placed her hands on her hips.

I funneled magic into both hands this time, willing it to blaze strong and waited for my opening; but she anticipated everything I tried. I faked left and went right, but she was probably noticing the same tell as Max had. Desperate to land a hit, I dodged left at the last second, trusting instinct alone. With everything I had, I threw my magic just in front of her, going for a direct hit.

To my sick delight, she wasn't able to stop her momentum in time and slammed right into my shimmering magic. She was flung back several feet through the air before she disappeared mid-flight. Then she landed in an ungainly heap on the mat in front of me.

"What the fuck! Oh, my gods! Are you okay?" I asked, rushing to crouch down next to her.

Reah burst into a fit of raucous laughter as she held out a hand for me to take. "That was brilliant, Aurelia! You've got some serious power, there. We can work with that."

With a relieved smile I helped her up from the mat just as a *crash* like broken glass sounded from the living room. I immediately tensed.

Would the sprites be so clumsy as to break something? Surely, they would be able to avert any slip-up with their magic?

Reah took a step in front of me and her silver magic coated her palms. "Hide, Aurelia. There's an intruder in the house." She squared her shoulders bravely, never once glancing back to see if I obeyed.

Who would be stupid enough to break into Grey's penthouse? Do they have a death wish?

My mind boggled at the thought of someone raising the wolf shifter's ire intentionally.

"Aurelia, hide now. That's an order!" Reah hissed under her breath.

I didn't want to leave her—she'd fast become the friendliest person I knew—but what could I do? I wasn't battle-ready yet, not by a long shot.

Who is in the penthouse and why?

I backed away from Reah but the room we were in was void of anything I could possibly hide behind. "Reah, there's nowhere to hide in here," I whispered back, filling my palms with magic.

"Fine. Follow me out the door and as soon as you're clear, run to the magicless training room and stay there." Reah moved to the door, anticipating action.

"Why there? I won't be able to use magic!" I asked, confusion furrowing my brow.

"If they go inside to look for you then you will have an advantage as they won't have magic either," Reah said, exasperated.

"All right, but you haven't seen me fight without magic." I shook my head but followed in her wake toward the closed door.

She pressed her ear to the door to listen, but our ears were met by silence.

What is going on out there? Where are Freya and Fiona? Are they okay?

"Focus, Aurelia," Reah snapped at me.

I glanced at my hands and breathed in deeply.

The magic in my hands had grown much larger than it had been before. With a conscious effort I stopped the flow of magic but kept the glimmering purple projectiles the size they were. I sure as hell wasn't getting rid of my only available weapon.

Reah frowned, opened the door a crack and scanned the hall. "On three," she said.

"What?" I asked.

"Three!' she announced with a cackle and jumped headlong into the hall like a Valkyrie from human legend.

"What the hell happened to one and two?" I grumbled as I sprinted out behind her, taking my chance.

Reah lobbed a gleaming silver ball of magic down the hall.

I gasped as I barely caught sight a hooded figure ducking out of the way.

Is that the man from my memory? What is he doing here?

"Now, Aurelia, go!" Reah screamed.

I shook my head to clear it and ran for the heavy metal door of the magicless training room. I needed to get inside, just as Reah instructed. It would be my only advantage against whoever was after me.

A crash sounded nearby, followed by a feminine grunt and I prayed to the gods that Reah and the sprites were okay as I pushed through the door with all my might. My knees nearly buckled beneath me as my magic fizzled out instantly, snuffed out by the wards of the room like a candle in a storm. I took a handful of calming breaths as I straightened my shoulders, adjusting.

I scanned the room for a weapon and cursed Max for not letting me practice with the bow. Now wasn't the time to opt for a close-range weapon. I'd already proven time and time again that I wasn't fast enough just yet. And I sure as hell didn't want to get close and personal with the intruder if I could avoid it. Taking my chances, I ran to the weapons wall and grabbed the bow down. A tingle ran down my spine with a strange sense of familiarity.

My instincts took over then and I nocked an arrow, pointing it at the only entrance to the room. I started at another crash that sounded closer than the last. Licking my lips, I altered my stance and prepared for the worst.

What is going on out there? Should I risk looking?

I took a step toward the door when the handle suddenly turned, and my stomach dropped.

A hiss filled the air as the hooded figure took a step inside and their knees buckled.

"Who are you?" I demanded, pulling back the string of the bow, ready to fire.

"What? You don't remember me?" the intruder asked, his tone one of hurt.

Why would he sound hurt that I don't remember him? Who is he to me?

Pushing the questions plaguing me aside, I tried again. "Did you kill my mother?" I barked ignoring his initial response.

The hooded figure stepped back out of the room, loitering on the threshold with his hands raised. "That witch was not your mother," he snarled.

It wasn't lost on me that he failed to answer my question.

"How did you know I was talking about the witch?" I growled, stepping forward as a sense of purpose and strength filled me.

He was in the hall now.

Will he be able to subdue me with magic from the outside?

"You have the wrong idea, Aurelia. I don't want to hurt you. I'm here to rescue you. It's finally time to go home," he said, his tone taking on a pleading quality, as if willing me to understand.

"I'm not going anywhere with you!" I yelled back with fire in my heart. "You were the man who left me freezing in the alley, weren't you? I told you I wanted to go home, and you left me there! I was just a child!" I accused bitterly.

"I was, yes," he answered, sounding somewhat remorseful.

But I refused to buy into his bullshit. I had no reason whatsoever to trust this asshole. "You need to leave, now. Grey will be back soon and if you've hurt any of my friends, I will hunt you down!" I held the arrow steady and took another step toward the door with conviction.

Please be all right, girls.

"You need to remember, Aurelia, and if you refuse, I will make you." The man lunged suddenly through the door, taking me by surprise as he knocked the bow from my hands.

The weapon slid across the mat, too far for me to reach. The air all but rushed out of me in a violent *whoosh* as he tackled me to the ground.

I brought my elbow up, intending to smack it against his temple; hopeful it would disorient him for a moment or two, allowing me the opportunity to clamber to my feet.

He dodged my maneuver with uncanny speed, thwarting my plan.

Pain crashed through me as my blow landed on his shoulder instead.

"You have to remember!" he grunted. "If you don't, all is lost."

"I don't want to remember," I shouted. "I don't want to remember being left in the cold or the fucking reason behind it!"

Shit. I'm talking too much. Just fuck this guy up!

My assailants hood never moved as he pinned me to the mat, his identity still predominantly a mystery to me. "You don't have a choice, Aurelia," he spat back as he swung his fist at my head.

I blocked him easily and it buoyed my inner pride. My training was paying off!

Where is everyone? Are they okay? If he hurt them then I will find a way to kill him.

I blocked another hit aimed at my face and managed to get my legs around his middle and bucked my hips, trying in vain to dislodge him. He felt like a lead weight on my body.

He pushed down into me again, dominating me with the clear advantage of his physical strength.

I lashed out with my fists, punching wildly, anywhere I could connect with.

His hands caught mine in a bruising grip and forced them above my head. "You are mine. You were promised to me!" he snarled in my face.

I laughed mirthlessly. "And you left me to die, asshole. I don't care about whatever claim you think you have on me. I will *never* be yours and I will never help you. Fuck you!" I snarled, thrashing bodily against him in frustration and rage.

"Remember me, damn it!" he roared, and pulled the hood from his head with his free hand.

Without warning memories assaulted me, and I gasped, my eyes growing wide. This man was with me in a vibrant, never-ending green field picking breathtaking wildflowers. Then he was sitting beside my bed, reading me stories from a book I didn't recognize. The memories shifted again and he was taking me from my bed, throwing his cloak over me as he stole me away from the castle.

Hold the hell up here! The castle?

I could hear the hounds being set free as he ran with me in his arms, shielded by his soft brown cloak.

"I wasn't given away by my parents?" I asked in horror through the memory, breaking through into the present.

He took me from them, then brought me here and left me to die?

"No," he said and loosened his grip.

Wrong move, asshole.

I broke his grasp on my wrists and punched him square in his overly pretty face. "I trusted you, Malcolm!" I hissed. "You were my friend and then you kidnapped me from my bed and left me to die? What the fuck?"

"You understood why, once," he said, nursing his jaw. "Our kingdom will never be safe if the other supernaturals are allowed to return. You understood what your role would be as a child." His words left me in shock, and he took the opportunity to wrap his hand around my wrists again before he lifted me and slammed me back down onto the mat.

Pain accompanied by dancing stars exploded behind my eyes and I found myself winded and reeling as darkness closed in all around me.

At the same moment a shout filled the air, originating from the living room.

"Go to sleep, my love," my once friend soothed. "I'm taking you home and then we will finish what we started all those years ago," he promised, sounding like an absolute deluded psycho. Not a heartbeat later Malcolm smashed his fist into my cheek.

Pain blinded me and my entire skull vibrated, the world tilting violently sideways before I was sucked into the welcoming embrace of sweet oblivion.

Chapter 18

Grey

THE ELEVATOR DOORS opened, and smoke billowed inside, making my eyes sting and my nose tingle.

What the fuck happened? How did someone get past my wards?

The usually lush and green moss-covered couch was covered in still-smoldering scorch marks, while vases and pots lay smashed, their water and soil spilled form asshole to breakfast. My heart twinged and as much as I loathed the way the girls redecorated my penthouse with plants; I missed the fragrant and colorful flowers that dotted the space. They made this lavish place feel like a home, while the odor of charred furniture and acrid smoke coupled with the devastation before me raised my ire and made me feel violated.

"Aurelia!" I shouted into the eerie silence of my smoldering high rise house, but there was no answer and my stomach lurched.

Has she been taken?

My wolf growled in my mind, his fury boiling to the surface like a geyser waiting to explode. He would hunt down the bastard who took her if that's what turned out to be true—and he would not rest until our mate was found.

Neither of us will.

"Fiona? Freya? Hello? Where is everyone?" I yelled and pushed through the destruction of my home, panic rising by the second.

A groan from the hall filled my ears and I raced to the lump on the ground, recognizing who it was immediately. "Reah, where's Aurelia?" I asked, dropping to a crouch by her side. The distinct scent of blood flooded my senses. She looked like she'd taken a brutal beating, which meant she'd done her job. She'd been loyal when it mattered most and tried to protect my mate with her own life.

"Safe, I hope," she groaned as she tried to sit up.

I pushed her shoulder down, encouraging her not to move, and pulled out my phone dialing Magna.

"On my way, now," Magna answered.

"Hurry!" I barked.

Blood continued to gush from Reah's head and though she was one of the strongest half-fae's I had ever met, she could still bleed out.

Shit.

"Where is Aurelia?" I asked again, removing my shirt and pressing it to the wound to try and staunch the blood flow until help arrived.

"Magicless room," Reah slurred, blinking repeatedly as she fought to remain conscious.

I propped her up against the wall and guided her hand to take hold of my now bloodied shirt. "Keep the pressure on as best you can," I instructed and nodded my thanks. "Help will be here soon."

It was a smart move, sending her to the magicless training room since no one else would be able to use magic against Aurelia while she was inside. She'd have stood a fighting chance at least against an older, and superior magic user on a levelled play field.

The destruction continued down the hall but there was no sign of an intruder or my mate. I roared as I raced to the door, but just as I burst through, it was clear no one was inside the room. The bow lay abandoned on the mat, and Aurelia was gone. I could smell her. She'd been here and it was still strong. I'd only just missed them.

If only I'd been faster!

A string of unholy obscenities spilled from my lips and my inner wolf howled in my head, pushing his way forcefully to the surface. My hands turned to anthropomorphic paws ending in lethal claws. As I clenched them into fists they dug into my palms, and I felt the telltale warmth of my own blood. I punched the wall in frustration and rage. Blood coated my knuckles as they split, but it didn't stop me from punching it again and again, until my hands were a macabre, scarlet mess.

A throat cleared behind me and I spun to find Magna. I glared at her with the rage of a thousand suns as I turned. "You knew this would happen!" I roared, unable to hold back the pain. "You *knew* and you still told me to go meet with Dan."

The seer was lucky that she was more powerful than me and that we had a working friendship, or I'd have painted the walls in her entrails.

Why did she tell me to go?

"No matter how uncertain the future, this was always going to happen. It was a trigger point in the timeline." Magna shook her head regretfully.

"And what is that supposed to mean?" I fired back, shaking my hand out to ease the pain. Blood still oozed from my battered knuckles, but they were already healing thanks to my shifter.

"It means that no matter our actions or choices leading up to this moment, this event was always meant to happen. The rest is up to Aurelia and what she decides to do," Magna explained with a sigh. "This acts as a catalyst for a great change."

"And you think I'm just going to let this fucking psycho keep my mate?" I scoffed.

There's a better chance Hell will freeze over. She's mine!

"Think about this, Grey. How did he know that Aurelia was here without you?" Magna asked.

"He's a bloody seer!" I threw my hands up in the air, my expression contorted.

"Is he? Are you sure? Or was he simply following Aurelia all this time and knew where to find people she had interacted with?" Magna raised a questioning eyebrow.

He's not a seer? Then how did he know that I was gone? Fuck!

"Someone told him," I snarled as the realization slammed into me with the force of a truck. "Only a handful of people knew I wasn't here. I've been betrayed!" I stomped past the old woman and back to the hall where Reah was propped up against the wall where I'd left her.

The half-fae's eyes widened at my angry glare and heavy approach.

"Did you tell this psycho that you were alone with my mate with only a couple sprites for company?" I raged, wrapping my hand around her throat and cutting her air off.

Reah choked, her eyes bulging in fear as she struggled against me in her already weakened state.

"It wasn't Reah, Grey," Magna called out from behind me, her voice firm.

I released Aurelia's magic instructor spun on the seer. "Well, that leaves you, Dan, Layla and Karma. And if I find out *you* did this, playing God for some favorable future outcome, I will find a way to end you, Magna!" I crossed my arms over my chest, my gaze narrowing into blazing pinpoints of gold as my wolf tried pushing through once more.

"I've already told you it wasn't me, Grey. And it certainly wasn't Reah. She tried to protect your mate. If you pause and allow your logic to overcome your emotions, you'll realize that deep down in your gut, you know who it was." She shook her head with a frown at my denial.

No. I refuse to believe it's who I suspect. It can't be! She's been with me forever, since I began the Syndicate.

"You have to be wrong, Magna. It can't be Layla. I won't believe it. She might have her faults, but she has been my second since we were exiled here!" I said and punched the wall nearest to me. Plaster rained down, covering the floor in fragments and dust as I pulled my fist from inside the wall.

"I didn't say it was Layla," she answered calmly. "She would make the most sense though, wouldn't she?"

"She's been acting strange since I found Aurelia. She seems almost jealous, but would she really be willing to sell us out in exchange for Aurelia to be kidnapped?" I ran a hand through my hair, matting it with my own blood. "Or, if it wasn't Layla, it has to have been Karma. She hated my mate from day one. She issued the challenge for sake! Or perhaps they're working together on this? I don't fucking know."

"This is all how it should be, Grey. And now is the time that you figure out the path you want to walk. Everything you do from here on out is shaping your future," Magna said, almost as though she were in a trance-like state.

"First, I need to find the sprites. Then we need to formulate a plan to find my mate and bring her home!" I stomped off and into the living room, kicking debris from my path. I turned over the coffee table that was on its side and scorched with elemental magic. A few of the plants were still smoking and as I walked past them, dread pooled in my gut. If the sprites were unhurt, Aurelia's plants would have already begun the process of healing.

This does not bode well.

"Fiona? Freya? Where are you?" I called out as I sifted chaotically through the rubble, worried I'd find them crushed like fragile dragonflies beneath the ruin.

Maybe they were in the kitchen when the bastard came in and were simply hiding?

I pushed through the door into the kitchen, only to discover that everything was in perfect order. My brow furrowed in consternation. Why had the intruder come through the hall and not even bothered with the kitchen if he wasn't a seer? How could he have known where to look for Aurelia?

Damn it. It has to be Layla, doesn't it?

I growled at the betrayal. How could she do this to me? Was she really so damn jealous that she would have organized to have my mate kidnapped? What was her angle? What did she want? My attention? My affection?

What the fuck! I've never been interested in her that way!

I opened the door to the pantry in frustration but there was still no sign of the sprites. I spun around and marched back to the hall to find Magna tending to Reah.

"Reah, did you see the sprites?" I asked as I rounded on her for the second time.

She was still slumped against the wall, wincing as she received care. "No, I didn't see them. I just figured they were in the kitchen."

"They aren't there," I grumbled.

"Did you look in all the cabinets?" Reah asked, her shoulders barely rising as she shrugged.

I turned around and stormed back to the kitchen. If I didn't find them hiding in the cabinets, I didn't know what I would do. I'd already lost Aurelia; I couldn't lose them too. I loved those flitty little critters more than I cared to admit. I flung open every cabinet in the kitchen, pushing aside pots and pans and dishes As I called out to them to let them know it was safe... but there was no answer.

"They aren't hiding in the kitchen." I hung my head as despair clawed at my insides.

Magna rushed to join me in the room as fast as her old bones could carry her and a grin parted her lips.

"What is it?" I asked, a part of me hopeful she'd seen something that could help us in this shitshow we'd found ourselves in.

"Those sneaky sprites," she chuckled. "They're with Aurelia!"

"How the fuck did they manage that?" I ran a hand through my hair as I paced.

"I'm not sure, but they are safe. And when the time comes, *that's* how we find Aurelia!" Magna said.

"What do you mean 'when the time comes'?" I growled.

I can't sit back and let them stay with that madman! What is she thinking?

"We have no way of knowing where he's taken them," Magna answered all too reasonably. "What do you suggest we do but wait until the sprites are able to escape and lead us there?" She planted her hands on her hips, her gaze stern.

She was right, of course, but I was loathe to think about what might happen to her while she was with that psycho hooded freak. He could hurt them. He could do anything, and I wouldn't be there to protect them.

My wolf snarled in my mind and thrashed inside my chest. He was *very* close to the surface and ready to shift right here and now.

I took a huge cleansing breath through my nose in an effort to push him back and a scent caught in it like a butterfly snatched up in a net. "That scent," I started. "Why is it similar to Aurelia's?" I asked as I followed it down the hall and into the magicless room.

"He's fae, they have similar scents," Magna called after me, returning to her injured charge.

"This is different," I called back as I investigated further. "It's like their scents are tied together somehow. I'm not sure. I can't make sense of it." I shook my head as I walked over to the bow on the floor and picked it up. I placed it back on the wall where it belonged and sighed as if the small semblance of order might somehow soothe my raging beast.

This blows! I can't just sit here, idle and do nothing... and why would their scents be tied together? Who is he to her?

My wolf snarled again and beat desperately against the cage I kept him in. There was no reason to allow him to lose control when there was no one to punish. It was pointless. No matter how much I hated this, I had to try and keep a clear head on my shoulders. I was the Syndicate. I was better than this.

Keep it together, Grey. For Aurelia.

Magna's soft footsteps followed me to the door but stopped short of crossing the threshold. She hated this room just as much as any magic user did. The wards were oppressive, heavy, and suffocating until you adjusted to them—and even then, it felt like a tangible burden.

"Dan needs to come and check this out," she said, a hint of anxiety seeping through into her usually stoic and wise voice.

"I'm not bringing any of them into my home! They caused this, and my wolf will go *insane*." I shook my head vehemently, clenching my fists at my sides.

My wolf already adamantly wanted to hunt Layla and Karma down and destroy them, along with the hooded fae who'd stolen our mate from us. He wasn't the only one, but we had to do this in such a way that none of them would ever see it coming. I couldn't have my prey fleeing before I had the chance to sink my claws into them.

They owe me blood and I will have it.

"Grey, are you sure it's wise not to call on them when you need help with something like this? You could end up making them suspicious. They may suspect that you know what they are up to. You'd lose the element of surprise." Magna raised a brow.

"They wouldn't be able to do anything here, anyway. It's a no-magic zone. Karma's mimic spell won't work in this room." I scanned the room with a frown, my gaze roaming over the empty space that should have safely contained my mate.

"It may be worth it to find out where he entered the property from and what he did in the moments before he came down the hall," Magna suggested thoughtfully.

She wasn't wrong, again, but I hated the thought of having traitors in my space. How was I going to keep my wolf from tearing them apart when they came in here? And how could I keep them away from Aurelia's surviving plants and flowers? They didn't deserve to enjoy her magic when they were the reason she was gone.

But she's right. Damn it.

"Fine," I huffed and pulled my phone from my pocket like it was a lead brick covered in thorns. I really didn't want to do this.

"Boss?" Dan asked on the first ring, sounding surprised.

"Are Layla and Karma still there?" I asked, keeping my tone as even as my emotions and inner wolf would permit.

"Yes, they wouldn't leave until you returned," he grunted back.

Like that's not suspicious.

"I need you all to come to the penthouse. There's been an attack and Aurelia was kidnapped. I need some kind of lead if I'm going to find her."

"We'll be right there." Dan hung up the phone before I could respond.

I punched the wall again angrier than ever.

Fuck! People need to stop doing that before I let my wolf out and he takes a chunk out of them.

"They're on their way," I growled, informing Magna and Reah as I paced the room. I was careful not to touch anything else until they arrived and Karma started the spell in case it hurt our chances of finding anything useful.

Fifteen minutes of pacing was getting on my nerves when the elevator door dinged and finally opened, revealing Dan and the others.

"What the hell happened here, Boss?" Dan asked with wide eyes.

"I told you we were attacked," I answered tersely as I turned and scanned the room. I had to turn my back on the women. My wolf was snarling at me, pushing his way to the surface; ready to tear both those bitches a new fucking asshole.

"Not that... I mean yeah, your penthouse is wrecked but is your couch covered in moss?" Dan covered his laugh with a cough.

"Aurelia has been learning some new skills and the sprites got a bit overzealous in supporting her." I shrugged, a pang of loss painfully needling its way into my heart again.

"Where is Aurelia?" Layla asked from behind Dan as she gazed about, drinking in the destruction.

"She was kidnapped!" I growled, rounding on her.

"What?" she asked with wide eyes. Clearly Dan had not communicated the details of our call; that, or she was playing dumb and insulting my intelligence.

"What about my challenge?" Karma shrieked, her eyes flashing, startling us all with the intensity of her vitriolic venom.

I glared at her, barely able to keep my wolf from launching for her god damn throat. "She's been fucking kidnapped; what do you think?"

Is this shifter-witch for real? She's making this about her. Seriously?

"You're here to do a job and you will do that job without complaint, or you'll find yourself no longer welcome at the facility or employed by the Syndicate." I punched the wall again to demonstrate my point.

They were quite happily pushing every button I had and doing a shitty job of convincing me they didn't do this. The women especially were just lucky I was biding my time for the moment, but their luck would run out soon enough.

Their days spent breathing and above ground are officially on countdown.

Chapter 19

Aurelia

"MISS," A SMALL TINKLING voice whispered next to my ear insistently with an edge of fear.

My eyes felt heavy and sticky, and I couldn't open them easily. I groaned in response, grimacing as I struggled to regain a firm grasp on consciousness.

"Aurelia, you have to wake up!" The shrill voice was followed by a small hand tapping on my cheek.

What the hell?

I cracked one eye open, blinking myself awake with all the energy I had.

Wait? Why was I asleep?

As if on cue my skull throbbed, and I winced. Everything seemed so hazy. "What happened?" I slurred as I fought to sit up. Someone had laid me in a bed and even tucked me in, but the room itself was unfamiliar. I forced my other eye open and rubbed them hard, trying to shed the sense of fatigue that clung to my mind.

Where am I? And why are the sprites staring at me with concern?

"Miss, you were taken from our home," Fiona said wringing her tiny hands in her lap. "It's not safe here!"

I shot up at that and the room spun violently, lurching like I imagined the crew on the deck of a ship at sea might during a storm. It made my stomach heave and I swallowed hard to keep the sour bile in my belly where it belonged.

Fuck. That was stupid.

My brain felt like mush as I glanced between each sprite. "What are you doing here?" I managed, the memory of my fight with Malcom surging back to me with dizzying clarity.

"We couldn't let him take you all alone!" Freya planted her hands on her little hips and glared at me like I'd asked the single most ridiculous question in the world.

"It's too dangerous for you," I argued. "Malcolm is delusional. He thinks the fae are in danger if we let the supernaturals back into Faery. You need to get back to Grey as soon as you can. He's going to worry about you." I shook my head as I pinched the bridge of my nose, trying to center my focus.

"But we are here to help," Freya said adamantly.

I couldn't let them do this. If they got hurt or killed, Grey would never forgive me. We all joked about the sneaky sprites, but we all loved them fiercely. Grey especially. "You can't help me," I said with a sad smile. "Grey will be devastated if anything happens to you two. He needs you."

"He will never recover if we don't make sure you come back!" Freya snarked before she flew up in my face and flicked my nose.

I swatted at her lazily. "That's bullshit. He just wants me for a job—for some plan of his." But even as I said the words, I didn't believe them myself... not entirely. The way he looked at me, and the way that he touched me showed me how he really felt, even if he hadn't told me in so many words.

Both sprites glared at me with renewed fervor.

"That's not true and you know it, Miss Aurelia!" Freya planted her hands on her hips and Fiona followed suit.

"Fine, but still you shouldn't have hitched a ride with me. It's dangerous." I threw my hands up. We had no idea what this guy wanted or what he would do to them if he found them. I touched my head and winced at the throbbing pain there.

Ouch. Did the fucker knock me out?

The sound of light footsteps alerted me to someone coming and I widened my eyes at the sprites to alert them of the approaching danger. "Quick! Hide," I whispered.

They buzzed their way into the open closet and hid as I'd instructed.

The door opened and Malcolm stood there with a radiant smile. He didn't have the cloak on now, his face was clearly visible, and he was just as I remembered him. He was an ethereal beauty, but I noted it as if from afar. I wasn't attracted to him at all, in fact, I scowled at him. If I ever had a soft spot for this guy, I certainly didn't anymore.

"You're awake," he said, his tone bright before his blond eyebrows drew down in a frown.

I continued scowling and remained silent.

Fuck you, Malcolm.

"Come on, Aurelia. Don't you remember me?" he asked.

"I remember you, but I don't know why you brought me here," I answered tersely and crossed my arms over my chest defensively.

"I brought you here because it's almost time for us to go home," he said and took a step into the room.

I scooted back on the bed trying to get away from him—trying to put as much distance between us as I could. I didn't want to go wherever he thought was my home. I barely remembered anything about this man. He was no more to me than a few disjointed memories at best.

He left me for dead. I can't trust anything he says.

"You hit me in the head and then kidnapped me from Grey's. Not to mention the fact you left me in a cold alley to freeze to death as a child. And now you want me to trust you?" I scoffed.

"It was all for a good reason. I wish you could remember our plans," he said and sighed. "What did you do to block your memories, Aurelia?"

"What do you mean, I blocked my memory?" I asked with a frown that mirrored his own.

Could I have done this to myself? Why would I do that? How does a child have enough power to create a block like that? Even Magna couldn't remove it!

"There's no way that pathetically weak witch successfully put a block that strong on you. Your old friend would have removed it easily if that were the case." He took another step closer.

"I don't want you to come any closer," I said as I leaned back into the headboard defiantly, denying him what he clearly wanted—to be near me.

"You are meant to be mine, Aurelia. We were tied together at your birth," he growled in frustration, losing his beautiful and treacherous mask of calm.

He can't be serious! Just no. There is no way I'm going to be with this psycho. I mean, what the fuck... an arranged marriage since infancy? Gross. What is wrong with these people?

"Good thing we aren't in the fae realm then, huh?" I snarked back, crossing my arms over my chest.

"Get up and follow me," Malcolm ordered as he skulked back to the door. He glanced over his shoulder, waiting for me to comply to his wishes.

"Where are you taking me?" I asked, refusing to move.

Like hell I'm going to make anything easy for him.

"Your magic is out of control and it's time to train. I can't believe you thought that mutt and his half-blood colleagues could teach you magic." He shook his head with a dark smile.

How bad would it be if I threw a ball of magic at this asshole?

"Mutt? How dare you? You think I'm going to do anything to help a fucking wanker who insults my friends, the people I care about, at every given opportunity?" I jumped from the bed glaring at him. My hands shook with the need to release my magic upon him. It was pooling readily in my hands and this time it didn't scare the hell out of me.

I wanted that magic at my disposal. I wanted to hurt him with it. He was just as prejudice as the Elders who kicked the shifters, witches, and half-bloods out of their homes in Faery in the first place.

Elitist prick!

"Aurelia, stop," Malcolm yelled as he encroached into my space.

"No, you are just like the rest of them. Fuck you. I won't help you!" I shook my head, trembling with the power of my rage and indignation.

"You won't have a choice, I'm afraid." He crowded me and reached up, pinching my chin like he owned me, the move far too intimate.

I ripped away from his bruising grip. "I will *always* have a choice. For the first time that I can remember, I had friends and a place that felt like home, and you just stole that away from me."

"Your parents will be so disappointed in you," he said with a bored sigh as he took a step back out of my space.

I laughed so hard it almost came out like a wild cackle. "Are you for real? Do you seriously think that I would give a damn about what the parents who I don't even remember, think of me? They obviously sacrificed me for some *supposed* greater good like I was a tool to be used and implemented at the right time, rather than their daughter. If they're disappointed in me—fuck them, too."

"What happened to the girl that knew what her job was?" he asked.

"She died when you left her freezing in an alley. She learned the true meaning of cruelty and became someone else," I shouted back as if that fact weren't blindingly obvious.

Where has he been this entire time? Not sleeping on a pile of blankets in a closet. being little more than a slave, that's for damn sure.

Based on the comfy bed I just woke up in, I would say he'd never suffered a day in his life.

Arrogant prick. He doesn't understand me at all and he's about to learn his actions have consequences.

"You understood it was for the best," he said, running a hand through his white-blond hair.

"Did I really?" I snarked. "Because I obviously did something to ruin your plan after that night. It's the *only* memory that comes easily to me. I can feel the chill in my bones when I remember it." I raised an accusatory eyebrow at him.

"What happened to you, Aurelia?" he asked softly, as if altering his demeanor was going to somehow successfully manipulate me or change how I felt.

I wasn't born yesterday, buddy.

"What happened to me?" I laughed without humor. "You have been in this nice warm house this whole time while I was either freezing in an alley or sleeping on the floor of a closet with threadbare blankets and scarcely enough to get by. What the fuck do you think happened?"

He reached up to cup my cheek.

I slapped his hand away without a second thought. "You don't get to fucking touch me," I snarled, the purple, shimmering magic in my grasp flaring with my emotions.

"Fine, if you want to be a brat, you can stay locked in this room until you remove that block on your memory and remember the stakes!" He turned on his heel and slammed the door behind him, leaving me once more with the sprites.

A soft click filled the room followed by the subtle but unmistakable buzz of magic. He wasn't taking any chances with the possibility of my escaping him.

I slumped back on the bed and put my head in my hands.

How the hell am I going to get out of this?

I refused to help him. I'd never submit to doing whatever it was that would ensure no shifters, half-bloods, or witches could ever return home. It was beyond cruel that they were exiled from Faery in the first place! If Faery was a place of magic, a realm especially for supernaturals, then we all belonged there as far as I was concerned. No one should be excluded. It was a racial prejudice, just like the humans demonstrated so often against others of their own kind. It was sickening.

The sprites buzzed out of the cupboard and back into the room, their glows dimmed more so than usual. Were they sad? Or was that to appear less obvious in the face of danger?

"He wants you to keep us all out of Faery?" Freya asked in her tiny voice.

"Yeah," I sighed. "For whatever reason, that's his master plan it appears."

"Why? I don't understand?" Fiona asked, adding to the conversation.

"I don't know why exactly. It doesn't make sense. He says it's for the greater good and that I used to understand. And that just makes me not want to remember the child I used to be." I shook my head and flopped on my back, staring up at the ceiling blankly.

Not having answers is infuriating...

"But why you?" Freya asked buzzing in front of my face. "Who are you?"

"I don't know that either, unfortunately. I'm afraid though. I mean, I caught glimpses of a memory of where I lived in a castle. What do you suppose that could mean?" I covered my face again.

What if I push through what's left of the block and I start to believe what I did before? I can't risk that. I don't want to believe that the pureblooded fae are any better or more worthy than any other supernatural. That's not who I am.

"Knowledge is power, Aurelia," Freya said as she landed her tiny feet on my stomach. "You need to have all the facts before you can decide what to do."

"I don't think you would follow him blindly just because you get your memories back," Fiona offered, tapping my hand with her own.

"But how do you know?" I asked peeking through my fingers and swallowing hard. "I don't want to become like him."

"You may have been raised to hate other supernaturals, Miss Aurelia, but you've learned through experience that we aren't all bad. And we certainly aren't as bad as that man who has locked us in here!" Fiona said.

I closed my eyes and sighed. She was right, but I still hadn't had the best of experiences when it came to the supernatural world either. But one truth remained. No race of people were inherently bad or toxic. Just like with humans and animals, there were always going to be bad eggs; those who did the wrong things, and hurt others with malicious intent. But they were far and away in the minority. And other whole races of life didn't deserve to be tarred with the brush of hatred and prejudice because of them.

Shoving my fears aside, I pushed into my mind with a renewed sense of purpose and went back to the first memory I possessed that wasn't too fuzzy. There was a castle in the distance as Malcolm ran with me across the grounds and into the forest.

Malcolm?" I asked softly. "What are you doing?" I could barely see past the cloak he'd thrown over me.

"Shh. The hounds will hear you, little one." He squeezed me tighter to his chest.

A familiar blue glow lit up the night and my eyes widened in instant recognition. Everyone in Faery knew what that was. Did he really intend to take me through it and into the mortal world? I panicked and struggled in his arms as the portal drew closer.

"Aurelia, stop," he whispered. "We must go to the mortal world. It's not safe for you here, anymore."

What does he mean it isn't safe here? This is my home, and we have the best guards in the realm!

"But, why?" I asked, pulling the cloak down so I could see his face.

"There was a prophecy, Aurelia. A prophecy that puts you directly in danger if you remain here," he said in a rush.

"A prophecy? What kind of prophecy?" I pushed as my eyes widened in fear.

Malcolm's expression was hard, but I could tell he was scared too.

He was my best friend And I trusted him... but what if he was wrong and I was in more danger in the mortal world?

How can he be so sure? Leaving Faery is dangerous, everyone knows that!

"I'll tell you everything, little one. I promise. But for now, we have to go." He covered me back up with the cloak and stepped through the glowing portal.

Pain shot through me as soon as we made it to the other side. I cried out at the terrible feeling that threatened to burn me alive.

Malcolm squeezed me tighter in an attempt to alleviate my panic. "You'll get used to it, Aurelia. The iron is draining, but it will hide you from the others who would seek to use you," Malcolm whispered in my ear.

Why would anyone want to use me? What isn't he telling me?

"Iron?" I questioned. "But that's a poison to us! Where have you brought me, Malcolm? It hurts." I sobbed through the unfamiliar pain that seemed to permeate me to my very core.

Malcolm whispered and kissed my forehead softly in a final goodbye. "It will be okay. You will be safe. And when the time is right, we'll go home—together—I promise," he said. And the memory ended there like a cliffhanger, leaving me none the wiser and infinitely more frustrated. I needed to backtrack and summarize and figure this all out.

Who am I, really? And what do I know so far?

I was a full-blooded fae who lived in a grand castle with guards, and the daughter of a couple Malcolm was obviously very well acquainted with. He was my best friend and they trusted me with him... even promising him my hand if he were to be believed. And then on top of all that there was a prophecy—one that threatened my very life—and spurred my childhood friend to spirit me away through the portal and into the mortal realm where I'd suffered to survive ever since.

My existence was like a great big puzzle, and I was missing a bunch of integral pieces...

Chapter 20

Grey

I GROWLED AT THE WOMEN, my temper fraying and close to snapping.

This is ridiculous. They're toying with me!

"Have you found anything yet?" I snapped.

They were taking their sweet ass time with this and the longer they took the less clear the picture would be. Memories, scents, and auras only lingered so long before they faded into the ether and were irretrievable even to magic.

Dan patted my shoulder, a grimace on his face. "Let them work, Boss. We aren't likely to find anything anyway."

My gaze ripped to his and another feral growl escaped my lips. My wolf was *so* perilously close to the surface my eyes were probably already glowing golden with his very aggressive presence.

Dan took a step back and held his hands up in immediate surrender. "Sorry, Boss. I didn't mean anything by it. This is all just a long shot... I think you know that."

"It's not a good idea to challenge me, right now," I said and exhaled in frustration.

Layla turned to me with a raised brow. "Why is your wolf freaking out?" she asked and crossed her arms over her chest, adopting a stance of authority and power.

"I need her back. Now," I spat, glaring right back at her.

"And it's just for the job, is it?" she scoffed.

I just told Dan not to challenge me and now she's doing it? How fucking dare she. Layla's lucky I haven't shifted and let my wolf have her. He'd tear her limb from limb inside of three seconds flat.

"Are you questioning my motives? I don't have to explain myself to you or anyone else for that matter." I stepped forward menacingly, closing the space between us until I towered over her.

"No, sir," she answered, dropping her show of bravado as she looked down and away in submission, once more deferring to my leadership without further question.

"Good. Now, I want you all out of my damn house as soon as possible, so go help Karma with her spell." I turned on my heel and strode into the kitchen, my rage lending me its strength.

"You're being overly hostile toward them," Dan note, following me into the kitchen.

"Someone told that hooded fae bastard that I wasn't here. It's the only thing that makes sense," I retorted as I spun to face him.

"What?" he asked, eyes widening in apprehension and shock.

"Only a select few knew that I left suddenly, and Magna suggested it was likely a mole. Someone has betrayed me. and the list of suspects is short." I sat down on a stool at the kitchen island, interlocking my fingers.

"And you think…" he trailed off and glanced to the living room. "Holy shit."

"Karma was supposed to be headed to the witch's house when she challenged Aurelia in the first place. That was why it took her so long to get there. Layla told her what happened, and together they devised a plan to get rid of her." I untangled my fingers and clenched my fist on the counter at the treachery. I was almost ready to go off like a bomb, but instead of fire and ash, it'd be raining blood and flesh.

Dan strolled to the fridge and opened it, grabbing two bottles of water and tossing one to me. "They thought they could control when the challenge took place and get rid of her quickly," he said, rationalizing it out and shaking his head as he cracked the lid on the bottle.

"And it didn't work," I added. "I told them it would happen when I was ready, when Aurelia had time to train. But it looks like they came up with a new plan to make her disappear on their schedule, anyway." I set my bottle on the counter and sat back on my stool.

"What do you want me to do?" Dan asked, his gaze hard and unwavering.

Maybe I should make him my second, he's much more loyal than Layla apparently. He might fuck up from time to time, but we all do. At least he's actually on my side!

I stood and moved back to the living room as Karma's chant filled the air. "Keep an eye on them while Karma performs the spell," I whispered.

Dan nodded surreptitiously and moved closer to the women.

Karma wandered around the space almost in a trance as she continued her chant.

Wispy figures took form around us and appeared to be fighting with magic; balls of silver light shimmered to and fro, sizzling through the air.

I moved closer to the hall to follow their progress as the memory of the penthouse was relived in real time thanks to the spell.

The man in the cloak threw magic at Reah again and Aurelia ran away from the intruder and toward the magicless room.

"Coward," Layla mumbled under her breath, but before I could react Reah was in her face.

"She was following orders!" Reah hissed and pushed Layla roughly in the chest.

"Who's orders?" Layla growled and her shifter eyes glowed in response.

"Mine, fuckwit! She was not ready to face an attacker with her magic. It's not quite stable yet. I made the choice and she tried to argue with me." Reah glared at her and took another step forward, ready to defend my mate's honor.

"Easy, Reah," I said and grabbed her arm.

"No! Why is this bitch so quick to judge?" she fired back, before turning her gaze on Layla once more. "What do you know about her kidnapper?" Reah asked before she ripped her arm from my grasp.

"What are you talking about?" Layla shouted with wide eyes.

"Don't you think it's strange that he showed up here within an hour of Grey leaving the penthouse?" Reah crossed her arms, correct in her deductions. But now was not the time.

Shit, she's going to blow everything to Hell.

"Reah!" I shouted, feigning outrage.

"He left unexpectedly. So, how did this fae know where to find Aurelia when Grey was gone?" Reah continued with a sneer, determined not to let her suspicions of Layla escape her.

"I got something!" Karma shouted, changing the subject.

I spun on the woman who was several feet away from the magicless room.

The intruder had removed his hood and Aurelia stared up at him with wide eyes as she was pinned beneath him.

My inner wolf snarled in outrage, and I completely concurred with his stance. Seeing that fucker on top of my mate had me trembling, the fuse on my temper almost spent.

We couldn't hear what Aurelia said, unfortunately, as the spell only mimicked what could be seen. But Aurelia fought back and thrashed before she was punched in the head and knocked out cold, going limp. Freya and Fiona buzzed into the room, but I didn't see where they hid before the man turned like he knew we were going to watch this very moment in the future.

Fucking prick!

Magna gasped as we all watched, holding a hand over her mouth in shock. "By the gods of Faery... I know him."

"What do you mean, you know him?" I asked, turning to her sharply.

"You don't recognize him?" Magna asked softly as she stared ahead.

The mimic spell cut out then, but his face remained clear in my mind's eye, and I thought about the long white-blond hair and slate gray eyes. "Fuck. The Captain of the King's Guard."

"What do you mean?" Reah asked with a frown. "What king?"

"The fae king. But what does that make Aurelia though?" Magna whispered in horror as the impossible truth settled upon us like a fine mist of doom.

No! It can't be true. She can't be the fae princess. The king that Malcolm serves is known to be calculating, brutal, and cruel beyond reason. Fuck!

Had Malcolm brought her here to save her from him or was there a more nefarious reason for it? Either way, it changed nothing right at this moment and time was of the essence. The longer Aurelia was with that asshole, the more likely she was to come to harm, and we would not allow it—not my wolf or I—not while we still had strength in our bones and breath in our lungs.

She's everything to us.

"Dan!" I barked, turning toward the living room.

He jogged over, quick to answer my summons.

"I need you to dig up everything you possibly can on Malcolm."

"Does Malcolm have a last name or is this like a Madonna thing?" Dan asked chuckling. Fucker sure as hell didn't know when to keep his sense of humor in check, despite his unwavering loyalty.

"Fae don't have surnames!" I growled.

Dan raised his hands up in surrender for the second time since he arrived in my penthouse. "All right, Boss. I'll ask around about a weirdo fae in a cloak named Malcolm. Got it." Without another word he ran to the elevator and stabbed at the button to get on with his mission.

"You two." I pointed to Layla and Karma. "Get this shit cleaned up and get back to the facility."

"You don't want my help to locate this fae?" Layla asked, frowning.

Not in this lifetime or any other.

"Dan has it under control. Do what I ask. I know where to find you should I need you." I waved them both off, dismissing them from my sight.

"You think I did this, don't you?" Layla asked angrily.

I couldn't answer without her smelling the lie, so I turned on my heel and walked away. "Magna, Reah, my office please," I called over my shoulder, maintaining my pace, my shoulder and head held high.

"Looks like someone is no longer the boss's favorite!" Reah said with a laugh.

"Watch it, Reah. You filled his head with some bullshit. He knows I would never betray him!" Layla said.

I took a deep breath through my nose and smelled the lie in her words. I turned sharply but instead of letting her know I caught onto it, I called out to Reah instead. "Move it."

Stomping feet followed me to my office, and I held the door open while both women walked in. I slammed the door shut behind them and stormed over to my chair behind my desk, sinking into the leather cushioning with a small measure of gratitude for the comfort it offered. "Magna, can you place a ward, please? I want privacy." I rubbed at my temples, the new information regarding my second giving me a tension headache.

I just got bloody clear confirmation that she would betray me... but did she? Why would she do that? Is it truly petty jealousy? Have I mistaken her loyalty all these years?

Magna waved her hands and chanted softly under her breath.

I waited for her nod and rounded on Reah. "I'm trying to keep Layla's deception quiet for now," I snapped and glared at her.

Magna took a seat in the chair across from me and raised an eyebrow. "So, you're sure it was her?"

"I scented the lie when she said she would never betray me," I said with a bitter sigh.

Rhea's face reddened at the confirmation of Layla's betrayal. "What are you going to do about it?" she yelled, outraged.

"I appreciate your loyalty, Reah, but I have to play this smart. They could spread lies through the facility about me wrongly accusing them to get Aurelia out of the challenge. It would cause mistrust among all of my employees." I clenched my fists.

And I know they'd do it, too.

"That's smart," Reah conceded. "I'm sorry. I can't imagine how angry you were just being in the same room with them. I was practically about to lose my shit and when she called Aurelia a coward..." The half-fae magic instructor snarled.

I could clearly feel my wolf's approval of her reverberating through my veins. True loyalty was hard to find, it couldn't even be bought for any amount of wealth. So, the fact Reah was standing up for Aurelia meant *a lot* to us both.

"We just need to play this smart, like I said. I don't want her figuring it all out and pulling shit at the facility," I said. "The last bloody thing I need a coup or a riot on my hands."

"I'm sorry to interrupt, but we need to talk about Malcolm," Magna said as she stared at me with trepidation. The mere hint that she was afraid meant we were in deep shit. Magna was ancient. If the King's Guard scared her...

"What do you know about him?" I asked, suppressing a shudder and leaning back in my chair.

"He's a brutal killer. He protects the royal family with his life, and before we were kicked out of Faery, he never would have been caught dead in the mortal realm. He hates the humans just as much as he hates all other supernaturals." Magna trailed off, staring off into space as if lost in thought or memory.

"So, what would he need Aurelia for and how does she know him?" I asked mostly to myself.

"I think you already know the answer to that," Magna answered raising a knowing and suggestive brow. "The truth is always straight forward, Grey. The most obvious answer is the often the right one."

No! I couldn't believe that the daughter of my greatest enemy was my fated mate, and also formally bonded to his greatest enforcer. It was beyond comprehension. It was the worst possible outcome of all.

The fucking fucker's fucking fucked!

"She can't be," I mumbled, a tight knot forming in my gut. "She just can't be."

"What if she is, Grey? You will have to figure out how to feel about that. She doesn't remember her family right now, but what happens when she does?" Magna asked sagely, always one step ahead.

"I will deal with it when I know for sure, but who her parents are means nothing to me." I shook my head. I couldn't allow it to mean anything.

She is what I want and need, nothing else. Finding your fated mate is everything... it happens once in a lifetime. There is only one and no replacing them. If Aurelia is mine, so be it. I will not jeopardize our union. We must find a way to save her!

I would even give up the plans I'd been formulating for decades for her if she asked it of me. I know my wolf would certainly demand it and there would be no denying him on that crossroads.

"What is this Malcolm dickhead even doing here?" Reah asked as she leaned against the wall.

"I don't know what his ultimate game plan is. I wish the mimic spell did more than just let us see. They were saying something to each other, but I couldn't read their lips." I slammed my fist against the desk in frustration.

Magna narrowed her eyes at me and leaned forward, an intensity to her that belied her old age. "About twenty years ago there was a rumor of a prophecy," she whispered. "I can't help but wonder if that has something to do with Malcolm and Aurelia being in the realm."

"A prophecy?" I asked, raising my gaze to meet hers.

How does she know about the prophecy? Who am I kidding, Magna knows way too much about everything.

"You already know what I'm talking about, don't you?" Magna asked.

"And you already know the answer to that." I couldn't hinder the grin that split my face at our banter. The prophecy was the reason I had been looking for a fae in the first place. I needed her to help with my plan, the only problem was she would have to *want* to help me.

What will I do if Malcolm convinces her that she belongs in Faery and we don't?

"According to the prophecy, there will be one who can either free us or keep us trapped here in the mortal realm forever," I said with a fateful sigh.

This is some heavy shit.

Reah straightened. "And you think Aurelia is the only one who can bring us all home to Faery?" she asked.

"I'm not sure if she's the one or not, but why would Malcolm bring her here if she was? Wouldn't they all want her to grow up in Faery where that kind of prejudice reigns? From there she could close the portal without ever knowing the difference."

"Probably, but perhaps not," Magna said thoughtfully. "They may have seen the possibility as more of a risk than they were willing to take."

"Do you mean to say that they would have killed a child because there was a *possibility* she might one day open the portal for us?" Reah asked, flabbergasted by the mere suggestion of such an atrocity.

I couldn't imagine killing a child, no matter what any damn prophecy said—even if there was one that threatened me, personally. It was just pure evil and despite my life of crime and questionable choices, it sickened me to my very heart.

"They aren't nicknamed the wicked fae for nothing, Reah. Any threat to their status quo must be eliminated ...even a child who hadn't even yet made a mistake." I stood and started pacing.

It still didn't make any sense in a broader sense. He'd brought her here and then abandoned her. He told her that there was a reason for it, and she had understood it at the time. What was I missing? It felt crucial.

What if she gets her memories back and decides that he's right after all and we never get to go home?

My chest hurt, my heart squeezing as if a damn elephant were sitting on top of me, crushing me with its weight. The thought of never returning to Faery *and* having to live without Aurelia—our mate—was too much to bear.

Chapter 21

Aurelia

I CLOSED MY EYES TIGHT and focused, trying not to allow desperation to overwhelm me. "We need to get out of here, girls."

Freya scoffed in despair. "The door is locked and sealed with magic!"

"You were able to sneak out the window. Did you see anything familiar?" I asked, then blew out a breath.

Stay calm, Aurelia.

I needed to center myself. If I let my magic get out of control, I was afraid of what Malcolm might do to me.

Who knows what he's capable of. I just need to breathe, like Grey taught me. In and out. Focus.

"No, nothing seemed familiar, and I couldn't explore far either," she said with a sigh.

"Is there a ward keeping us in?" I asked, cracking an eye open. "Is that really a thing?"

"Yes," Freya said. "Of course. Wards can keep people in or out, the same way they can allow or mute magic," she explained. "I can probably get through it now that I know it's there, but it's going to take some time."

"Time isn't something we have, Freya," I answered as I flopped onto my back once more in frustration. "He's going to start growing impatient soon. It's already been two days."

Fiona tapped her foot on my knee to get my attention. "What if we all go out the front door?" she suggested.

"Fi, you know that's not possible," I said, pressing my hands to my head.

"Hear me out," Fiona pressed. "All you need to do is pretend that you are ready to train. He will open the door and we can use that opportunity to attack him."

"You want to attack a pureblood fae who is much older and more experienced with magic than me?" I sat up again, wringing my hands. That was a seriously bad idea, but I didn't have a better plan to offer, and I'd been wracking my mind for the past forty-eight hours straight.

Freya chewed her lower lip anxiously. "If we catch him by surprise, it just might work."

"You are both insane. I mean... our chances of success are almost painfully non-existent!" I threw my hands up.

"What do we have to lose? He won't kill you—he needs and wants you; you are his promised—and even if you can't get out, maybe one or both of us can! Then whoever makes it can fly back to Master Grey," Fiona argued. "We could lead him to you and organize a rescue, Miss Aurelia!"

"I can't believe that I am actually going to agree with this," I huffed in exasperation.

Am I completely out of my head? Grey will never forgive me if the sprites get hurt... but can I just sit here and not *do whatever I possibly can to get back to Grey?*

Fiona clapped her tiny hands together in triumph and flew up to sit on my shoulder.

Freya did the same, alighting on the other.

"So, all you have to do is get his attention and then when he opens the door we will fly up in his face and distract him. Then, you hit him with the biggest blast of magic you can and hopefully that will knock him out and we can make a run for it," Fiona said with a comically malicious grin.

"Actually, that just might work," I admitted with a heft measure of admiration. The sprites might be tiny, but they were like pocket rockets where their pluck and courage were concerned. They were loyal to a fault, and I couldn't help but love them for it. I nodded with a small burst of hope filling my belly. "All right, so when are we going to do this?"

"There's no time like the present!" Fiona announced as she flew up next to my face.

I stood from the bed and stretched my back in preparation for our escape attempt. I'd been in this damn room going stir crazy for two days. The only time the door ever opened was when a servant came in to feed me. Even then the magic held firm, like it was made specifically to keep me in. Whatever ward was on the door would only be lifted if Malcolm believed I was coming out and ready to give into his demands. I shuddered at the thought.

Just as well this is nothing more than a ruse!

The mere notion of agreeing to fulfill his wishes and likely becoming his wife was enough to cause a hot surge of bile racing up my throat.

Screw that for a joke. I'll never join him—not in this lifetime or the next!

"All right, girls. Wait for my signal and stay out of sight until he opens the door," I whispered. I approached the door and sucked in a deep breath before banging on the door loudly. "Malcolm. You win! I'm ready to start training. Please just let me out of here," I yelled. I was met by nothing but silence, so I tried again. "Malcolm! Let me out."

Footfalls sounded from the other side of the door. "Aurelia, what are you screaming about?" Malcolm asked, stopping on the other side of the door though there was no indication that he was moving to open it.

I glanced at the sprites out of the corner of my eye.

They were hiding behind where the door would open, fluttering silently and preparing for action on my signal.

"I'm ready to train. Let me out. I feel like I can't breathe in here!" I said again, my voice raised.

"Are you really? You are willing to come home with me, finally?" he asked, sounding almost hopeful.

Crap!

I couldn't believe it. I felt almost bad for my deception.

Can I lie about this when he has that painfully hopeful note in his voice? I don't want to go anywhere near Faery.

And then I remembered my Grey. His beautiful, ripped human body, his intense gaze, the way he made me feel, and even how soft his incredible snow-white fur had felt under my hand when he defended me at the facility. My sense of resolve strengthened at the memories, and I focused on my mission to get home, back to the penthouse and Grey, with the sprites safely in tow.

"Yes, I will go back to Faery with you." I said with a grimace and glanced at the sprites. "I'll go," I added, "but I'm not making any more promises than that. I still can't remember much…"

They both gave me encouraging nods even though the lie made me feel every inch the wicked fae that Malcolm was.

"All will be well, Aurelia. If you will only just trust me like you once did, everything can return to normal," he said, his voice soothing and encouraging, as if he were talking down a jumper who might change their mind at any second.

The familiar sound of buzzing magic could be heard on the other side of the door as the ward was lifted, and I breathed deeply as I took a step back.

This is it. He's taken the bait. It's now or never. Please let this work...

I put my hands behind my back and let my purple magic pool in them before I nodded firmly at the sprites, giving them the signal.

The doorknob rattled before clicking open and the smile on Malcolm's face was brilliant—he almost looked as beautiful as I remembered him from my time spent in the castle—until he was dive bombed by the sprites.

"What is this treachery?" he shouted and covered his head with his hands, swatting at Fiona and Freya in annoyance.

While he was distracted, I seized my chance and pulled my hands out from behind me, hurling my magic at him with the intent of knocking him out. The shimmering purple blast struck Malcolm in the chest and sent him soaring back until he crashed into the wall at the opposite end of the hall.

All the breath left him in a shocked *whoosh* just before his eyes rolled back in his head and he slumped to the floor.

"Go, go, go!" I yelled to the sprites, and we all took off down the hallway. I had no idea where I was going but based on the view through the window, we were definitely on the second floor, at least, so looking for stairs was going to be my best bet.

"This way, Miss Aurelia!" Fiona urged as she tugged at my hair.

I changed direction on a dime and followed the sprite to a long stairway. Without hesitation I sprinted down the stairs, taking them two at a time as a roar filled the air. "Shit. He's awake already! We need to find a way out of here, *now*." I pushed myself faster down the stairs, glancing backward over my shoulder at Freya who was watching my back.

"I don't think he is up yet, Miss," Freya squeaked as she watched the landing above. "I'll stay and hold him off!"

"Oh no, you won't Freya," I hissed as I snatched her out of the air much to her displeasure. I would take her with me!

"Miss Aurelia, please! I must protect you. The master is probably out of beside himself and out of control without you!" Freya's tiny fists beat against my hand.

I ignored her as the front entry way came into view, relief flooding through me.

"Aurelia, where are you?" Malcolm roared from the top of the stairs, before he spotted us.

"Miss, let me go hold him off! There's no time," Freya pleaded.

Fiona glanced back between us before she zipped past me so fast I didn't have time to catch her. It was clear she had every intention of sacrificing herself for her sister and me.

"Go, Miss. Get out of here. Take Freya! Hurry," Fiona cried as she flew up the stairs directly toward danger.

"No, Fiona. Come back here!" I cried out as I lobbed another purple ball of magic at Malcolm where he stood at the top of the stairs.

He dodged out of the way at the last second and landed on the floor by the stair's banister with an *oomph*.

I spun on my heel. "Come on, Fiona," I screamed. "Let's go!"

Malcolm shot up faster than I could have anticipated, and a wicked smile crossed his face as he vanished from sight. A second later, he reappeared right next to Fiona, only to snatch her roughly from the air.

"No!" Freya screamed with a yelp, biting my hand in desperation and forcing me to let her go. She flew back to her sister, buzzing angrily around Malcolm but he just snatched her from the air too.

"Let them go, Malcom," I demanded and held up my hands as I pushed magic into them. Purple swirls filled the air and my wings fluttered to life at my back. He would *not* take my friends from me. I refused to let the asshole hurt them.

Not on my watch, bucko!

"I'll let them leave," he bargained. "But you have to come home with me. You have to train to use your magic and then you must close the portal once and for all."

"No, Miss Aurelia," Fiona cried out as Malcolm shook her roughly.

"Don't do it. You are not allowed to sacrifice everything for us!" Freya shook her head.

Malcolm's fist tightened around her, crushing her small body and making her choke.

"What is your answer, Aurelia?" Malcolm boomed before he cocked his arm back and threw Freya against the front door like he was pitching a baseball.

I cried out in agony, tracking Freya's body as she slid down the door into a little heap on the ground. Her glow dimmed and a tear trailed down my cheek, hot and filled with emotion too heavy to bear.

She's not dead. She can't be dead! No!

I turned back to Malcolm with a scowl.

Fiona was thrashing furiously in his hand. Failing to break free, she bent her little face down and bit into his finger with all her might.

"Fucking vermin!" Malcolm shouted in disdain. "How about I pluck your pesky little wings to show you your place among purebloods?"

"No, you said you would let them go," I screamed back, my magic flaring in response to my panic.

I couldn't bear it if he took her wings.

What kind of monster is he? How can he be so deluded as to think that I would have ever helped him?

"That was before they showed what pests they truly are. Being here so long, I almost forgot what vermin sub-fae are." Malcolm sneered, viciously handsome and wicked all at once as his blond hair spilled over his shoulders.

"You said you would let them go. So, just let them go and I will do whatever you want." I held my hands up and took a deep breath, willing my magic to disappear. To my utter shock my magic dissipated, and I breathed a sigh.

Finally, my magic has learned to listen to me even when I'm panicking.

"No, Aurelia. Don't do it. I'll be okay!" Fiona shouted, but the terror in her eyes mirrored my own.

Malcolm shook her and pinched her wing with unbridled cruelty in his gaze. He raised an eyebrow at me. "Perhaps I should keep them, so I know how to keep you in line." He grinned. "That would be most convenient."

"If you don't let them go, I'll never help you," I growled in response, my face burning with anger.

Fiona yelped as the pressure on her wing increased.

I glared at Malcolm, allowing my magic to fill my palms once again.

He tugged sharply on her wing, delighting in the tiny sprite's pain.

With nothing on my mind but preventing the tiny fae's destruction, I threw a ball of blazing purple magic at his head, willing it to fuck him up in any way possible.

He flinched, but not fast enough, my magic singeing his ear.

The odor of burned flesh reached my sensitive nose and I smiled with dark satisfaction in return. It wasn't a perfect hit, but it had landed, nonetheless.

Fuck you, asshole! I hope it hurts.

"Fuck," Malcolm yelled and cupped his ear with his free hand. "Fine, I'll let them go, but you're staying with me, or I *will* kill them! And I'll make you watch."

Malcolm stormed down the stairs and grabbed my arm in a bruising grip. He dragged me across the foyer where Freya was still lying in a heap by the front of the door.

I cried out at the sight of Freya's broken little body, praying to whatever gods were listening that Fiona would be able to get Freya back to Grey before it was too late. Surely, he had a healer at his disposal.

Or perhaps Magna can help?

"I'm not leaving you, Miss Aurelia," Fiona shook her head vehemently, still in Malcolm's unforgiving grasp.

"You have to get Freya to Grey," I said through my tears. "She needs you."

Fiona glanced at her sister with sadness and then back to me, obviously torn on what to do. She was so loyal that my heart broke for her.

"Make up your mind, quickly vermin. I don't have all day." Malcolm shook her again. and

I gritted my teeth to the point of pain and clenched my fists by my sides. This mother fucker was going to pay dearly. I didn't know how or when, but I was going to find a way to destroy him for what he'd done. He was the very definition of a prejudiced, wicked fae. And now I truly understood why we were named the way we were, especially if the majority of my kind acted and thought the way he did.

"Go, Fiona. Please, get her out of here," I begged. "I'll be okay."

"Fine," Fiona sighed, miniature glimmering tears staining her cheeks.

Malcolm opened his hand at hearing her response, keeping his word and releasing the tiny sprite.

Fiona flew down to her sister, picking her up gently in both arms and cradling her against her chest like a mother would clutch her precious child.

I felt so incredibly proud of her at that moment. She was truly a little hero.

They are lucky to have each other. Fly strong, little one!

Malcolm squeezed my arm even harder as he shoved open the front door.

I lunged forward in a desperate, if not futile attempt to break free of his grasp and run.

At the last second, he wrapped his hand around my throat and pulled me back roughly to his chest.

To my revulsion I felt something distinctly hard pressed into me from behind as I squirmed against him.

Sick, psycho!

"No," Fiona's tiny voice cried, but then she was gone from my sight.

Malcolm slammed the door closed with his foot, gripping me even more tightly and without a shred of remorse.

"Can't breathe," I gasped. Panicking, I clawed at his hand and tried to loosen his grip. I needed to get air into my lungs, but it was no use. He was physically too strong and soon I could see stars, and several heart racing moments later darkness began to encroach on the corners of my vision as my pulse throbbed in my ears.

Malcolm laughed; his breath hot against my ear. "You shouldn't have tried to run from me, Aurelia. This is only the beginning, my love. You are mine now."

What have I gotten myself into? What is he going to do to me? If this is how he treats the woman promised to him, I can't imagine what he intends for his enemies...

As fear warred with revulsion, I could only hope the sprites would make it back to Grey before this insane asshole choked me to death—but I wasn't counting on it. So, with my last conscious breath as Malcolm lewdly ground against me and ran his tongue down my ear, I thought of Grey and focused on recalling the time we'd spent together.

If I die today, he would have been the best thing that ever happened to me.

The beauty of the simple truth bolstered the fragile flame of hope burning in my heart and offered me a small measure of comfort as oblivion surged in to claim me. Whatever took place now was beyond my control, at least for the moment...

Chapter 22

Grey

"ANY NEWS?" I ASKED Dan as I impatiently paced my office.

It's been two days since Aurelia was taken... and I'm losing my mind here!

"Nothing at all, Boss. How did that fucker just disappear with her, anyway?" Dan asked and scrubbed a hand over his face. We were all tired but wired and it showed. We'd barely slept a wink in forty-eight hours.

"You have never been to the fae realm before so you wouldn't know," I explained. "Pureblood fae have the ability to sift as long as there are no wards preventing it." I ran a hand through my hair trying to maintain my hold over my growing frustration. I'd never thought to ward my home against the ability because there were so few purebloaded fae around outside of Faery itself.

"Sift?" he asked with a frown. "Is that what they call vanishing like that?"

"It's like teleporting from one place to another, basically, but they *have* to have been to the place before," I said. "They can't just sift somewhere they've never been."

"Well, shit. They could literally be anywhere. If this guy is as ancient and powerful as Magna fears, then he's likely been everywhere in his time." He sat back in his chair with a scowl on his face.

"Exactly. And I have no bloody idea of where to even start looking. They could already be through the portal and in Faery for all I know." I clenched my fists at my side, my lips pursing in irritation.

Please don't be in Faery, Aurelia... that's somewhere I won't ever be able to follow you.

Magna had said we would never find them without the sprites' help, but my wolf was thrashing inside me. He was losing control of himself, and I was losing control of him.

"Fuck. It's been two days and there's still no sign of Freya and Fiona yet. I know Magna said we would need them to find her, but I want her back now!" I stopped pacing to glare at Dan. It wasn't his fault, none of this was, but our general inaction and inability to do anything fruitful was eating me up inside.

"I'm doing everything I can, but there's nothing more we can do. I've gotten all the information I can and we're just coming up at a stalemate." He straightened his spine, clearly not willing to take my shit lying down when he knew he'd done all he could, just as I'd asked.

"It's not enough!" I roared, gripping my head.

My wolf thrashed in my chest desperate to get out and go look for her himself, but he couldn't. A huge white wolf wandering around the streets of Dallas trying to sniff out his mate—shifter, witch, or mortal side—would raise some eyebrows. My phone buzzed on my desk. I stomped over and picked it up. "What is it, Magna?" I asked, putting her on loudspeaker and trying to keep my temper in check.

"The fae note just held a warning. It simply said that he was coming for her and that it was time," she said in confusion.

"That doesn't help us," I said with a growl.

Dan shook his head. "Nothing makes sense though. If she was passed out in the hallway at the witch's apartment when he came to get the book, why didn't he just take her then? He would have been able to avoid everything that went down here in the penthouse. He would have had no opposition whatsoever and Aurelia was tranq'd, so it would have been easy for someone like him to just sift her out of there."

"The bit that confuses me is that he assumed she would know how to read the fae language," Magna added.

Did she know how to read the language? Was that something she's forgotten with the block?

"The memory I was pulled into, it was clear she knew the man. She spoke in fae to him so maybe she also knew how to read?" I proposed and scrubbed a hand over my face in a fresh wave of frustration.

"Dan has a good point as well," Magna said. "Why didn't he take her before? What was the purpose of him leaving her on the floor and endangering her further?"

"What was the purpose of leaving her starving and freezing in a dirty alley when she was just a small child?" I yelled, unable to bite back the remark. Nothing this asshole son of a bitch did made any sense at all.

He is bound to her in some way, and yet he knowingly and willfully allowed her to suffer. I could never let her suffer like that.

She was mine and I was hers—we were fated mates—and if I had to kill the wicked fae to get to her then I would.

"That's a good point too," Magna agreed. "Though he may have needed something else to happen or had something else to do before he could take her."

"Have you seen anything at all that will help us find her?" I slammed my fist onto the desk. I needed to get her back like *now*. I couldn't take care of the fucking moles in my organization until I did.

"No, the sprites are still our best bet for rescuing her, but you need to be ready, Grey," Magna said with a sigh.

I paced over to the window and stared out into the cloudless night sky. We didn't see many stars in the city given the ambient light, but the full moon hung high in the sky and the sight made my heart hurt. I missed Aurelia terribly.

Is she okay? What does that psychopath want from her?

Dan's and Magna's voices turned to white noise in the background as I stared out the window, lost to thought. Before I realized what I was seeing, a faint green glow caught my attention in the distance, and I squinted, leaning closer to the glass. "Dan! Come here. Is that…?" I asked, trailing off, not daring to hope that I could be right.

"It's definitely a sprite," he said leaning closer to the window beside me. "But I can't tell if it's them. Plus, there only appears to be one."

"Fuck!" I growled and slammed my open palm against the window. The glass rattled in its frame, and I flinched. It probably wasn't the best idea to go smashing windows.

"Wait a minute! It looks like it's carrying something," Dan said as the sprite continued to move closer toward the building.

I squinted into the darkness and called upon my wolf vision, my heart skipping a beat. "That's Freya!" I announced, recognizing her instantly.

What the hell happened to them?

Fiona was flying in a tired and chaotic zigzag pattern, like she was barely managing to maintain her altitude as she held her sister in her arms.

I raced from the room and into my bedroom, flinging open the doors to the balcony wide. "Fiona!" I called down to the sprite, my heart in my throat as hope blazed within me. She needed to fly higher to reach me, but I wasn't sure she had the energy left in reserve to achieve it.

"Master Grey!" she yelled excitedly, her tiny voice like music to my ears. She flew a little higher but fell again, unable to stay up with the precious burden clutched to her chest.

She's not going to make it.

"Dan," I yelled into the penthouse. "You're going to have to go downstairs and get them. Careful that they aren't seen."

"I'm on my way," Dan called back and rushed down the hall without a moment's hesitation.

"Fiona, it's going to be okay! Just stay there. Dan is coming for you, okay?" I called out, beyond relieved to see my sprites again.

"Okay," she said her voice fatigued as she jerkily maintained her hover.

How long has she been flying with her sister in her arms and what the hell happened to them?

If I wasn't already planning on killing Malcolm—which I was—this would have been the nail in the coffin that would put an end to his miserable life. I raced back into the office and picked up my phone. The call with Magna was still connected. "I think I'm going to need your help," I said. "It looks like Freya is in pretty bad shape."

"I'll be there shortly," she said, and the line went dead and this time I wasn't even annoyed someone had hung up on me.

I wandered into the living room to wait for Dan. My eyes caught on the black leather couch, free of all traces of Aurelia. I'd nearly strangled the meddling bitches, Layla and Karma, when I'd realized they'd destroyed the last of Aurelia's plants that had survived the home invasion and magic battle between Malcom and Reah. Even if the moss had irritated me at first, they had no right to destroy the plants. This was my home, not theirs, and if nothing else it proved just how petty they were and how much they truly hated my mate—which would be dealt with in future. I wasn't going to keep people in my employ who were a danger to Aurelia.

I clenched my fists at my sides and breathed deeply to calm myself. Being angry wasn't going to help Freya and Fiona. Turning on my heel, I paced the living room for several long minutes before the *ding* of the elevator alerted me to their arrival. I spun to face the door, my heart lurching in my chest.

Please be all right my little sprites.

Dan stepped out of the elevator with his jacket bulging with his precious concealed cargo.

Magna stepped out from behind him a moment later wearing a worried frown.

I ate up the space between us in two giant steps, holding my hands out to him.

He opened his jacket and an exhausted Fiona flitted out.

"What happened?" I asked, swallowing the lump in my throat as I waited to hear what had transpired, finally, after what felt like the longest two days of my entire life.

She wobbled in the air then landed on my open palms. "My wing's a little torn." She grimaced and glanced away. "We tried to escape with her, Master Grey, but she was caught. I'm so sorry. I wasn't given a choice—he was going to kill us or hold us hostage to control Miss Aurelia." Fiona hung her tiny head in shame, a single tear trickling down her rosy cheek.

She just flew who knows how long carrying her unconscious sister with a torn wing and she's apologizing to me? What the actual hell is going on here?

"And I bet Aurelia told you to leave her, didn't she?" I asked shaking my head.

My mate is far more courageous than she gives herself credit for.

Fiona swiped at her eyes and nodded. "He was going to start torturing me... he almost ripped my wing off, and he threw Freya into a door! Aurelia bargained with him to save us, to let us go free."

"What?" Dan barked as he laid tiny Freya out on the leather couch to be attended to. Her small body was broken; it was a miracle she was still breathing. Malcolm was a monster, that was for damn sure.

"You did the right thing, Fiona. Now, we'll be able to go and rescue her." I ran a hand through my hair as I pondered my next course of action.

What kind of sociopathic bastard tries to rip the wings off a sprite and slams another into a solid door? I would *really* enjoy killing the bastard now. The sprites were just as much my family as Aurelia was destined to be. They were my chosen family, those loyal to me, those who cared for me.

And no one fucks with my family and gets away with it.

"Magna, can you heal Freya?" I asked spinning to the half-fae woman.

"I'll do my best," Magna said with a nod before sitting next to her on the couch.

I looked away sharply, gritting my teeth and clenching my fists until they shook at my sides. The sprites had been with me forever and seeing Freya like that burned all the way to my damned shifter soul.

"I don't know how long we have before they leave, Master Grey. It's bad! She only agreed to train and help him so that he would let us go," Fiona babbled in panic.

"What is he planning?" I asked with dread, my insides twisting.

"He wants Miss Aurelia to go with him to Faery so she can close the portal. He wants to make sure we can never get back!" Fiona cried.

"It can't be done, can it?" Dan asked with wide eyes.

Magna hummed softly by Freya, the green light of her healing magic glowing over the sprite. "I think it's the prophecy," she answered. "Aurelia must be the one the prophecy is all about. She can either set us free or leave us to rot, forever exiled from our home. Malcolm played into her purity and used her kind heart against us." Magna shook her head in exasperation as her hands completed slow circuits in the air above Freya.

"But she only did it to save us," Fiona said softly and sniffled. "Maybe it would have been better for us to…"

"No!" I snapped. "It would not. Don't even think such a thing! Aurelia's not going to close the portal. We know her better than that! We're going to get her out of there no matter the cost. And we're not going to let this asshole succeed." I turned to Dan, filled with renewed purpose.

"What do you need, Boss?" he asked as his shoulders straightened.

"I need you to go keep an eye on Layla and Karma. I need to organize a team that I can trust to help me get Aurelia back, but I can't have those bitches alerting Malcolm that we are coming for him," I ordered.

"But Boss! I want a piece of this guy too," Dan complained.

"I can't have Aurelia seeing you, Dan. Remember the whole you shot her with a tranq dart thing and got us all into this mess?" I raised a questioning eyebrow at him.

"I didn't mean to fuck up... but fine," he grumbled. He turned and stalked to the elevator without another word.

It was time to call in some reinforcements. I would show Malcolm what happened when he stole what was most precious to me.

He's going to pay. Big time.

"Fiona, you need to rest while I get a rescue team together," I said.

She followed me into my office. "I can't rest knowing what is happening to her, Master Grey. He had his hand around her throat and was choking her when he slammed the door in my face." Fiona chewed her lip nervously, fear in her eyes.

"He what?" I yelled, rage bursting within me like an erupting volcano.

The bastard was already on my shit list for punching Aurelia in the head and kidnapping her... but leaving Fiona to wonder if Aurelia was still alive as she worked desperately to save her sister made him worse. He wasn't just a wicked fae.

He's a dead fae.

"He hurt her a couple times and I'm afraid of what he will do to her if she doesn't do as he asks," she said, her lip trembling as she landed on my desk, slumping down on the smooth surface.

"We won't let that happen, Fiona. But we can't find him without you. We're relying on your help, so I need you to rest until my team gets here," I said sternly. "That's an order little one."

Fiona's face fell but she nodded and took off, still flying in a chaotic zigzag though due to her damaged wing.

"If Magna is done healing Freya, ask her to fix your wing! You can't fly like that!" I called out after her. With my heart thumping in my chest, I picked up my phone and opened a text conversation that I'd hoped I wouldn't have to engage until my end game plans were well underway. But drastic times called for drastic measures, and time was not on our side.

Aurelia needs me, now more than ever.

And every supernatural, whether they knew it or not, was counting on me to stop that fucker from sealing us out of our true home, forever. It was time for the big guns.

I need your help.

I typed into my phone and hit send, pulling the trigger. Then I turned the phone off and slumped back into my chair, exhaling a deep sigh. I wasn't expecting a response. I knew I wouldn't get one from them.

It's done. There's no going back now.

A moment later I grinned maliciously, the flames of my ire rekindled with blazing glory. Malcolm had *no* idea what was coming for him. With the Riders of the Wild Hunt after his ass, not even Faery would be safe.

I will do whatever it takes to rescue Aurelia, even if it means calling on Death himself.

My wolf howled inside my head in triumph. He was just as ready for blood, carnage, and revenge as I was. And one way or another, we were damn well going to get it.

Soon. Very soon.

Chapter 23

Aurelia

"NO," I SAID, DEFIANTLY crossing my arms over my chest and glaring at Malcolm.

"You said if I allowed the vermin go free you would do whatever I asked," Malcolm reminded me through gritted teeth.

"I lied," I said with pleasure, and I shrugged out of his grip. "Well, I wasn't raised by fae and who's fault is that?" I raised a brow in silent accusation.

"You will do what I ask, Aurelia, or you will be punished," Malcolm roared, fast losing his patience. He grabbed me again and dragged me behind him, his rage buoying his stride to speed.

I tripped over my feet just trying to keep up with him and fell to my knees, my breath whooshing out of me with an *oomph!*

Malcolm let go of my arm in frustration and fisted my hair, pulling me roughly up with it. "You don't get to be a brat when you don't even remember who you are! You will help me, or you will learn the true meaning of suffering, my love."

"You taught me that already when you stole me from my bed in the castle!" I snarled back at him as fire danced across my scalp at his grip. My eyes widened at my own words.

Shit, I lived in a castle.

I'd known it since I attempted to retrieve my memories and relived Malcom spiriting me from my room. But knowing it and *saying* it aloud were apparently two very different things. This time the fact really registered with me, sinking into my consciousness, and I my mind reeled at the impossible.

Who am I?

And it seemed there was only one logical answer to that question. I'd been in quiet denial of it, but now the truth was unavoidably clear.

Holy shit.

"My parents were the king and queen, weren't they?" I asked in no small amount of horror and disgust. My parents were the elitist, prejudiced wicked fae who hated all other supernaturals. The realization made me feel sick to my stomach in the space of heartbeat.

"Your parents *are* the king and queen, and you will meet them as soon as we close the portal," Malcolm said tightening his fist even more tightly in my hair.

"I don't care to meet them, asshole. They never looked for me, so I why should I care about them at all?" I yelled and thrashed, not expecting an answer.

"Is that what you think, is it?" He shook his head, his eyes hard as they stared down at me. "They sent warriors looking for you for years! And even though you were hidden with the witch, they never gave up on their search."

My real parents actually searched for me? That doesn't sound right... Why wouldn't they have been able to find me?

It didn't make sense. Aside from a bit of glamour to hide my wings, I wasn't living underground or skulking about like a shadow. I avoided trouble, but I was out and about. I ran errands for Mother, I brought home groceries. I partook in daily necessities like everyone else. I was despised and unwanted, but people saw me around...

Surely, elite fae warriors would have been able to find me?

I stopped in my tracks and glared at Malcolm. My head screamed in pain at the pressure on my hair, but I didn't care.

Malcolm stopped and loosened his hold, watching the emotions flash behind my eyes.

He had to be lying. He was trying to make me *want* to go back, but I would never willingly go back to a people so prejudiced that they purged entire races of people from their realm based on nothing more than some stupid notion of blood purity.

"Your plan backfired, asshole," I said. "I will never condemn the supernaturals to a life of hiding if I can help it. They deserve their home back! We had no right to do what we did."

"Why do you care so much about them, anyway?" Malcolm asked with another shake of his head. "Your friend, Grey's most trusted beta, is the reason you are here right now. They can't be trusted. They sold you out at the first given opportunity."

What? Layla is the reason he knew when to come after me.

My gut roiled with hate, and I fumed with an instant desire for revenge. She was the reason I was in this mess, not to mention the sprites being harmed.

I'm going to kill that bitch.

Malcolm grinned at the defeated expression on my face. He obviously assumed that meant I would help him. Unfortunately for him, he couldn't be more wrong.

I hadn't met many benevolent supernaturals in my life but there were a precious few and I wouldn't want to condemn them. Having never had a stable home of my own since early childhood, I knew just how much losing one could mean to someone. Living in exile, hiding among humans was not what we were destined for. It couldn't be!

"It doesn't matter. She has hated me from the day she met me. I would expect nothing less of her." I slapped his hand away.

"They are a scourge, and you would bring them back to our realm?" Malcolm ground out. "Your parents will be so disappointed." He wrapped his hand around my arm again and flung me through an open door.

I crashed to the floor but held in the cry of pain that threatened to pry its way from between my lips and expose me. I wouldn't show weakness. Not now and certainly not to him. My back screamed from brutal landing on the stone floor, and I blinked back tears, unwilling to let them fall.

Fuck him. I'm going to get through this.

This wasn't the room he'd locked me in before when I first arrived. It was musty and dark, and a chill ran down my spine as he slammed the iron door closed.

"I showed too much kindness to you before, apparently. So, you will stay here until you agree to do as I ask," Malcolm snarled through the door. "I've waited this long to fulfil our ask. I can wait a while longer."

I scooted back, away from the door until my back hit a wall. The room couldn't have been bigger than six feet wide. There was a small, dirty cot in the corner and the only light in the room slipped in from under the door. Otherwise, he'd left me in complete darkness. I brought my knees to my chest and wrapped my arms around them, praying that the sprites had made it back to Grey and that they were okay.

I quietly attempted to call my magic to myself so that I could attempt to blow a hole through the damn wall, but it fizzled out as quickly as it was summoned. The iron in the cell was draining my magic away, like water through the many holes of a colander.

"Shit, this isn't good," I said to myself and rested my chin on my knees once more.

"Who's there?' a rough voice asked unexpectedly, startling me.

There's someone else in here? How the hell did I miss that?

"Oh, just Malcolm's latest prisoner," I groaned.

"I'm no prisoner, girl. He dumped you in my living quarters," the voice answered.

It was too dark to see more than a small shadow on the other side of the tiny space. Scuttling sounds filled the tiny room, and I flinched back.

A small man stood about three feet tall in front of me and by what scant light there was, I could see he wore a scowl.

"What?" I asked and reared back in surprise, hitting my head against the wall.

"What did you do to the master to make him to throw you in here?" He raised a huge bushy eyebrow, his face mostly hidden in shadow.

"I refused to be his pawn," I said simply, raising my chin in defiance.

I don't owe this little man anything.

The small man gasped and leaned forward, suddenly more inquisitive than perturbed. "Who are you?" he asked.

"I'm a prisoner and that's all you need to know." I straightened my spine and sighed, not willing to cave and divulge my life story to this nosey little goblin.

"You're the princess!" The miniature man gasped. A second later he snapped his fingers and a flame sparked to life in his hand.

"I don't know what you're talking about." I retorted.

"By the gods. The master has been looking for you for years, why would he put you in here?" he asked, almost speaking to himself.

"I don't care. He's an asshole and I just want to go home," I said glancing away into the darkness in the corners of the room.

Home? Is that what Grey's penthouse has become in such a short time? I've never really thought of anywhere as home. But it is…

The realization floored me. Grey and my small group of acquaintances had come to mean more to me than anything or anyone else I'd ever known in a very short space of time—but the feelings, the love? They were real. I knew it in my bones.

"If you want to go home, I'm sure the master will take you to the portal," he said and patted my knee.

"You misunderstand, I *don't* want to go back to Faery. That's not my home." I shook my head and pursed my lips.

The little man gasped and took a step away from me, his face a mask of horror and confusion. I could practically see the questions on the tip of his tongue. "You… how? Why?" he stuttered out. Clearly, he was on the wicked fae's side of the argument if he thought I was the one in the wrong.

I sat in silence, refusing to answer his questions. I didn't owe this man my history. He could come and go as he pleased, while I was a prisoner. He worked for Malcolm and for all I knew Malcolm put me in here so the little man could get information on me or convince me of the virtues of Faery.

He stared at me, waiting for a response and when I didn't give him one, he huffed. "Fine, keep your secrets," he grumbled and walked away. "You would do better to do as the master asks. He's not terrible." He laid on his cot and snuffed out the flame in his hand.

As a result, I was plunged into darkness again, but it didn't bother me. I liked the dark. I'd dwelled in the dark my whole life and it hadn't broken me. Hell, I was used to living like this. There was no way Malcolm would be the one to break me.

Not a chance.

I curled into a ball on the grimy floor and closed my eyes. Grey would come for me, I had to believe that. And when he did, I would tell him what a traitorous bitch Layla was.

He'll have a field day with her!

I MUST HAVE DOZED OFF at some point because a shout had me straightening in the darkness and I was instantly alert. "What was that?" I asked the small man, assuming he'd been woken by the noise too.

"I don't know," he answered as he shot up from the cot. He peered at me for a moment then vanished into thin air.

Soon after there was another shout and then a crash. I jumped up from the floor and took two long strides toward the door and beat my fists against it, hope swelling inside of me.

Yes! It's Grey. It has to be. He came for me.

"Grey, I'm in here!" I yelled at the top of my lungs, still beating against the door.

"Step back," a gruff voice answered from the other side.

Who is that? Did Grey bring reinforcements?

I sidestepped away from the door just in time and ducked, holding my arms over my head as the door flew across the room and hit the opposite wall with an almighty *thunk*.

The man on the other side of the door was so wide I doubted he could even fit through the door without having to turn sideways. He had a long scraggly beard and a scar above his left eye. He was obviously a man that had seen many battles.

"Who are you?" I asked, taking a wary step away from him.

"I'm an acquaintance of Grey's. Come, we need to get out of here." The man turned on his heel and stormed away, expecting me to follow.

I wasn't stupid. No matter who this guy was, he was huge, strong, and he'd broken me out of Malcolm's clutches. He was without doubt the better option. Without hesitation I jogged to catch up to him and followed close to his back, keeping my eyes peeled for danger as we went. As soon as I was out of the iron laced room, my magic came back, and purple shimmering glory crackled across my palms.

"Where's Grey?" I whispered. Was I stupid for following this surly man that I knew absolutely nothing about?

Probably, but he got me out of that poison-laced room, so perhaps it's a case of looks can be deceiving.

"He went after Malcolm, but we need to go." He grabbed my arm far more gently than I would have expected from a bear of a man and nothing like the way Malcolm had treated me. It was an urgent gesture, but guiding and protective at the same time.

"Asher!" a man yelled in the near distance. "Did you find the princess?"

I stiffened and glared at my rescuer, immediately on edge.

How do they know that I'm a fae princess?

"Don't look at me like that, princess. Grey figured it out quickly because of Malcolm's involvement," the man, who I now knew to be Asher, said as he led me to the entryway of the building.

Tears misted in my eyes as I looked at the front door, recognizing it immediately. My gaze dropped to the floor, and I swallowed hard. "Freya?" I ventured softly.

"She's healing," he answered before putting his hand on my back and leading me out into the early dawn light.

I squinted as my eyes adjusted and breathed in a deep sigh of relief. I'd hated seeing her like that, crumpled and dim, unconscious with the shock of the sudden impact. I shuddered at the thought as I relieved it in my mind. Just knowing that she was healing lifted a huge burden from my shoulders.

I scanned the forest with a smile, my heart filling with relief until I saw the motorcycles parked in the driveway. "You want me to get on one of those?" I asked in shock, pointing at the huge hunks of metal on wheels. I'd never been a fan.

Asher grinned and nodded. "Are you scared, princess?" he teased.

"No," I shot back and stomped my foot. "Those things are just bloody death traps and I have a healthy respect for my life."

"Well, it's either that or you walk back to Dallas but that's nothing short of a recipe for disaster if Malcolm isn't caught." Asher shrugged. "Your choice. Far be it for me to order about a princess," he added.

Shit, he's right. I don't really have a choice. Fuck it. Smart ass...

"Fine," I sighed. "Let's go then."

The truth was I didn't even know which way to go to get back on my own and there was no telling where the hell Grey was at this point in time.

Is it even safe to head back to the penthouse?

I moved toward the motorcycles with trepidation, when out of nowhere, pain shot through my back, and I was knocked face first into the hard-packed dirt. A surprised, clipped shriek escaped me as I hit the ground. I tried to move the boulder of a man off me but couldn't. I was pinned.

"Stay down, princess," Asher warned. "Looks like Malcolm is back." My burly rescuer rolled off me, staying low to assess the situation.

"What the hell happened?" I asked against the ground, gasping for air.

"He attacked you with his magic, but I tackled you down before it could touch you," he said scanning the trees intently.

What the hell? I thought he needed me to close the portal. Not to mention the psycho wants to claim me for his own. Why would he try to kill me now? And where the hell is Grey?

Malcolm stepped out from the trees and there was a shimmering quality to him. He was using some kind of magical shield. "I killed your wolf, my love!" Malcolm taunted, his eyes blazing with malice as his blond hair whipped around him in the morning breeze. "Now that mutt is out of the way, you have no reason not to help me."

"No!" I screamed, unable to hold back my instant, natural reaction.

He can't be dead!

Magic erupted in my palms as I jumped to my feet, pain and rage fueling my power like too much gas poured on a bonfire.

Asher was on his feet in an instant and stepped in front of me ready to take a hit for me.

But I wouldn't be stopped. I stepped to the side, twirling around him to throw everything I had at him. I screamed in defiance when it bounced off without harming him. His shield shimmered on impact, but otherwise there was no outward sign of any damage.

"He's lying, princess. He's trying to bait you. Ki... *Grey* is much harder to kill than that!" he said and stepped in my path again, acting a physical shield of flesh in my defense.

This man was truly willing to give his life for mine and though I was humbled, I couldn't help but frown at him.

What was he about to call Grey? What doesn't he want me to know?

"Am I lying, hunter?" Malcolm asked with a raised brow and took a step closer. "Why would I lie about killing that mongrel? It serves no purpose because after I kill the rest of you, I'll take her home anyway." Magic, unlike anything I'd ever seen before, blasted from his fingers like bolts of raw, unbridled lightning.

I gasped and once again I hit the ground with a jarring *thump* as I was tackled to the ground by Asher.

A bolt of Malcolm's magical lightning struck a tree and it exploded into an inferno of flames before falling on the motorcycles, totaling them in a heartbeat.

"Shit! That bastard is going to pay," Asher snarled as he got up into a surprisingly swift crouch. "That was my favorite fucking bike." Shadows suddenly gathered and swirled around Asher out of nowhere like they were living, breathing entities. His arm shot out and the shadows hurtled toward Malcolm with frightening speed.

Malcolm's eyes widened as the shadows broke through his shield like it wasn't there at all. They slithered and wrapped around his body, pinning his arms to his sides, as a rustling sounded in the bushes from behind him.

"Grey!" I whispered, tears of relief pooling in my eyes as an absolutely beautiful white wolf lunged for Malcolm, his maw wide and his teeth bared.

Malcolm smirked, seemingly unperturbed. "I'll see you again soon, Aurelia," he promised, and then disappeared from sight.

"How did that fucker sift with my shadows on him?" Asher growled, scratching his beard.

Grey's breath-taking huge, white wolf raced forward and nudged my cheek with his wet nose.

I wrapped my arms around his furry neck and sobbed my heart out in relief, unwilling to let him go. He felt so soft, and strong, and smelled like mine—like home. Everything about his presence instantly comforted me and soothed the ache that had steadily grown like a thorn in my soul over the past two days. "He said you were dead," I cried, burying my face in his thick coat and breathing deeply. A pair of pants hit the ground beside me, and I startled, before looking up into Asher's kind eyes.

"As touching as all this is, we need to find a way out of here," he grunted. "This shit isn't over."

My lovely, brave alpha wolf whined but backed away from me and started to shift.

I shivered when he returned to his human form, naked as the day he was born. Without shame I scanned his tan, toned body, nearly groaning at what I saw. He was beyond mouth-watering, and an ache bloomed to life between my thighs in response. Biting down on my lower lip, I teased it between my teeth and sighed aloud.

"There will be time for that later," Grey assured me with a chuckle, following my obvious gaze. "But right now, I need clothes."

My cheeks burned with embarrassment as I crouched down and grabbed the pants from the ground and handed them to him reluctantly.

He was just *gorgeous*, and he made me feel all kinds of things I probably shouldn't, given how little I truly knew about him. Was this likely a recipe for disaster? Probably, but as I peered up at him the fire in his eyes matched mine, and I decided that I could deal with a disaster just fine. We were fated mates after all and given the benefit of time I was sure there wasn't anything we couldn't overcome together. He was my wolf, and I was his god damn fairy princess.

Chapter 24

Grey

THANKFULLY, AFTER AURELIA'S immediate rescue we hadn't encountered any further complications. With the bikes smashed up, we called in alternative transport and got back to my building in one piece. We bid our friends a goodnight, offering our thanks and gratitude for all their help and then headed for the only home we had outside of Faery.

I picked Aurelia up in my arms as soon as the elevator doors opened to the penthouse. I knew there were others there who wanted to see her, those who had helped and were now waiting... but I didn't care. They could wait. It had been Hell on Earth without my fated mate for days, and my wolf had reached the limit of his patience. He had been going mad with panic and anger in her absence and he now that we had Aurelia back, there was no way he was waiting a moment longer. Though I wondered how it could feel like that for us after only having known her for such a relatively short time.

It has to be the fated mate bond we share.

It was the only feasible explanation. The only thing that made any sense at all.

"What in the gods... What happened to my poor plants?" she asked with a frown as she surveyed the remains of our once lush and green apartment.

"Later!" I grunted, inhaling the scent of her as I stomped past Magna and the sprites. There would be time for words, but that time wasn't now.

Magna opened her mouth to say something, the words dying on her tongue a heartbeat later.

I glared at them. She wasn't stopping me. No one was. My wolf was thrashing inside of me to get to his mate. We'd suffered long enough.

"Hi!" Aurelia called back to them apologetically as I whisked her away. "Grey, where are we going?" she asked with an amused giggle, the sound like music to my ears.

I nuzzled her neck and kicked open my bedroom door. It slammed into the wall with a loud *thunk*! I stopped just inside the room and set her down on her own two feet. Her body slid against mine in the most delicious of ways and I licked her neck possessively. "I need you," I groaned. "I need to feel that you are here and *mine*."

She shivered at my touch, her stunning emerald-green eyes gazing up into mine.

I gripped her hips, pulling her back against my body with feral desire. My already rock-hard cock rubbed through my clothes and against her belly.

Shit, I don't know how long I'm going to last with these wickedly tempting curves.

Aurelia reached up with a smile and wrapped her arms around my neck, standing on her tiptoes to plant a sensual, drawn-out kiss on my lips.

The door clicked shut behind me and I broke the kiss to glance over my shoulder and raise an eyebrow at her.

Did she just do that with her magic?

"I've been practicing," she said in response to my unspoken question, a grin on her beautiful face.

I slid my hand around to her back, then underneath her tank top. The skin-on-skin contact made me shudder with anticipation and yearning.

Her lips came up to my neck and she kissed and licked her way back to my mouth, pulling me down to her. "Grey, I want you," she whispered, rubbing her thighs together, no doubt heightening the pressure of her need.

I pulled her tank top up and trailed my fingers over the exposed skin before I ripped the shirt over her head. Staring down at her voluptuous, lace-covered breasts, I groaned.

She's perfect.

Her hands tightened in my hair at my touch, and a moan slipped from her lips.

I leaned in and licked along her collarbone, then trailed kisses down to the swell of her breast, reveling in the taste of her flesh as I nipped the sensitive skin there.

Aurelia's back arched, her warm body pressing against mine with obvious desire.,

"Go lay on the bed and take the rest of your clothes off." I took a step back, waiting for her to do as I commanded.

Heat tinted her cheeks a breathtaking shade of pink as she reached behind her back and unclasped her lacy bra. She slid it from her arms and let it fall silently to the floor, averting her gaze as she sucked in a deep breath.

Fuck, and I thought she was beautiful before. Her curvy body is a work of art and it's all mine.

"Wait," I objected.

She stopped with a frown; her fingers looped into the waistband of her leggings.

I prowled toward her like a wolf ready for the kill, or more accurately a wolf ready to claim his mate. I picked her up and threw her over my shoulder, racing to the bed with her.

She giggled and flailed playfully, pummeling my back with her fists. "Grey!"

I tossed her onto the mattress and leaned over her glorious body, taking a nipple into my mouth.

Her giggle soon became a moan as she dug her fingernails into my shoulders, her head thrown back in ecstasy.

I nipped at her luscious flesh and attended to her other nipple, lavishing it with the same level of attention before slowly trailing kisses down her soft belly. And then I moved on to the waistband of her leggings.

"Grey," she whimpered, her voice breathy and ripe with need.

"What is it princess?" I asked with a wicked grin. Unwilling to wait for her response, I tugged on her leggings, pulling them slowly down her creamy, thick thighs. She was perfection incarnate and I was dying to be inside her. One taste of her wasn't enough. It would never be enough.

With a casual flourish I threw her leggings on the floor, adding it to the pile along with her bra and shirt. Then turning back, I trailed my fingers up her inner thigh. Eagerly I followed my finger with my lips, keen to pepper her beautiful skin with my hot lips.

Aurelia's hands sunk into my hair, and she cursed under her breath at my languid, slow, and purposeful ministrations.

I shuddered at the sting of pain as she gripped the strands of my hair too tightly, trying to forcibly tug me up her body.

Aurelia wriggled her hips in frustration and attempted to rub her thighs together, no doubt to expel me from my position of power of her.

I gripped her hips, holding her firmly in place as I ran my nose over her panty-covered center, breathing her in. She was soaked through, and the delicious damp scent of vanilla and jasmine filled my nose.

I need to taste her. She's so perfect. She literally even smells like a fairy princess!

I glanced up at her flushed face with a dark smile and brought my hands to her hips. Gripping her underwear in a tight fist, I ripped the flimsy fabric down the middle, destroying them in a single brutal moment of passion.

Aurelia gasped and tightened her grasp on my hair, her whole body trembling with wanting.

I lunged forward, plunging my face into her heaven and licked her all the way up her slit and to her clit and sucked on it, savoring the sweet flavor of her slick.

Her back arched, her muscles tight, a scream tearing from her throat as she held me to her soaking pussy.

I couldn't breathe but I didn't give a damn if she smothered my face into her dripping wet pussy. If I died right here and now, it'd be the way to go—a death worthy of a king.

"Oh, my gods, Grey," she breathed as her thighs fell open. Like a cut snake she squirmed and thrashed beneath my touch, as if fighting her desire, unwilling to succumb to the deviant pleasure afflicting her curvy form.

I thrust my tongue inside her, scooping up her desire and lapping at it greedily before making my way back up to her swollen and sensitive clit. Without warning I thrust a finger inside her, my digit gliding in effortlessly and without resistance into her tightness.

She thrashed her head from side to side, biting her lip all the while until I saw blood bead there. "Fuck, Grey!" she shouted, her voice trailing off into a needy whine that made my cock ache. Her whole body shook as she climbed higher and higher toward her inevitable climax. She was so responsive.

I'm going to fuck my golden princess every day for the rest of my damn life!

Smiling wickedly, I curled my finger inside her at the thought as I pushed a second finger inside her pussy, pumping several times hard and fast as I flicked her clit with my tongue.

"Grey!" she screamed my name like an anguished prayer as she shattered, unable to hold herself together under my relentless onslaught.

Her sweet cum coated my fingers and tongue as I devoured her like a man starved, feasting upon her until she finally stopped bucking and swearing at the ceiling, her fists tangled in her own hair.

When she finally relaxed, having come down from her orgasm, I crawled up her body, trailing kisses along her stomach and over her breasts until I was directly above her. Her expression as I leaned down and sealed my lips to hers was priceless.

She moaned into my mouth and wrapped her leg around my hips, pulling me toward her. Aurelia broke the kiss, frowning in confusion. "Wait, why the hell do you still have clothes on?"

I chuckled at her delicious enthusiasm and kissed her again before sitting up and scooting back off the bed. I removed my pants with ease and my mate's gaze burned into me, setting my insides on fire.

"Like what you see, princess?" I grinned as I crawled back over to her.

"That stupid nickname isn't so much of a nickname anymore," Aurelia growled, twisting her lips into a delicious pout.

"Shh, we aren't talking about that anymore," I soothed as I leaned down and kissed her roughly, stealing her breath away and bruising her lips. I would need to know what she'd learned while in that bastard's clutches... but not now. Now, I just needed to make her scream for me again. I wanted her to scream my name until it was engraved on her soul.

I rolled on top of her again and gripped her hip tightly, fitting our bodies together while rubbing the head of my cock against her wet entrance. But I stopped short of burying myself inside her. With her warm breath against my face, I simply rocked my hips, just dipping in and out of her puffy, slick lips.

"Grey! Are you teasing me?" she demanded, thrusting her hips up at me.

I gripped her waist, maintaining my control—keeping her my prisoner—and trailing my lips down her neck, nicking her flesh with my teeth. "I would never dream of teasing you, princess," I drawled, enjoying the scent of desperation and need a while longer. To be so desired was a heady and delectable drug, indeed and I wanted more. As much as I could possibly get.

"Then please!" she cried, begging me for a reprieve. "I couldn't bear it if you stopped again." She threaded her hands into my hair and tugged my mouth back to hers in a bruising kiss. "Just fuck me, wolf," she whispered, breaking the kiss to breathe against my lips.

I growled. The demand turning me and my shifter on even more. "As you wish, princess," I snarked softly, overwhelmed by desire. With a satisfied grin, I positioned myself at her entrance. Then, calling upon all of my resolve and self-restraint, I pushed in slowly; remembering that she was a virgin. And the last thing I wanted to do was to hurt her in my need for her.

Damn.

It was almost like mission impossible. She was hot and wet and so tight that every inch of me yearned for nothing more than to be hilt deep in her.

She hissed in pain and arched her back, biting down on her lip from the inside, her bows knitted.

I froze, studying her face as I hovered, not daring to move another muscle until she offered me some indication that she was all right to continue. I wanted her, but after everything she'd been through, I'd fucking *kill* myself if I hurt her. I never ever wanted to be the cause of her pain. I couldn't bear the thought, and neither could my wolf.

"I'm okay, Grey," she whispered, suddenly, cupping my cheek and breaking through my reverie. She pressed her lips softly to mine, encouraging me to claim her, to make her mine.

And so, I did. I didn't need more than that. I pushed forward, forging inside of her, levelling out until my sac rested against her thick ass.

Fuck me.

She fit me like a glove and my body shuddered from the tips of my fingers to ends of my toes at how *perfect* she felt. She was mine, now. Forever. I'd claimed her and taken her virginity. My cock was the only one that would ever taste the heaven that resided between her luscious thighs.

And I'll kill any man or woman that tries to take her from me.

I rocked my hips forward and grunted as I reached the deepest parts of her again and again.

"By the gods," she breathed, arching her back, her fingers tightening in my hair.

I gripped her hip and withdrew to my head before slamming back in. "Fuck, Aurelia, you feel *so* good," I groaned as I thrust in and out of her hard and fast, pumping her so hard that I felt the wicked sensation of our pelvises colliding with each stroke. "I don't know how long I'm going to last," I hissed, before I shifted my weight onto forearm so that I could trail my fingers down her belly to her clit and circle it roughly.

Her legs tightened around my hips as her body thrust back against me, desperate to feel everything all at once. Our bodies moved in sync, and she gave as good as she got. She was without doubt the keenest and most earnestly passionate lover I'd ever had.

My spine began to tingle with my impending orgasm, and I pinched her clit between my fingers, making her yelp aloud. "Can I mark you, mate?" I asked, my wolf shining through my eyes and his husky gravel taking over my voice.

"Yes," Aurelia moaned as her back arched and she willingly and instinctively bared her neck to me.

There would never be anything sexier than my beautiful mate submitting to my bite. I licked up the column of her neck, my wolf howling in my head like a beast on crack.

Mine.

"Grey, please, make me yours," she moaned, the unmistakable note of desperation not lost on me.

I'd never heard anything sexier in my entire life. I lunged forward, my heart in my throat as I sank my partially shifted fangs into the spot on her neck that met her collarbone. I froze as euphoria unlike anything I'd ever experienced before tore through me, triggering my orgasm. It hit me hard and fast, almost knocking the sense out of me. I came on a roar, unleashing my hot load deep inside her, filling her with my shifter seed.

Aurelia screamed in ecstasy and her pussy rippled around my cock, milking me until there was nothing left to give.

I released her neck and lapped at my mark on her skin. My shifter saliva had healing properties and would encourage the wound to heal faster. Exhausted and sated beyond my wildest dreams, I pressed my forehead to hers and took a deep steadying breath. "Are you okay, princess?" I asked as I disengaged and rolled carefully to my side, then pulled her back to my chest.

"Yes. That was... incredible," she whispered.

I squeezed her tight and nuzzled her neck. I'd missed her so much when she had been gone from the apartment. But my wolf was finally calm with my mate in our arms. As protective as I was feeling, a deeply disturbing and unsettling thought washed over me in our post coital bliss. "Did he hurt you?" I growled; my voice low as I pulled her closer.

"It was nothing, Grey. Nothing I couldn't survive. I'm stronger than you think." She shook her head and turned into my arms to face me.

"I will fucking kill him one day," I said as I glared into her eyes, unable to hide my passionate desire and fervor for revenge. My declaration was a promise, and it was one I would keep no matter what. I would have Malcolm's bloody head even if it killed me.

"I know you will, my love," Aurelia soothed. "And then we will go home to Faery, together, and take our place back in the world." She kissed me softly, her lips lingering on mine as our hearts beat as one.

And I could only hope that she was foreseeing the future, because there was nothing more, I wanted than to make her my queen.

Chapter 25

Aurelia

GREY PACED THE ROOM, anxiety clear in his every move as I got ready for the challenge, or at least what was supposed to be the challenge... "Are you sure about this?" he asked softly for the third time.

"Yes, this is the only way." I reached out to him and laid a hand on his arm, halting him in his steps.

"But what if everything goes to Hell? They are all my employees, but Layla and Karma know them much better than I do, they're with them every damn day." He gripped my arms, his brow creased as concern and love for me warred on his features for pride of place.

Asher stepped into the locker room and shook his head. "The princess has the makings of a fine and brave warrior. Stop being the nagging mate, Grey," he chastised. "It doesn't suit you."

"I'll kill you next, hunter!" Grey growled; his lips downturned.

I smacked Grey on the arm and groaned at the feel of his taut muscles beneath my palm. We hadn't left the bedroom for *days*, but we needed to deal with Layla and Karma sooner rather than later. "Asher saved me. You will not kill him, wolf." I frowned at Grey in playful warning.

My mate sighed and rolled his eyes. "As you wish, my love." He grinned and kissed me softly in return.

Asher coughed. "Sickening," he remarked with a wink at me. "All this affection is enough to turn the stomach of even the most seasoned soul."

I put on a brave face and smiled at the hunter's joke, but inside I was nervous—really nervous. What would happen if they found out that I was aware of what they had done, or their betrayal of not only Grey and I, but the Syndicate itself?

Did Malcolm tell them what he told me? Has he given them a heads up so they can cause chaos at the challenge?

I hoped not. So far there didn't seem to be any unrest that was out of the ordinary and everything was quiet, but I'd certainly learned that in the world of supernaturals anything could change at any moment. Ours was a world of survival, deceit, underhanded dealings, and crime and that attracted a certain type of individual—ones with flexible morals and loyalties.

"Are we sure that Layla doesn't know anything?" I asked chewing on my lower lip.

"As far as we can tell, based on our work inside the facility, she has no clue what's about to go down," Asher confirmed with a grin.

"You were spying from inside the facility?" I asked with a raised brow, intrigued.

"No one in the facility or anywhere else in this realm would question the Riders of the Wild Hunt." He crossed his arms over his chest, clearly more than a little proud of his prestigious position.

I couldn't see what everyone else saw. He didn't seem that scary to me. The other riders didn't seem that scary either, to be honest. Sure, they were big, imposing, and lethal, but... they had hearts, they were kind to those deserving of it, and fiercely loyal.

But I guess it's all just a matter of perception. Perhaps others have not seen the side of them that I have?

"Are the guys in position?" Grey asked Asher. "It's almost time."

I bounced on the balls of my feet nervously, buzzed with equal measures of energy and fear. This was the challenge everyone had been waiting for. And even though I'd been working relentlessly with Max to hone my physical prowess, my anxieties remained.

Karma was the best the Syndicate had. She'd been a point of pride for years... until she chose the wrong side and revealed her true colors.

What if she tries to kill me

A challenge was only meant to end in defeat, but sometimes things went too far. Deaths happened in the ring, and I knew that had been Layla's plan all along. It was why she sold me out to Malcolm in the first place. The cocky bitch thought we would never find out.

Dumb bitch.

She thought she was so good and had played the long game so successfully that no one would ever guess, let alone believe that she would betray Grey. But she was wrong, and she was about to find out just how wrong she was.

I checked my knives were secure on my body and ready for action before I blew out a breath to steady myself.

Grey squeezed my shoulder and sent an encouraging smile my way that made my heart skip a beat. "You're going to be great, princess, don't worry." He wrapped an arm around me and pulled me against his chest.

It was beyond comforting. I *loved* it when he touched me. His lips on my neck made me shiver. "Thank you," I whispered. With stoic resolve I stepped away from him and gave him what I hoped was a confident smile before doing exactly what Reah had encouraged me to do. I schooled my features into an unreadable mask, adopting my poker face.

In this battle, I will not allow my enemy to read me like a book. I will give away nothing. I will be hard, strong, fast, and smart. You can do this, Aurelia.

The crowd outside the locker room started shouting. They were already baying for blood. Their feet stomped on the ground, causing vibrations to shiver through the floor. I took a cleansing breath. This was it. They would be savagely thirsting for a bloody battle, and I would do what I could to give them what they wanted without actually killing anyone... even though a part of me wanted it to go that far. I wouldn't become what they said I was. I'd leave the outcome of their lives to Grey or fate—whichever came first.

"All right, let's get this show on the road," I said with more confidence than I felt. I mentally pumped myself up and stomped to the door and stood there, waiting until Grey came to open it. He'd drilled into my head the importance of him doing that for me in this fight. We had to present a united front, or I would be seen as weak and without allies. It needed to be seen that I had the Syndicate's favor; that it was me who was in the right. It us against the traitors.

I am not weak. I am a damn fae princess, as weird as that is to say.

I strutted out the door with my head held high with Grey and Asher at my back. The room was practically an industrial-sized basement with bleachers set up next to a ring for blood-thirsty spectators. The magic pouring off the ring made my stomach flip-flop. It was just like the warded, magicless room in Grey's penthouse that I used for training for this very moment.

Layla stood next to Karma on the other side of the ring and smirked at me, her eyes narrowed and expression rife with venom. She thought this was a done deal and that I would be gone shortly, her problem erased and out of her hair. The dumb bitch really, truly believed that she'd won; that she'd walk away from this the victor.

I grinned menacingly at her obvious challenge and nodded subtly to Grey.

Grey squeezed my hand before stepping in front of me—my love, my man, my wolf, and my shield.

My mate.

"It's come to my attention that we have traitors in our midst," Grey shouted over the screaming voices looking for a fight, his voice carrying a terrifying air of authority and power. It was clear he was in his element. He commanded obedience like he was born to it.

All the yelling ceased, and the employees of the Syndicate whispered among themselves as they glanced around at the people nearest them.

"What are you talking about, Grey?" Layla asked, stepping forward.

Yes, please step into the ring!

There was nothing I wanted more than to take Layla down a peg or two, but this was technically Grey's battle. She'd fucked with me, but she'd betrayed him.

"Someone in this room betrayed me," he repeated and raised a brow at her, daring her to deny it.

"Who would dare betray the king?" she sneered aloud and scanned the room, as if it was really anyone else at fault but her and Karma.

King? What the hell is she talking about? Does she mean the King of the Syndicate... or something else?

I peered over at Asher remembering his near slip outside Malcolm's house of horrors and something inside my gut twisted, but I maintained my poker face. I wouldn't forget Reah's training.

Is Grey a king of some kind? If so, why didn't he tell me?

"Cut the bullshit, Layla!" I spat, pushing the thought aside for the moment. "Everyone knows you've hated me from the day I set foot here. You're jealous as hell."

"You bitch. What are you accusing me of?" Layla screamed back, her eyes blazing.

"Betrayal, treachery, handing me over to the enemy, and getting Reah and the sprites and injured just for starters," I quipped with a nonchalant shrug.

"That's a lie," Layla screamed.

"Is it?" Grey asked as he stepped menacingly forward. "Because that sure as hell smelled like a lie to me."

"What?" she asked in shock.

"Step into the ring, Layla. If you really are innocent, step inside the ring. You should have nothing to fear." Grey crossed his arms over his chest, standing tall, broad and beautiful. He was an absolutely imposing figure.

Layla took a step back and bumped into one of the Riders of the Wild Hunt. She wasn't going anywhere.

He glared down at her with his arms crossed over his chest like an immovable mountain.

The crowd sat in complete, sterile silence now as they watched the betrayal unfold before their eyes. This was no doubt a far juicier show than even they had hoped for. But who were they most loyal to?

Will they retaliate against us when this is all over?

They thought they were getting a bloodbath, namely mine. But they were getting an entirely different kind of show instead.

Karma took a step away from Layla. It was kind of cute how she thought she was off the hook.

"Where do you think you're going Karma?" I asked sweetly as I felt the thrill of justice surge through my veins.

"What do you mean? I didn't betray the boss!" Karma spat as she crossed her arms over her chest.

"You see, I know that's a lie, kitty cat." I grinned. "Layla may have been second in command, but at the end of the day she is still *just* a shifter. How could she have possibly known who Malcolm was or where to look without the half-witch who performed the first mimic spell in the first place?"

"No, you're wrong! I had nothing to do with this you lying bitch," Karma screamed, as clearly guilty as her partner in crime.

I think thou doth protest too much!

She tried to turn and flee but was caught easily by one of the riders.

Grey stood next to me; his hands folded behind his back as the two women started bickering with one another. It was pitiful to see. Even at the end they couldn't present a united front. They were truly traitorous to their filthy cores.

"You all know what happens to traitors, do you not?" Grey shouted over the shocked gasps of the crowd.

"No, Grey!" Layla turned her pleading eyes toward him. "We've been together forever and you're going to throw all of that away over some fucking wicked fae?"

"Yes. You should have known better than to move against me," he said flatly. "I might be your boss, but you know I'm so much more."

"I wasn't moving against you! I was just trying to get her out of the way," she shouted back desperately before she lunged, making another escape attempt. But again, she was caught by the ominous rider behind her.

"At the expense of your own people?" I asked, my brows furrowed.

What a selfish cow. She can't see past her own damn nose!

Layla sneered at me. "My people have nothing to do with it. How could sending you to Malcolm hurt the shifters at all?"

"Did Malcolm share his plans for me with you? Did he inform you that he wanted me to seal the portal forever and leave you *all* stuck here?" I asked. "Of course, he didn't. Otherwise, I don't think you would have done this. No matter how much you hate me and the rest of the fae, I doubt your petty jealousy would have won out over your desire to go home to Faery."

"You lie! You're an evil, wicked fae and I wish you were dead!" Layla screamed and thrashed in the arms of the rider behind her. In the next instant her body convulsed, and bones cracked and reformed as she shifted into the form of a huge black wolf. The rider holding her lost his grip on her and she jumped forward into the ring, stupidly daring to thwart justice and attempt to prove herself innocent with a lie.

Just as quickly as she had shifted and landed inside the wards, she was forced back in her human form. Her naked body convulsed violently as blood spewed from between her lips, painting the floor in a ghastly splash of bright crimson. She writhed in her own blood as more red leaked from her ears and nose; the spell upon the ring slowly boiling her from the inside out.

The acrid metallic scent of blood and the odor of cooked flesh filled the large space, and I turned my face into Grey's chest not wanting to witness any more of the carnage. Guilty or not, it was a truly horrific and fucked up way to go.

When her whimpers faded, and silence again descended upon the oppressive training grounds I glanced up and saw someone I never expected to see at the facility. "You!" My eyes widened and I tore myself out of Grey's arms.

The man who shot me with the tranquilizer and started this whole mess was standing a mere ten feet away from me.

His eyes widened as my purple, swirling magic lit my palms.

If he hadn't shot me the witch might still be alive! Malcolm never would have been able to kill her and set me up.

I turned to Grey and the first night we met played over again in my mind like a broken record. He hadn't found me randomly. That man was there.... And the pieces of the puzzle finally fell into place. They had been working together from the start. *Grey* was the reason everything had changed. He sent that man after me because he needed me for his grand plan.

Betrayal sank into my stomach like sour rot as I took another heavy step away from the man who had become so much to me. The whole situation was played out on his order all along. It was all a lie. My heart sank and my insides ached.

You'd lied to me...

Grey reached for me. It was clear he understood exactly what I was thinking. I'd finally figured it all out and the penny had dropped. And now he was going to try and smooth it over.

I shook my head, my nose scrunching in anger. "Don't fucking touch me!" I said through gritted teeth.

Grey turned to the man I was staring at, then back to me. "I can explain all of this. Don't go jumping to conclusions." He made to reach for me again.

My magic reacted to the feelings of my betrayal and threw up a shield between us. "You had him follow me!" I accused. "The only mother I remember is dead because I was passed out from being shot with a tranquilizer dart. You're the cause of all my suffering these past weeks! How could you? I thought you cared about me?"

"Just listen, Aurelia, I can explain. I didn't know that he shot you until you told me. That was never a part of the plan. I'd never do that to you. I just wanted you for a job at the time and asked Dan to bring you in—that's all. And I honestly ran into you by accident on my way back to my penthouse. I wasn't trying to corner you, but my wolf claimed you as his mate immediately. So, I kept Dan away until I could find the right way to tell you." He reached for me again, but my shimmering shield knocked him back ten feet, right into his buddy, Dan. They could have each other.

Betrayal threatened to drown me along with a new fresh sense of despair. I had no idea where I was going to go, I just knew I had to get out of there. Again, everything I loved was gone, taken from me between one breath and the next. And I was sick of it.

I don't want to hurt anymore! Why can't anyone just be honest with me? I'm not a fragile flower. I deserve better.

"I don't ever want to see you again, Grey," I said with a finality that chilled my soul, before I made a run for the elevator. No one stopped me as I hit the button and stepped inside.

But Asher suddenly appeared and stepped in beside me. "Going down?" he asked.

"What are you doing?" I asked with a frown, struggling to hold myself together as the doors began to close.

"I was going to offer you a ride," Asher said with a shrug of his enormous shoulders.

"I don't need a bloody ride," I mumbled. "I don't even know where I'm going." Pain lanced through my chest, sharp and cold, and I gasped.

Why does it hurt so much?

It's like the betrayal was a physical weight crushing my body, and I had no idea how to relieve it.

How could he do this to me? How?

My mind reeled and I began to hyperventilate as panic overwhelmed me. I'd trusted Grey—I'd loved him. How could he be behind it all? I met Grey's gaze once last time and I felt everything and nothing all at once. My heart was a cacophony of raw emotion, and I didn't know if I could take it. As Grey's expression crumpled, so did my future. I never imagined I'd be forced to reject my fated mate. It hurt so much I thought I would die.

Asher patted my shoulder as the doors closed to the elevator with an insulting and ridiculous *ding*. "I know of a place you can stay," he said as he pushed the button for the ground floor of the building.

I didn't want to have to accept the kindness of a stranger again, let alone a stranger that had such close ties to Grey... but ultimately, what choice did I have? I didn't have anyone else.

I had no place to go. I had no friends. And now I was losing the few people I thought I cared for and cared for me in return. It seemed like my whole life was a vortex of nothing but lies, deceit, and betrayal. This was the third home I'd lost inside of two decades. How was I supposed to go on? Where did I belong?

And who am I, really?

An exiled princess? A nobody mated to a traitor? Just a young woman who'd grown up in the foster system to discover the world was truly as dark, remorseless, and fucked up as she'd always believed it to be?

Maybe the supernaturals are as bad as Malcolm says. They call us wicked... but they have shown their true colors time and time again! Witches, shifters, half-fae... the whole bloody lot of them!

With my heart racing and fury clouding my judgement, I wracked my mind for hope. For something, anything to grab onto. An anchor in a sea of turmoil and despair. A glimmer in the dark to guide my way.

Maybe I should just go back to Faery and see what happens? It can't be worse than here, surely?

Perhaps I could rediscover who I was. Maybe I could meet and hear my birth parent's side of the story. I could return home—to my real home—and become who I was born to be, a Princess of Faery, the daughter of the reigning king and queen.

I swallowed the lump in my throat that seemed intent on choking me and took several calming breaths the way Grey had taught me; the irony not lost on me. Licking my lips, I stood tall once more beside the Ride of the Wild Hunt as we waited for the elevator to reach the bottom.

Maybe I'll find the happily ever after to my fairy tale in Faery...

It was a desperate hope, but I clung to it like a lifeline. Come Hell or highwater, I was going to face the next chapter of my life with courage and an assload less naivete than I'd done so far.

I mightn't be the fastest learner, but I learn, and I am NOT going to be burned again!

Aurelia's story continues...
in Book 2 - **Shadow Fae** and is AVAILABLE NOW: HERE[1]!

---

1. https://books2read.com/u/mVAz95

Printed in Great Britain
by Amazon